she

was

wronged . . .

I AM

HER

REVENGE

I AM

HER

REVENGE

MEREDITH MOORE

razor
bill

An Imprint of Penguin Group (USA)

A division of Penguin Young Readers Group
Published by Penguin Random House
345 Hudson Street
New York, New York 10014

USA / Canada / UK / Ireland / Australia
New Zealand / India / South Africa / China
Penguin.com
A Penguin Random House Company

ISBN: 978-1-59514-782-0

Printed in the United States of America

1 3 5 7 9 10 8 6 4 2

For Mom, my best friend and my biggest cheerleader.

I miss you every day.

And for Dad, for being proud of me no matter what.

I love you.

CHAPTER 1

This land is barren. Windswept. A heavy mist hangs over the earth, shrinking the world to only a few yards of space. I feel as if I have entered an enchanted place. My home in upstate New York was filled with tall pines creaking up toward the sky, lush grass biding its time under blankets of winter snow, houses and concrete and people.

Here, short clumps of green-brown heather cover the ground. Every so often, a tree ekes its way out of the soil, its trunk having curved back toward the land under the pressure of the wind until it stuck that way. It reminds me of a person hanging on to the edge of a cliff, this stubborn clinging to life.

Madigan School, though, doesn't look like it would bend to any force of wind. Its four buildings are clustered together in a square on top of a hill, surrounded by a high stone wall. The main school building stands tall and proud at the forefront, surveying the wild moors of Yorkshire, England, below it. It's taller than it is wide, its windows piling on top of each other. The gray stone facade—Georgian, the catalogue called it—only grows larger and more intimidating as the cabdriver and I approach it. If I were to draw it in my secret sketchbook, it would tower over the viewer, immense and imposing.

We wind our way up the hill to campus, and something feels like it's flipping around in my stomach. This is the scenery of my new life, but it appears to be just as foreboding as my old one. I can picture Mother looking down at me from one of the windows, waiting for me. Lying in wait for me.

The flipping in my stomach intensifies, and I close my eyes and picture myself hidden away in my bedroom at home, up in the attic where Mother rarely ventured. Breathe in, breathe out. I can do this. I have to do this for her. Mother relies on me.

The driver passes through the imposing wrought-iron gate, emblazoned with *Madigan School* in twisty cursive across its top, and stops the car in front of the main building. He turns in his seat to look at me. "You all right back there?" he asks, his Yorkshire accent so thick that I can barely understand him. But I can still recognize the uncertainty in his voice. He doesn't know how to deal with a hyperventilating girl.

I calm my breath and put on a dazzling smile. "Just a bit nervous, that's all," I simper.

He smiles, relieved. His watery blue eyes stare at me for just a touch too long, and I know I have him. I have nothing in particular to do with him, but this is still reassuring.

There are people milling about the lawn, girls and boys about my age glancing at the car out of the corners of their eyes. As soon as I step out, all of the useless motion stops. People stare. I've engineered my appearance for this specific reaction, and Mother will be so pleased that it worked.

I wear the uniform I was required to buy, but I know it looks nothing like anyone else's. I shortened the red and black plaid skirt and ripped the hem, making it jagged and frayed. I paired it with black tights and sparkly gold ballet flats, to soften the edginess of the skirt. My white shirtsleeves are rolled up to my elbows to show off arms cluttered with bangles: gold and red and black. I've bared my throat, having unbuttoned my shirt until you can see just a hint of cleavage, though there's not much there to show. The pale skin of my neck and the vulnerable cut of my collarbones will be the focal points. I painted on a thin dash of black eyeliner, making my deep blue eyes pop. I skipped the blush and added dark red lipstick to contrast with my pale skin.

My hair, though, my best feature, I've left alone. It hangs long and black down to the middle of my back, a thick mass of glossy hair that tempts you to run your fingers through it.

I am irresistible.

And everyone notices it.

As I pass my eyes over the crowd, a slow smirk on my lips, the buzzing starts. Kids turn to each other and ask who I am. I grab my bags from the driver as the girls begin judging my outfit and the boys make bets on who will get me into bed first.

I'm used to it all. During my one year of public school, back home in upstate New York, I showed up as the sweet girl next door at first, the type who wore pale pink cardigans and pearl bracelets. This made some girls want to be my friend, but none of the boys seemed particularly interested. So Mother and I cooked up a new persona: the edgy confident girl. This girl was friendly enough and desirable, but unimpressed with boys who just assumed I would fall all over them. I wore clothes Mother could hardly afford along with my slash of red lipstick. And suddenly everyone was talking about me.

I'm not pretty. My eyes are too wide and my mouth too small. But I've learned ways to soften these traits and become something even better than pretty: fascinating. I am someone who earns double glances, someone whose eyes trap you, someone otherworldly. Once Mother had figured out how to alter my uniform to match that captivating quality, she pronounced me perfect.

I pay the driver without giving him a second glance, straighten my shoulders, and march toward the front door. Students move out of my way to let me pass, but no one speaks a word to me, despite the fact that there's only a slight hint of condescension in my smile.

I open the massive wooden door and enter a foyer with a sumptuous marble floor—white shot through with tendrils of somber gray. A wide slate staircase rises in front of me with depressions in the center of each step, revealing how many thousands of students have traveled on it. The walls are paneled with dark wood, and, despite myself, I let my eyes drift up to the ceiling, several stories above. It has carvings I can't make out on its white surface.

It's an entrance designed to awe. I can relate to that.

"Sorry, do you want the admin office?" a small British voice asks.

I snap my eyes back down to find a girl as small as her voice looking at me like I might bite her.

"I just—you're the new girl? From the States?" she asks, tilting her head to one side as she considers me.

She's pretty, a blonde ringleted thing in a freshly ironed uniform. The kind who offers everyone genuine friendliness and is probably well liked. Someone I should engage with, not treat with disdain.

I focus on making my eyes light up as I smile widely at her and stick out my hand. "Yes, hi! I'm Vivian," I say. "And I have no idea where the admin office is."

She beams back at me, her smile of perfect white teeth stretching even wider than mine. "I'm Claire. Come on, I'll show you." She beckons for me to follow her. "I think you're going to be my roommate?" she says as our footsteps echo down the hall. "Emily used to be, and since you're replacing her, I guess I have to give up my single."

Emily. So that's the name of the girl Mother got rid of so that I could take her spot a month into senior year.

I laugh along with my new roommate at her weak joke, and we stop in front of another heavy wooden door. Its top half is nearly covered by a gold medallion bearing the school's crest: a torch rising out of an open book. Above it, a marble plaque declares that this is the headmaster's office.

"Thanks, Claire. See you soon, I guess," I say before squaring my shoulders and pulling the door open by its oversized brass doorknob.

The room is bare except for a generic painting of a green hill on the back wall and a desk with an expensive laptop and carefully ordered piles of paper. The secretary, a woman with frizzy brown hair and bifocals, looks up sharply when I fling open the door. Her look only intensifies as she takes in my carefully disheveled appearance.

"Vivian Foster."

I nod. My last name was stolen from the father I never knew so that my name would be different from Mother's, though she's never told me what her name is. My fate has been planned since before my birth.

"Your skirt is too short," the secretary declares, looking me up and down again.

"Oh, is it?" I ask, feigning concern as I look down at my skirt. "I measured it to make sure it would comply with the dress code, two inches above the knee." I look back at her with horrified pleading in my eyes, hoping she's the forgiving type.

She purses her lips. Not so forgiving, then.

I straighten, examining her. "Should I get my schedule from you?" I ask, my voice a tiny, meek thing.

The meekness doesn't seem to appease her. "The headmaster wants to meet you first." She's staring at me now like I'm a revolting bit of spoiled fish. I bite my lip, waiting until she finally sighs and presses something on her phone.

"Vivian Foster is here to see you."

"Send her in," a gruff voice orders.

The secretary cocks her head toward the headmaster's office, and I sail past her. It's time for the true performance.

I widen my eyes into those of a soft, uncertain little girl and walk into an office of dark carved wood and overflowing bookshelves. A bald man sits at a mahogany desk, hunched over a sheaf of papers. Mother drilled me over and over about him, so I know what to expect. George Harriford is forty-seven, divorced, no children. He dreams of being an author and has published a few insipid poems in journals no one has heard of. That sheaf of papers might even be his novel, the opus he's been working on for more than two decades. The one he's probably never going to finish. He loves Nabokov, red wine, and complaining about his ex-wife, though how Mother knows that, I have no idea.

"Sir?" I ask, my voice a whisper in this cold space.

He looks up, and his eyes take me in. I press my back against the door, sealing the room off from the prying ears of the secretary.

He gestures for me to sit in one of the red leather seats, and I sink into one, crossing my ankles primly and leaning forward to seem eager. My seat is rather low, and the desk and its occupant loom over me. A bronze bust of Nabokov, with his round face and piercing eyes, rests in one corner, and I feel as if I'm sitting in judgment.

"Miss Foster, I'm Headmaster Harriford. Welcome to Madigan School," he begins, his squinty brown eyes still locked on me. He's one of those men who is bald but shouldn't be—the bulge on the back of his head makes him look somewhat alien, and his forehead towers above his scrunched face.

"Thank you," I murmur, widening my smile. "It's kind of intimidating, but I think I'm going to like it here."

He rushes to assure me that I'll love it here, that I'll fit right in, that the students are ever so friendly. I smile at the appropriate moments and twist my hands together to show a nervousness that I no longer feel.

"I'm sure you're tired after traveling all night, yes?" he asks.

Though my head feels heavy and my eyes threaten to close, I shake my head. "I'd actually love to get to class and meet everyone," I say, filling my expression with hope and excitement. "I've missed a month already, and I don't want to miss anything else."

He laughs, utterly charmed. "That's the kind of enthusiasm we're looking for in students here at Madigan," he declares. "If you want to go, I won't stop you."

"Thank you so much, Headmaster Harriford." I bite my lip, as if my excitement is too much to contain. Really, I might be overdoing it. He seems to love it, though.

"Do you have any questions before you go?" he asks, folding his hands over the papers on his desk.

"Just one. Does Madigan have a creative writing club?"

He leans forward. "Are you a writer?" He imbues the word with a sense of reverence, and I smile inwardly.

I try my best to blush as I look down at my hands, but I don't know if I'm successful. "I'd like to be," I murmur. "Writing is one of my passions."

I sneak a glance up through my eyelashes to find him beaming at me. "Well, we have a literary magazine, *Open Doors*, that's very well respected. You can ask Ms. Prisby, your English teacher, about joining. They would love to have you."

"Thank you, Headmaster Harriford."

He glances at the grandfather clock ticking away in the corner, its face painted with the school crest. "You'd better hurry if you want to make your first class. Ask any of the students the way—we're very friendly here at Madigan, as I told you. And if you ever have any questions or concerns, you'll come speak to me, yes?"

I nod, smiling. "I will."

He sends me back out to the prissy secretary, who sniffs as she hands me the schedule I requested earlier. "You only have a few minutes until the bell," she declares. "You'd better hurry. Tardiness is not acceptable at Madigan."

"What should I do with my bags?" I ask, gesturing at the duffels I left in the corner.

"Leave them be. I'll watch over them until the end of the day, when your roommate will show you to your room."

I do my best to smile politely at her sneer and head out into the hall. Wooden lockers line the walls, most of them covered with brightly colored signs proclaiming "Go #42!" or the like. Books and papers spill out of every crack, and the marble floor gleams in the bright golden light from the large crystal chandeliers hanging from the ceiling and the ornate sconces on the wall. I hold my head high and make my way through this swarming hive of red plaid and shouts and laughter, searching for room 211, where my first class will be: history with Dr. Thompson.

I needed to pick three or four subjects to study at Madigan, since I enter as a sixth former and have to take A-levels at the end of the year. Mother picked English literature for me first, then rounded it out with history and psychology, reasoning that those were the fields I had the most knowledge in and wouldn't need to spend too much time on.

"You need help?" someone asks as I sidestep sharp elbows and overstuffed book bags. A boy, of course.

I look at him, taking him in with a brief glance. Dull brown eyes, cocky smile. Popular, clearly. It's in the way he holds himself, feet planted apart as if he wants to take up as much space as possible.

"Where's room 211?" I ask, my tone curt and unfriendly.

"You know, I don't like giving directions to pretty girls whose names I don't know."

I refuse to play along. "Look, you can help me, or you can get out of my way."

His cocky smile fades a bit, and he looks at me with even more interest. "One floor up, take a left, third room on the right."

I push past him without a word. I hope I've made him curious, because if he's curious, he'll talk about me.

I make it to 211 just as the bell rings and the hallways empty out. I stand for a moment in the doorway as everyone stares. Dr. Thompson, a grizzled man in his late sixties, nods at me. "Vivian Foster, everyone. Introduce yourselves individually later. Vivian, sit down in the front here next to Claire."

The blonde girl from earlier, my new roommate, waves at me, smiling hopefully as I slide into the wrought-iron desk next to hers, its wooden surface polished and shiny. I learned last year that only overachievers sit in the front row. It looks like I pegged Claire in the right slot.

The class is studying the Italian Renaissance, something I know plenty about. Lucrezia Borgia is one of Mother's role models, and I learned everything about her world as a consequence. She was the illegitimate daughter of a pope, and it's rumored that she poisoned those who got in her powerful family's way.

I remember Mother telling me about her and all of the terrible things that she supposedly did. "She did what she could for her family. Nothing is more important than family," Mother said, concluding the lesson. She rested a hand lightly on my shoulder, and there was almost something like a smile on her face as she looked into my eyes. I find myself nodding at the memory. You have to do whatever you can for your family. It's the only thing that matters in this world. It's the only bond that lasts.

I zone out, and my eyelids grow heavy. I jab my pen into the palm of my hand every few minutes to stay awake until the bell finally rings and I can head to English literature.

Which is much more interesting. Because it's there that I first see him.

CHAPTER 2

I notice him almost as soon as I walk into the room. He sits in the back of the classroom with the other confident kids, and his golden popularity shines through every pore. He wears the required boys' uniform: gray slacks, white shirt, black blazer with the school crest on its lapel, and red and black plaid tie. His tie is loosened and his shirt is wrinkled, but somehow he looks more insouciant than sloppy. He leans back in his chair like a king on his throne with an easy, self-assured smile. As soon as I spot him, it's as if the whole room starts spinning, revolving around him. Everyone's waiting to see what he'll do next. He is the center of everything.

I feel my breath stutter in my chest, and I know this is the beginning.

I only let myself glance at him, my eyes slithering over him in an open show of indifference as I sink into a chair in the middle of the room. I turn my back toward him coldly, hoping he notices.

My pulse races, ripping through my skin. My breathing grows shallower, and I take a few deep breaths to regulate it. I keep my spine straight and proud and focus my attention on the twenty-something woman at the front of the class.

"Who's the new girl?" a boy—him?—asks behind me.

Another boy laughs. "No idea, mate. She'd look good in my bed, though."

The first boy, the boy who has to be him, answers with a hefty dose of disgust. "Try not to be such a wanker all the time, Liam."

I cling to that, the voice of the boy who has drawn me to him.

The teacher, Ms. Prisby, clears her throat. "All right, everyone, we've got a new student. Vivian Foster, yeah?"

I nod slightly.

"Well, good, then. I'm sure we'll do our very best to welcome you to Madigan. We've been reading Tennyson's 'The Lady of Shalott.' Have you read it?"

"Yes." Of course I have. Mother made sure I read everything on the syllabus before I got here. But I knew this poem long before that, and the story behind it. In the poem, the lady will be cursed if she looks down on Camelot, so she spends her days weaving a tapestry and watching a magic mirror that shows her events of the world outside. It's only when she sees Lancelot in that mirror and hears his voice below her tower that she looks down, and in doing so, she has to sacrifice her own life, putting herself in a boat that carries her dead body down to Camelot. When she's found, all Lancelot says about her is "She has a lovely face."

The Arthurian legend the poem is probably based on is even more pathetic. Elaine of Astolat develops a crush on Lancelot, nursing him after he's injured in a tournament. But his heart belongs to Guinevere, and he leaves Elaine, who is so distraught that she boards a boat and dies of a broken heart. The ending is much the same, with Lancelot simply paying for her funeral. Hardly caring about her at all.

Ms. Prisby's voice calls me back to the present. "Then you can jump right in." She offers me a smile briefly, before it falters under the weight of my disdain, the disdain that only she can see. She looks back at her book, suddenly unsure. She's young, not much older than I am. She's almost too easy a mark.

"Right, well, we're looking at the theme of art in isolation versus art that confronts the real world," she says, continuing on to point out that the lady creates a wonderful tapestry when alone, but once she looks down to Camelot, her loom breaks, and all of her artistic talent is forfeited.

I keep my head down, scribbling nonsense in my notebook and trying to sort out my first impressions of the boy and what his first impressions of me might be.

He has light blond hair that curls slightly at the ends, making him look boyish. His eyes are warm and brown-green and observant. His jaw is square and firm. He's attractive, the kind of boy teenage girls hang posters of in their rooms.

And he's noticed me. He's maybe even already attracted to me, or maybe he just doesn't like the way his friend speaks about women. I'm not yet different enough from the girls who must throw themselves at him daily.

As soon as the bell rings, the other kids jump out of their chairs and dive into the hall. It's the last class before lunch, and everyone seems to be in a hurry to eat.

I take my time, gathering my notebook and stretching my long legs before standing up. The boy and his cronies are taking their time, too, watching me.

When he walks up beside me before I reach the door, I'm prepared.

"Hey," he says, placing a strong hand on my shoulder to stop me. "I'm Ben."

I turn to find him beaming a wide, confident smile at me. He's a bit taller than I am and much broader, with the body of an athlete. His nose is crooked, as if it's been broken before.

Probably playing sports; he seems too affable and easygoing to get in a fistfight. There's no coiled spring behind his eyes, the sure sign of a hothead.

I expect him to let those hazel eyes drift down and back up my body, but he doesn't. He keeps them on mine. "I know it, uh, has to be difficult being the new girl, but I wanted to offer my help. You know, if you have questions or anything."

I raise my eyebrows, trying not to show how my thoughts are scrambling. I thought he would be cocky, maybe give me a pick-up line, something I could decline with derision to show how different I am. To make him want me even more.

I can't reject him, not when he's being kind and considerate. And I can't fall all over him. So I take a gamble, tucking a strand of my hair behind my ear in a show of self-consciousness. "Thanks," I say, my voice small and shy, before turning and hurrying out the door.

I spend lunch exploring the main building, too tired to face a room full of my peers. The dining hall, a few lockers, and the administration offices that I visited earlier take up the first floor. The next four floors are made up of unending hallways of sameness: lockers and classroom doors and slightly scuffed floors.

I head for the top story, hoping for a view. For a new perspective on this place I've come to. And I'm not disappointed.

There are a few classrooms up here, but almost half of the floor is taken up by a room with a marble sign above the doorway, the words "Student Lounge" carved into it. I peek in and see only a couple of girls reading in armchairs in one corner, so I walk inside. I throw the girls polite but uninterested smiles and head for the wall of windows opposite.

I can see the whole of the hilltop below, with three large gray stone buildings that form a quadrangle with this one, a courtyard in the middle. The courtyard is cluttered with wrought-iron benches and gas lampposts and a few ornamental trees. They stand stubby and straight, but only because there are ropes on each side of them tying them to the ground. Otherwise, I'm sure they would be like the trees I saw on the way in: curved and bent, but not yet defeated by the force of the wind.

I can't see much beyond the high stone wall that surrounds the campus, though the fog from this morning has dissipated a bit. Up here it feels as if I'm in a dome, as if I'm cut off from the world outside. I watch a few students meander along the courtyard paths, flickering in and out of sight beneath the branches of the trees below, but I'm too high up to recognize any of them from the bustling halls. I wish I had a pencil and paper so I could draw them, show them as they really are. They are mere ants, waiting to be stepped on.

A giggle from one of the girls behind me breaks me from my reverie, but when I look back, she's pointing to something in her book, sharing a harmless joke with her friend.

The rest of the lounge is like an overgrown living room, muddled with brown leather couches, overstuffed armchairs, a few dark wooden tables, and tall brass lamps. The walls are lined with rich crimson wallpaper, and a thick golden-hued carpet covers the floor. A daunting stone fireplace takes up most of one wall, a fire crackling in its mouth. I examine the books in the low bookshelves that line one of the walls, dragging a finger along their cracked spines. There are beautiful volumes by Dickens and the Brontë sisters and Shakespeare and the like. Yearbooks dating back to 1947 rest on the bottom shelf.

I take one last look at the room before I have to head to psychology. If I had that pencil and paper, I would sketch the air here, the feeling of this place. It is warmth and ease and the sharp scent of money.

After I suffer through psychology, where the teacher drones on about human behavior experiments I already know, I go back to the administration office to find Claire waiting with my bags.

"I was right," she says brightly when she sees me. "You *are* my new roommate."

I nod, forcing a smile onto my face.

Claire picks up one of my bags, the heavier one. "Come on," she says, "I'll show you our room, roomie." She nudges my arm, inviting me to laugh along with her.

I follow her with the lighter bag through the wood-and-marble hallways to the back entrance of the school. We step out into the chilly early October air, and I look for the details that I missed from my vantage point in the lounge. The hilltop the school sits on is not very wide, and it's covered in short brown grass and mud that squelches underneath our shoes. The side-walks between the buildings are red cobblestone, with large gaps between the bricks and a healthy covering of mud. The gas lamps lining the walk are already lit, their flames dancing in glass cages.

"Boys' house," Claire says, pointing to the building on the left, which has the name Rawlings Hall etched over its small portico. "And our house." She points to the one on the right, Faraday Hall. Both are built from the same rough-cut gray stone blocks that make up the main building, with ivy grasping onto their sides, reaching nearly up to the top floors. Ebony-trimmed windowpanes peek out through the ivy, several of them glowing with soft lamplight.

The building directly opposite us completes the quadrangle. It's almost as large as the main building, with a set of wide stone steps leading up to a pair of wooden doors that seem much too large for one person to open by herself. Ornate Corinthian columns line the porch that spans the entire front of the building, and I realize that it's the only structure on campus that is untouched by ivy. It's too grand to be covered. "Canton Library," Claire says, noticing my gaze. She stops in the middle of the courtyard, forcing everyone else to stream past us. "Madigan has one of the most extensive book collections of any secondary school in England. Canton is a good place to study."

I nod and hitch the duffel bag from my hand to my shoulder.

Everything is clustered together on top of this hill. It doesn't seem enough space for the hundreds of students and teachers who live and work here. When I remember that just beyond the rough gray stones of the ten-foot wall surrounding us there are brown moors stretching for miles, the tightness in my chest loosens.

"The playing fields are down at the bottom of the hill off the right side, closest to our house, out the back gate," she tells me. "What sports do you play?"

"None," I answer. Mother got me out of Madigan's athletic requirement by telling the administrators something about a heart condition. "I'm not really a sporty person."

"I play lacrosse in the summer term, but I work for the news-paper this term," Claire offers, her voice rising at the end to make it more of a question, the way most of her sentences end. It's like she wants to make sure what's she saying is acceptable.

I nod as if I'm interested, but say nothing, and we remain silent as we cross the rest of the yard.

We enter Faraday, my new home. As soon as we set foot on the worn brown wood floors, I hear a symphony of girls' laughs and shouts and conversations. The hallways are dim, their navy-wallpapered walls lit mostly by the lights shining from the open doors of the bedrooms. Girls tumble in and out of these rooms, everyone friendly and happy. Most have changed out of their uniforms now that the school day is over, and though some are in sweatshirts, most have covered themselves in skinny jeans and soft cashmere and wool sweaters or brightly colored silk tops. They dance by us like exotic birds, leaving us in clouds of their cloying perfumes, most of them smiling at Claire and offering me a tentative "Hi."

I take a deep breath and pretend this is all normal for me.

Claire leads me to a room on the second floor. It's small, more of a closet than a proper room, with two truncated beds shoved into it. One tiny desk faces the window, while the other faces a blank wall. I toss my bags on the bed that's not covered by an explosion of pink. "I took the desk by the window?" Claire says behind me, her voice vibrating with nervousness. "It used to be Emily's. If you want it . . ." Her voice trails off.

"The other's fine," I chirp, putting my hands on my hips and looking around the room with a smile as if it pleases me. I don't look at Claire. I don't want to see the emotions passing across her face. She's so open, so vulnerable. Ready to be eaten alive.

"I'll introduce you to Mrs. Hallie, then," Claire says, her default brightness restored, walking out of the room before I can answer.

Mrs. Hallie, the housemother, is a plump, gray-haired woman who wraps her arms around me as soon as I meet her, and I bite my lip and force myself not to push her away. I learned at public school last year that I'm not very good at enduring hugs. This embrace lasts an interminably long time, until she finally gives me one last squeeze and lets me go. "You're just going to love it here!" she declares as she shows me the bedding and other necessities Mother shipped for me.

Claire grins and heads back down the hallway, leaving me alone with Mrs. Hallie, who tells me the house rules, all of which I already know: No drinking, smoking, or boys, ever. Curfew at nine on weekdays, midnight on Fridays and Saturdays. The gates to the playing fields are locked every evening at seven, and all other gates to the outside are locked at all times unless a student is given special permission to leave by a faculty member. Internet is shut off promptly at ten o'clock each night. She explains that there's no cell reception in this part of the country unless you're very lucky, so there are landlines set up in each hallway. "With international plans, dear, so you can call your mother whenever you like," she says.

I keep smiling and pretending to care until this interview is over and I can retreat to my room with my boxes.

Claire and the rest of the chattering girls have disappeared to their afternoon activities. After that they'll go to dinner, and then the library to do homework, which the teachers pile high onto all of us. I shove the textbooks Mother bought me in the corner of the room and concentrate on unpacking and transforming myself. I find a box of cereal among Claire's things and munch on that for dinner.

I think about Ben, replaying the conversation we had after English class. And an image begins forming in my mind. I start by taking out my black eyeliner and defining my eyes even more, until their blueness is electric. I tear holes in my tights and rip stitches in my skirt to make the seams and hem even more jagged. My only school shoes are a pair of ballet flats, but I use red nail polish to scribble lines of poetry on their gold surface, the chemical scent eclipsing the faint floral perfume that permeates the air from Claire's side of the room. When it's dried, the lines of my favorite Catullus poem are scrawled around the sides of both shoes.

Odi et amo. Quare id faciam, fortasse requiris?
Nescio, sed fieri sentio et excrucior.

There. Everything about me reflects a passionate, tortured soul, in need of saving.

I'm setting up my desk lamp when Claire comes back. Her ringlets seem deflated, as if the long hours in the library sapped some of her blonde energy.

"Hey," I say with a soft smile and an uncertain voice.

Claire smiles at me, raising an eyebrow as she takes in my new black-rimmed eyes. She notices the open box of cereal on my side of the floor, too, but says nothing.

"How much homework did you get done?" I ask, approximating a sincere tone.

"Not nearly enough," Claire says with a dramatic sigh, flopping onto her pink marshmallow bed. "I swear, they're being bloody sadistic this year. Did you do that history reading? We're supposed to learn about a hundred years in one night."

"Haven't started," I admit. "Is it that bad?"

She nods, then smiles. "The teachers will probably give you a little leeway for a few days, since you're a new student and all that? But they're pretty demanding, just to warn you."

"I'll get it done." Mother taught me speed-reading almost as soon as I learned to read. My time is meant for more important things than homework.

"Can I ask you something?" Claire says, tilting her head in that observant way she has, her eyes intently absorbing me.

I steel myself. "Sure."

"Why did you come a month into the year? Wouldn't it have been easier to finish it out back home?"

I shrug, bending to plug in the lamp. "I've been on the waitlist for a long time. When this spot opened up, I couldn't pass on it."

"What about university? Have you already applied?"

"I'm applying to places in the States," I lie. Mother told the administration that I would be using a college counselor in New York for all of my college applications. Hopefully no one here will notice that I won't actually be applying anywhere. "I'm not really worried about it."

I can feel Claire freeze up behind me. "You're not really worried about it?" she repeats. "And your parents are okay with that? Mine would chain me up and torture me if I didn't get into Oxford or Cambridge."

"My mother doesn't care," I say. My tone is clipped, and she takes the hint.

"Well," she says, bouncing off the bed and rummaging in one of her dresser drawers. "I'm going to take a shower. The bathroom's at the end of the hall, and it's for the whole half of this floor, so there are thirty of us sharing it. It can get rather crowded at night and in the morning."

I offer up a smile. "Thanks for letting me know."

As soon as she's gone and I'm alone in the room, I sit on my hard bed and rub my temples.

Before I can decide what I should do now, someone knocks on the door. I open it to find an unfamiliar brunette girl with a pixie cut and a bored expression. "You're Vivian?" she asks, her tone matching her expression perfectly.

I nod.

"Your mum's on the phone for you," she says before walking away.

I peek out into the hallway and notice a monstrously large black phone on the wall. I walk to it slowly and close my eyes as I pick up the receiver. "Hello, Mother."

"You were supposed to call as soon as you arrived." Her harsh, icicle-laden tree branch of a voice crosses the Atlantic as clearly as if she were standing next to me, her cold gray eyes staring into mine with an almost tangible distaste. I can picture her face so clearly: the porcelain skin, with only the faintest hints of lines at the edges of her eyes and wide, thin-lipped mouth. The heart-shaped mole on her cheek. The prematurely gray hair curling at her forehead.

"I had no time alone," I say. "The hallway has been crowded."
I wince at the lie.

"Then you should have figured out a way to get some privacy.
You know the rules." She speaks slowly, deliberate as always, her
brutal words seeping through the telephone line.

Her reproach is a birch switch on my back. "Yes, Mother."

"The report?"

I hold my head up, trying to overcome the lump forming in
my throat. I've disappointed her, and I hate myself for it.

"Everything's going great here!" I say brightly. There's no one
in the hallway, but I've already discovered how thin the doors
and walls are, and I want to sound like a normal girl giving her
doting mother her first impressions of her new school. My voice
in its feigned cheerfulness bounces around the navy walls. "My
roommate is really sweet, and I think we'll get along great. And
there was this very cute boy in English class." I say this last sentence more quietly, though it's innocuous enough.

"Your impression of him?"

"Popular and cute. I'm sure he's got lots of girls swooning
over him already. He seems very nice, though. Kind."

"What is your plan?"

I laugh, a laugh that is high-pitched and clearly fake. I cut
it off quickly. "Oh, I remember what you told me, Mom. But I
think I might be a bit more vulnerable than you think I am."

"Fine. Play the vulnerable girl if you think it will work on him. As long as you are sure. If you are wrong, it could cost us everything. Remember, I want email updates every night and a phone call every Sunday. No exceptions."

"Of course, Mom," I say, as if the lump in my throat is not growing larger.

She clicks off before I can say anything else, and I dock the receiver back in its cradle.

A hundred memories press down on me, and I stumble back to my room, sitting on the bed and closing my eyes tightly, hoping to push the unbidden recollections away. Still, these images of my mother flying into a rage crowd my thoughts. If I ever made even a whisper of a mistake, she would be overcome with anger so startling and violent that it would leave her almost incoherent. And it would leave me cowering in the corner of the room.

I'm still struggling to control my breath when Claire comes back in pink cotton pajamas and a towel wrapped around her head. It makes her light brown eyes seem even larger, like the open, trusting eyes of a baby doll.

I focus on that weakness and let a mask of nonchalance fall over my face. "I guess I should follow your example," I say, getting up off my bed and hunting for my shampoo and towel.

I let the hot water in one of the old marble showers ease the stress out of my shoulders, ignoring the long line of grumbling girls waiting for their turn. When I'm done, I saunter past their scowling faces with hardly a glance.

When I get back, Claire is on her laptop, hanging out with her Ava avatar. Her Ava, who has blonde hair in ringlets just like Claire's, is picking out an outfit for her from some online shop, showing her how to pair a mustard-yellow wool jacket with a brown tweed skirt. I start combing out my long hair in the mirror, glancing at Claire's reflection. "What's your Ava called?" I ask.

She meets my eyes in the mirror, startled. Then smiles. "I named her Victoria. After the queen, you know? Because she's so strong and independent?"

I nod, as if I find this fascinating. I don't understand the obsession with Ava avatars. But those digital dolls that you can install on your computer or phone have become increasingly popular since I was a kid, and Mother made sure to mention them to me in her lessons.

They serve many purposes. An Ava can model different outfits from shopping sites for you, showing you how to accessorize or the best poses to show off certain features. She can dispense advice about how to deal with bullies. She's programmed with a plethora of clichés and positive can-do spirit. Everything she says or does depends on which model you buy—there's an Ava for the glam girl, for the shy girl, for the lovelorn. A few years ago, they came out with a boy model so that shy boys could have best friends, too. They named him the Adam, which, though the name isn't as catchy, sold just as well.

But the most intriguing feature of these avatars is that they can have conversations with their human companions. The more you talk to your Ava, the more intelligent and custom-designed she becomes. Soon, she knows her companion's secrets and crushes and troubles and can tailor her questions and responses and suggestions accordingly. She mirrors her companion's attitude and becomes the best friend she ever had.

It's always struck me as a bit frightening.

"This is going to sound pathetic, but . . . I didn't have many friends in primary school," Claire explains, "so Victoria became my best friend. She taught me how to open myself up to people and be myself. I guess I'm too old to keep interacting with her, but she was just such a big part of my life, you know?"

"Sure," I say encouragingly.

"Do you have an Ava?"

I shake my head. Aside from the fact that Mother was never very good with computers, she's always hated Ava. She wanted me to interact with real people instead. Real people with secrets and facades and ulterior motives.

"You know there's a boy in our class whose father invented them? Ben Collingsworth?"

"Oh, really?" I say, as if this means nothing to me.

"Mm-hm." Claire focuses back on her computer. "Goodnight, Victoria," she says.

"Goodnight, Claire!" Victoria says with an impressive amount of enthusiasm and a British accent. "Sleep well, and remember that tomorrow is a brand-new day! I'm sure your new roommate will see how fantastic you are in no time!"

I try my best not to roll my eyes. "So you told her about me?"

A blush is already staining Claire's pale cheeks. "Yeah, I hope you don't mind? I tell her everything."

I smile a tight smile. "Of course I don't mind."

Later that night, I pull out my book of Tennyson's poetry and begin rereading it. Claire is lying on her stomach reading a biology textbook, taking notes and kicking her feet in the air. At ten o'clock we turn off the harsh fluorescent light and leave only our desk lamps on, which creates a warm, hazy-rose atmosphere.

Here in this room with Claire, I'm feeling something I can't quite define, but I think it's contentment. I snuggle in my sheets, pretending they're softer than the coarse, cheap cotton Mother sent, and dive into the familiar pages.

CHAPTER 3

I must have fallen asleep, because the next thing I know, I'm startled by some kind of rustling noise, followed by a decisive bang.

"Claire?" I ask, pushing my way out from under the covers. "What's going on?"

"Come on!" she calls. "Put your coat on. You're going to miss it!"

I sit up to find her throwing on a pink coat and rubber boots, her eyes shining in the moonlight.

"Just trust me," she says.

I nearly laugh at that but keep my lips pursed tightly together. I throw the covers off, intrigued, and follow her example, pulling a thin black coat over my white cotton top and black pajama pants. I add a slash of red lipstick, just in case, before

Claire ushers me out of the room, a finger to her lips. We tiptoe down the hall to the top of the worn wooden staircase, where a group of seven girls have gathered, crouching and cautious in the moonlight streaming in from the windows. Their faces are pale and shadowed, almost ghoulish, and I swallow a lump in my throat before Claire pushes me forward into them.

"What are we doing?" I whisper. My knee presses against the molding of the wall, painfully, as Claire shoves me back before I can peer down to the bottom of the stairs. Someone steps on my foot, but I can't turn my head to see who did it.

"Jenkins guards the halls at night," a girl I don't know says into my ear. "But she goes out for a smoke break every night at midnight and again at three. So we have a window."

I give her a slight nod to show that I understand.

There's a creaking below, and everyone tenses. Then footsteps. A woman, stocky and short, materializes. I can see only her back. She heads for the front door, twisting the knob. Then she's outside, and the door is closing softly behind her.

At once, everything is motion. We all patter down the stairs, taking a sharp right at the bottom and heading for a door in the back. Then we're outside and scurrying to the stone wall. The girls line up in front of me, each of them placing their hands and feet in the same well-worn spots as they climb up and over the wall. Claire points the footholds out to me, and I'm soon sitting on the top, staring out at the wide expanse of the moors beyond. The other girls have already clambered gingerly down the other side, but I leap down, landing in a crouch in the mud at the bottom.

We all sprint down the hill. The moon flickers in and out of the clouds, creating vanishing pools of light. The tall wet grass lashes against my ankles, left vulnerable by my tennis shoes. I'll have to buy rubber boots like Claire's. The valley below is bare, open to the eyes of the school, but up another hill and into another valley, we are hidden. And we nearly run over a group of a dozen guys.

"You made it!" one calls as we catch our breath.

I look around me, at the girls whose group I've somehow joined. We're a coterie of pajamas and coats and broad smiles. Electric lanterns, the kind used for storms, light the scene, and the light they give off is harsh and white. Many of the girls drop onto the towels the boys have laid out, and I turn to find Ben standing next to me. I nearly recoil.

"Hallo, Viv."

I do flinch at that. Only one person has ever called me Viv. Only one person is allowed to. I resist the urge to correct him, and glance down to the ground, hoping to look flustered. When I look back up at him, I make myself stare at him like he's a puzzle I'm trying to figure out. He reflects that same look back at me, and for a moment, we stand there staring at each other. "Hi," I say, hardly more than a whisper, settling down on the nearest swath of towel. The wet ground seeps through it unpleasantly, but I remain still, my head now bent away from his.

I can feel him stand next to me for a moment, the air around him swirling in confusion, before he moves to sit with his friends across from me.

I learn from snippets of conversation around me that, for some of these kids, this is an almost nightly ritual. They sneak out here to gather for gossip and alcohol and other illicit activities when the boys' house guard goes out to meet Jenkins at midnight for a nightly smoke break.

"And then he's always checking the bathroom from three to four," a friendly, dark-haired boy tells me with a snort, leaning much too far into my personal space. There's some thread of a joke that I can't quite catch, and I don't bother to. I just glance at him, as if I don't understand why he's talking to me.

The girl next to me, who would be pretty if not for her over-pronounced nose, introduces herself as Arabella. She has shucked off her coat and sits in nothing but pink silk shorts and a tank top, her freckled skin rising in goose bumps in the cool air. Someone should have told her that redheads shouldn't wear pink—her face is washed out by the bright color contrast. But by the way the boys and girls buzz around her, I know she's important. Maybe even the queen bee. "I need to paint my nails neon. Something noticeable, yeah? My Ava recommended it." This is met with a chorus of nodding heads. As is "Meggie is such a slag. Right? She'll flirt with anything that walks past her."

Then, later into the night, she turns to me and says, "New girl." Her words meld together as if her tongue has grown too large for her mouth. "I don't know you, but I think I could make a project out of you. If you looked not so—like, *severe*, you would be . . . brilliant, you know?"

I just nod and roll my eyes. She somehow takes this as encouragement and hugs me close to her with one arm.

I stiffen and pull away as soon as I can.

The whole night, as a cloud settles over us—a mixture of fog and cigarette smoke—I pretend to take long pulls from the bottle of rum being passed around and let the boredom show on my face. I'd inadvertently joined a three-hour session of sitting on damp ground, getting drunk, and flirting.

I keep my eyes firmly pointed away from Ben but still try to keep track of his every move. He smokes a joint with his friends but declines the pills being passed around. I listen to his laughter and to the unsubtle attempts of several girls trying to flirt with him.

There's one girl, though, who plays it a bit smarter than the others, and I'm soon watching her closely. She has long reams of golden hair cascading down her back, which she tosses and twirls in elegant coils with her fingers. She smiles knowing smiles at Ben whenever anyone around them makes a joke, and she keeps making a point of passing him the joint she's just taken a hit from.

Her efforts pay off toward the end of the night, when she rises and totters to him a touch unsteadily. Then she falls, gracefully, landing neatly in his lap with her arm slung around his shoulders. He looks amused but not surprised to see her there, and when she lifts her lips to his, he complies. But only for a moment. He pulls away with a friendly smile and pats her on the back. Then he looks up. He looks for me. I let him catch me staring.

The coat Mother sent me here with is too thin, and without the warmth of alcohol, I'm shivering. I hug my knees closer to my chest and bury my face in them, breaking my eye contact with Ben. I open my mouth a touch to keep my teeth from chattering and take a few warming breaths.

Suddenly, something heavy is covering my shoulders, settling around me. I twist my neck up to see that Ben has covered me with his coat. He looks down at me, his hazel eyes pale in the moonlight, with nothing but a long-sleeved gray tee and navy pajama bottoms on. The tee is molded to a chest that has more muscles than I would have predicted. I snap my eyes back to his.

"Thank you," I say softly.

The expression in his eyes is full of something so soft that it takes my breath away.

Our gazes stay locked for a long moment, until finally he nods and steps back. Without a word, he returns to his friends. Everyone is watching us, some more openly than others. Arabella stares at me with an undisguised look of confusion and distrust, and the girl who has been deposed from Ben's lap is glaring at me with such intense hatred that I half expect my skin will start boiling.

I pull Ben's coat closer to me. It smells of the sticky sweetness of his joint, but also something spicy, like cologne or shampoo. I have to stifle a sneeze.

Then the pointless conversation of a wasted night resumes around me.

After a while, when I'm sure it must be time to go back to the dorms, the dark-haired boy from earlier nudges my shoulder. "Pretty boring, huh?" he whispers into my ear, his breath reeking of alcohol.

I shrug at him. I haven't talked to this boy much tonight, but I've learned that the others call him G-Man and slap him on the back, laughing heartily at his frequent jokes. He seems pretty popular, though his face is too tiny for his head and his ears stick out.

"I've got something that will make it more fun for you, if

you'd like." He opens his hand beneath my gaze, revealing two small white pills on his palm. And suddenly his popularity makes sense.

I snap my eyes to his. "What are they?" I ask, breathless and feminine, as if I don't know.

"Molly."

The version of Ecstasy that's so popular at ritzy boarding schools. Perfect. I open my hand for him to drop those little illicit pills into. "I think I'll save them for a rainy day," I murmur, letting my arm brush against his. I lean even closer to him, my breath caressing his ear as I whisper, "Can I come to you for more?"

He looks into my eyes, suspicion touching his gaze. But I give him my most innocent, admiring expression and watch as the suspicion fades. "I'm your guy," he says, his voice artificially low. "I've got anything you could need: Adderall, Oxy, name it. Everything to make boarding school in the middle of fucking nowhere bearable."

I beam at him and settle back. Across the circle, Ben is watching me. I wonder what he thinks of me, though it's easy enough to read the curiosity in his eyes.

Finally, everyone checks their watches and stands up, gathering the soaked towels and laughing their last laughs. It's time for the next covert operation.

I walk slowly to Ben, shrugging his coat off of my shoulders and holding it out to him. I say nothing as he takes it, but I meet his eyes, letting my gaze linger there. He nods, pulling the coat on over his snug T-shirt, and I bite my lip as I turn away and follow the crowd.

The boys turn the storm lanterns off, so we are shrouded once more in darkness, the moon now secreted away behind a cloud. The fog has grown thicker than I thought, and I stumble forward, trying to keep up with the group of whispering girls in front of me. I feel as if I would disappear if I lost them and become swallowed up by this strange place.

As we climb the hill to the back of the school, our figures cutting through the fog, a tall, dark figure begins to take shape above us. It's not until we can almost touch it that I realize it's a person. A few girls squeak as they catch sight of the shadow, until a young guy steps out into a sudden patch of moonlight. Then everyone around me relaxes.

He stands in front of me. Broad shoulders and tousled dark hair. I can make out the chiseled cheekbones and square jaw in the pale moonlight. Something about him—there is something . . . .

Arabella pulls me past him just as I'm opening my mouth to say something to him. I swivel my head to keep my eyes on his, and his follow me. Those eyes. They are the darkest and deepest ones, the ones that know how to see the insides of my soul.

"We don't speak to the help, silly," Arabella tells me while we're still in earshot. I wince for him.

The fog has now cloaked him behind us, as if he were never there at all. "Who is he?" I ask, when breath returns to my body. Though I know. I already know.

"Just Tom, the gardener. He's fit, yeah, but not socially acceptable. It'd be death to your reputation if you dated him."

It can't be. It can't be him.

But it is. I saw it in his eyes.

We make it over the wall and into the building just as Jenkins steps out for her second nightly vice and creep into our rooms.

"Wasn't that brilliant?" Claire asks, her eyes shining brightly. She stumbles a bit as she crashes toward her bed.

I nod. Nothing will come out of my throat.

As soon as Claire stops babbling and snaps her light off, I burrow into the covers, my eyes wide open. All I can see is him. Boy. The only person allowed to call me Viv. The one who used to be my only friend in the world.

CHAPTER 4

I don't fall asleep until just before dawn, but my dreams swirl with him.

I haven't seen him since I was fourteen. But now he's here. He found me in the dark corners of the night and stared into my soul with those eyes. How can he be here?

I can't focus on anything all day. I drift through my classes, enduring people's stares and attempts at friendliness.

I tell Claire I'll meet her for lunch in the dining hall, but as soon as the midday bell rings, I hurry out into the open air. I see the gardener's shed just behind Rawlings: a shack made of wide wood planks with one smudged window, which must be where he lives. I find him standing outside it, just as I knew I would. He's waiting for me.

My eyes catch his as soon as I have him in sight.

As I walk hesitantly toward him, I let myself examine his face: so strange and so familiar, all in one stroke. The high cheekbones, the warm skin, the sinfully long lashes—all features he inherited from a Native American mother who left him with his father when he was four years old.

Now he's beautiful and terrifying all at once. And he's older, of course. Bigger, stronger, and more world-weary, somehow. He wears jeans and a black jacket that matches the raven black of his hair, even darker than my own. He stands with his feet planted firmly, waiting for me to come to him. Like I'm prey that he's luring.

"Why are you here?" I ask once I stand before him.

At the sound of my voice, there's a flash of something in his eyes. Something like pain. "I knew that your mother would send you here to find him. I got this job a couple of years ago." He's watching me so closely. "I was waiting for you."

It takes a worrisome amount of strength for me to turn my face away, but once I manage to, I scan the windows of Rawlings Hall, making sure no one is looking out at us. "You've come to stop me?" I ask softly.

"Yes." His voice is lower than the last time I heard it. And more powerful. He must be twenty now, and a man.

I bite my lip. "You can't. I'm a weapon." He knows this. He knows everything about me. Just as I thought I knew everything about him. I'm the one who gave him his name, after all.

Boy, or so Mother called him, was the son of the man who always helped Mother. Helper, as I named him in my head, had been attached to Mother since as long as I could remember. I used to think he was my father, actually, but when I called him that, Mother laughed her winter chill laugh and declared me an idiot.

Boy and his father lived in the guesthouse in our backyard. Boy was three years older than me but never went to school. I taught him how to read and write as I learned it, but we had to do it secretly. Mother had forbidden it. Boy was her servant, was made to cook meals and take care of the house and the yard.

Helper was used for other things that I never quite comprehended. He would often be gone for weeks at a time, coming home to enclose himself in a room with Mother and have whispered conversations.

Eventually I came to understand that Helper was part of Mother's plan and was the only man she ever trusted. Their relationship was a strange one, filled with silent glances and mystifying words. It was as if they spoke a different language, one I had no hope of deciphering. Helper never smiled. I took that as a warning.

When we were young, maybe around nine and twelve, Boy and I changed his name to Arthur. But it was a secret, something to whisper and guard. We decided on it when I told him the origin of my own name.

"Vivian is one of the names of the Lady of the Lake in the stories about King Arthur," I recited as Mother had taught me. "But it's also sometimes what they called the enchantress who destroyed the greatest sorcerer of all, Merlin. That's the Vivian I'm named for. Merlin fell in love with her and told her all of his secrets, revealed all of his magic. She used it to weaken him and trap him in a tree."

"She sounds cruel," Boy said. We were in our usual hiding spot behind his guesthouse. Boy leaned against the fence, crossing his arms as he watched me. I remember the smell of the soil and the first buds of the gardenias that Mother loved, their perfumed scent waxing and waning with the breeze.

"She's as cruel as I'm meant to be," I said, shrugging my shoulders. "Mother always says that all's fair in love and war." She would say it with perfect bitterness, spitting the words out with a vehemence I didn't understand.

Boy's deep brown eyes watched me. "I have no name," he pointed out. "I have no example to follow."

"Whose example do you want to follow?"

He stopped, considering that. He looked down at his hands, the lines in his palms caked with dirt, then looked back up, his face bright and hopeful. "Someone strong. And brave. And nice."

"You should be a leader," I told him. "You should be Arthur." Arthur, I explained, was the king of Britain and the flower of chivalry. He represented everything that was good and true.

All men were evil if you didn't control them completely, as Mother controlled Helper. I knew that, even then.

But I couldn't quite put Boy in that category. Boy wasn't the enemy. The enemy wouldn't sneak flowers from the garden into my room because he knew I liked the way they lit up the gloom. The enemy wouldn't smile with such pure joy when he finally read a paragraph out loud without stumbling over the words. The enemy wouldn't be the one bright bolt of light in my world.

"Arthur," Boy repeated, savoring it.

And from then on, the name was his.

Now, at Madigan, he crouches down a bit to look me in the eye. He's searching for something, but I don't know if he can find it anymore. "What has she told you about any of this? Has she told you *why* you're supposed to ruin his life?"

"I told you everything. You know everything I know." I snap my lips back together to stop the stream of words that threaten to come pouring out.

"I want to hear you explain it now that you've met him. I want you to say it out loud."

I shouldn't play along with his game. But he's the boy who

always understood me. I want to make him understand me now. So I begin at the beginning. "Ben's father, William Collingsworth, broke Mother's heart. He was her first love, and he used her. He drew her into his world when they were teenagers and then just pushed her out of it when he found some other girl. Mother went back to New York, to the city. She was heartbroken and desperate, so she tried to lose herself in the crowds, in whatever made her feel less alone. When she got pregnant from some worthless one-night stand, I was the only thing she had. Her father had died when she was little, and then her mother died in a car accident, leaving her the house upstate but almost nothing else."

He bites the inside of his lip as if he wants to say something, but decides not to, taking a deep breath. Instead, he asks, "But why *couldn't* she have been happy? Why couldn't she have found a job, raised you, lived a normal life?"

I stare at him, at his furrowed brow and piercing brown eyes. He doesn't understand at all.

"Don't you see how twisted she is?" he continues, his voice wavering somewhere between desperation and amusement. "How insane?"

I step back from him. "She deserves her revenge. He broke her heart, so now she'll break his."

He steps forward, destroying the space I'd put between us.

Those brown eyes are cold and serious again. "By using you. By controlling your life."

"She's given me everything. I owe her *everything*." I've leaned too close to him, and I pull back, straightening my shoulders. I remember what I am.

I am seventeen and enchanting and poised to destroy.

Soon after Mother had me, she learned that William and his wife, the girl he left her for, had had a son named Ben. So she came up with a way to rip apart the seams of time and relive the past. This time, though, she would be the victor.

Like a Siren from the Greek myths Mother made me read, I will seduce Ben to my side. I will make him fall in love with me, and then I'll wrap him around my finger and snap his heart in two, until he is broken completely. And his father will know my mother's wrath.

Mother has become a mere fragment of a person because Collingsworth broke her. Countless nights I would hear her keening wail behind the locked door of her bedroom. I would stand at the door, helpless. She needs revenge, craves it with an intensity that only destructive love can muster. I have to do this for her.

Starting when I was very young, she taught me how to flirt. How to captivate. A boy was an easy target, she taught me. A being swayed by desires that she understood completely. If I learned how to manipulate those desires, I could make any boy my slave.

And I must never become a victim of love. Love dismantles you. I'll never let it break me apart.

Not again, at least.

Arthur knows all of this, because I told him. Back when we were friends. And then something more.

The way he examines me now, though, it's like he doesn't even know me. "What changed you?" he asks.

"I haven't changed."

For a moment—just a moment—there is a flicker of inexpressible sadness in his eyes. Of grief. I blink, and it's gone.

Arthur puts his hands in his pockets, his old tell. He always used to do that when he had something to say but was thinking of just the right way to say it. He wasn't allowed to speak in front of Helper or Mother, so when he was allowed to talk, with me, he would take time with his words. Make them count.

"You can control yourself."

I shake my head. "I can't disappoint her."

"I won't let you hurt him, then."

There's a sudden rustling behind me, and I turn, my hand encircling my throat. But it's only a black bird hurtling into the air from the ground. When I turn back to Arthur, he raises his eyebrows at me. I'm not usually so skittish. I'm not afraid of anything.

"Have you met him?" I ask, taking a deep breath and making sure my face is wiped of emotion.

He knows who I mean. "I've seen him."

I pause, trying to find a way to frame my question.

But he answers it before I can ask. "He doesn't deserve to be destroyed." His cold voice is an admonition.

"You can't know that." I look him right in the eye when I say it, but I see no doubt on his face. His deep brown eyes bore into mine.

"I can. His dad may be an asshole, but Ben doesn't deserve the things you're capable of."

I flinch at his harsh words, at the way he growls them. This warrior in front of me is part of the new, unfamiliar side of him. "Why do you call yourself Tom here?"

"Because it's common. No one takes notice of a gardener named Tom." He pauses, watching me. "And because I'm not Arthur anymore." He steps closer to me, suffocatingly close. So close that the world around us fades into dull brown murmurs.

"Who are you?" I ask in a choked whisper. I feel myself leaning forward, closer to him, until I feel the warmth radiating from him. I crane my neck further so that I can keep my eyes on him. He is so tall now. It thrills me.

He shakes his head slightly. "Viv, don't you see what she's turned you into? You have to get rid of her."

I step back, and the spell is broken. The world is back. "She's all I have." I make the words cold, hard, unyielding.

That stops him, makes him look down at the ground.

My mouth opens before I can help it. "You left me." My voice has morphed into something wild, broken. I've never heard it this way. I stumble back, creating even more distance between us. "You left me," I repeat.

He doesn't look back up at me. "I had to."

I turn, walk away a few steps, turn back. "I need to accomplish my task. You can either help me, or you can stay out of my way."

The determination in my tone makes his neck jerk up, his eyes meeting mine again. I see then that I am unfamiliar to him, too, and that gives me strength. I lift my head high and walk back to the dining hall. By the time I reach it, I'm trembling.

CHAPTER 5

The rest of the day passes in a blur, until I find myself alone in my room before dinner in front of the laptop Mother sent with me. I need to give her an update. I can tell her about the outing last night, show her that I'm researching the school's social spheres and have identified the girl who will become my enemy, as she requested. But I can't tell her about Arthur, or Tom, or whatever he wants to call himself. And I can't tell her how I've wasted my day, how I looked at Ben without seeing him when he teased me lightly in English class for staring out the window. Or, I can, but I'll have to put a calculating spin on it.

I continue to engage Ben's interest, I write. *He seems fascinated by me. I have adopted a damaged, shy-girl persona to keep his attention.*

Mother sends me a reply right away. *Fine. But begin to bend. Let him in a bit, then push him away. Then he'll be yours for the taking.*

I stare at her words for a long moment.

When I was growing up, there was a girl about my age who lived in another big house a few blocks away. Mother would take me for walks past her yard, and I would peer through the bars of the gate at her and her magical life. She spent her afternoons playing in the huge playhouse her parents had bought for her, one with real glass windows and lace curtains and flags fluttering at the top. From my vantage point, I could see that her world was one of big smiles and expensive toys.

When I was six, she got a new doll. Even through the gate, I could tell how special that doll was, with its long, wavy black locks like mine and pretty pink silk dress. It would cry if you tipped it over, which the girl did often, cradling it in her arms afterward like it was a real baby.

It was beautiful, and for weeks, I coveted that doll more than anything.

One day, we walked by and the girl wasn't in her yard. But there, right by the gate, was her precious doll. Mother stopped when she saw the expression on my face. "Take it. Quickly, while no one's looking," she told me.

I remember looking up at her in confusion. "But it's hers," I said.

"If you want it, it should be yours," she hissed. "You want it more than she does, right? Take it."

I reached through the bars of the gate and grabbed the doll's tiny hand with my own, pulling her through and hugging her to my chest. I remember the rush I felt, the elation.

"Some people get whatever they want, without even trying," Mother told me as we hurried back home. "But if *you* want something, you're going to have to fight for it."

The next time we saw the girl, she was skipping around the yard with a new doll under her arm, smiling and carefree. Mother was right. I wanted her old doll more, so it was rightfully mine.

When the batteries ran out and the doll could no longer cry, I put it in a dark corner in my tiny closet and forgot about it. But I didn't forget the lesson Mother had taught me.

Claire bounces into the room, and I shut my laptop quickly.

"I . . . hate . . . homework," she declares, throwing her book bag on the floor. "This year is going to kill me."

"It's worse when you don't get any sleep, huh?" I ask.

"True," Claire says, smiling ruefully at me. "I usually don't join the sneak-out, to be honest, but this is the last year. No time like the present, yeah? And, actually, it was a lot more fun than I remember it being." Her eyes light up as she remembers the night before, when I saw her smiling, laughing, drinking long sips from the communal bottle of rum.

I shrug. "It was kind of boring."

She settles into her desk chair and pulls out her laptop. "I guess."

I decide to pry further. Claire is probably the best source I'm going to get, and my questions will seem like nothing more than the queries of a curious new student. "Arabella seems like the queen bee around here."

Claire nods, not looking up from her computer. "She is. And she gave you the sign of her oh-so-glorious approval last night, if you want to join that group." I learned a lot about sarcasm in my year at public school, and Claire's tone seems to match it.

"You're not a part of her group?"

"I like to think I do my own thing. I have plenty of friends, but I don't limit myself to one clique, you know?"

I suspected as much. She and Arabella seemed friendly enough last night, but I didn't see them talking much by themselves. And every time I saw Claire in the halls, she was chatting with someone new.

"Emily, my old roommate, was best friends with Arabella," Claire offers, looking up from her computer. I try not to look too interested.

"What happened to her?" I ask. Mother never gave me details.

"She was expelled. Someone called the administration and said she was having an affair with her chemistry teacher in exchange for *A*s." She sets her jaw.

"Was she?"

"No," Claire says, shaking her head vehemently. "I don't know who would lie like that. Emily was the smartest person at this school. She didn't need to cheat. And she definitely wasn't the kind to sleep with a teacher. I mean, she went to a lot of tutorials, yeah, but it was because she really liked chemistry, not because she liked Mr. Park! And they were always chatting and joking or whatever, but he was friendly with tons of other students, too." I nod, though it seems like Mother picked the right teacher to accuse. Helper must have done his homework well. "They had this 'official investigation,'" she says with sarcastic air quotes. "Emily said someone had planted these notes, like love letters, supposedly between her and Mr. Park, and one of them, one from her, said she would do whatever he wanted as long as he gave her an *A*. So he was fired, and she was expelled. It was so disgusting. There was nothing going on," Claire continues, "no matter what Arabella says."

"Arabella accused her?" I ask, surprised.

Claire shrugs. "I don't know if she was the anonymous caller or the one who planted the letters, but she definitely believed the rumor. She stopped speaking to Emily and started spreading lies about how much of a slag she was, which I think hurt Emily more than being expelled, because she'd been friends with Arabella since primary school."

"Arabella's really concerned about her reputation, huh?"

Claire shuts her laptop and crosses her hands over it. "Emily told me once that Arabella's parents were a lot like mine, like super disapproving? Her older sister got pregnant while she was here at Madigan and had to drop out. The father was some tosser who was way less popular than she was and refused to help with the baby. Arabella has to prove to her parents that she won't turn out like that, that she's got the perfect reputation, so she only dates, you know, socially acceptable boys, ones her parents approve of? Sleeping with a teacher to get a good grade is basically the opposite of that, and so Arabella decided she couldn't be friends with someone who was accused of that. She totally ditched Emily." Claire rolls her eyes. "Just be careful around her."

"Got it," I say, trying not to let my satisfaction show. "So what are the other cliques at this school?"

Claire looks at me closely. "What kind of group did you belong to at your old school?"

I keep my voice casual. "No group, really. I was pretty much on my own."

She narrows her eyes, considering that. "Why?"

Because I had no other choice, I think. "Didn't really find any friends," I answer instead.

"I'd like to be your friend," she says brightly.

Of course she would.

I give her a thin smile and nod. "That'd be nice."

"So you've got Arabella's crew," Claire says, ticking off her fingers. "There are the hard-core jocks, who kind of belong to that crew, too. And then the super smart people, who pretty much live in the library. They're harder to befriend, since you have to be quiet around them. And the slackers. And then just—everyone. I mean, I guess everyone can't be defined by one thing? That's what I like to think, anyway."

In public school I learned that even if you don't feel like you can be defined by one thing, in high school, that's all anybody will do to you. Everyone wants to pigeonhole everyone else in one neat little category, because that makes them easier to dominate and destroy.

Still, I nod and smile at Claire now. "I like that idea."

I guess I'll have to discover the true social secrets of this school on my own.

After classes the next day, I put on a tight black sweater and a short black skirt, along with my ripped tights and poetic ballet flats, and head for the student lounge for the weekly Thursday meeting of *Open Doors*, Madigan's literary magazine, just as I told Headmaster Harriford I would. But the main reason I mentioned my great passion for writing was not to win Harriford's support; it was because Ben is the editor-in-chief.

Ms. Prisby, the faculty advisor, is waiting alone outside the door of the lounge, greeting everyone as they come in. Perfect opportunity.

When she sees me, her smile fades a bit but doesn't disappear. "Vivian," she chirps, "it's so good to see you here."

"Headmaster Harriford suggested I join the literary magazine," I say, as if the entire prospect bores me.

Mother instructed me carefully on how to earn Ms. Prisby's hatred, while hiding my provocation of her from Ben. "She's his favorite teacher," she told me. "You have to make her seem petty and mean."

I didn't understand how that would help me seduce Ben, but I knew better than to ask Mother any questions.

I watch Ms. Prisby struggle to decide how to respond. Finally, she nods, her smile dropping off her face completely. "We're going over some submissions we received in the summer, if you would like to come in."

I push past her and don't take off my sneer until I'm past the threshold.

Ben is sitting at a round table in the middle of the lounge, and I feel his eyes on me. He, like everyone else at the table, has an impressively high stack of papers in front of him. As I take a seat across from Ben, Ms. Prisby enters the room and clears her throat. I meet her eyes, but she doesn't meet mine.

"Well, okay, then," she says, clapping her hands together as she settles into the seat farthest from me. "Let's get started."

Ben shoves a pile of papers toward me, and I look up at him. "Thank you," I say softly. My eye contact catches him off guard, and he stares at me for a second. I hold his gaze, then drop my eyes like I'm confused. Like I don't know exactly what's going on.

We spend the first hour of the meeting debating themes for the next issue. Or rather, Ms. Prisby and the other students debate themes while I watch Ben as closely as I can without being obvious. I do catch his grimace when Ms. Prisby suggests, "What about Avas? You know, best friends from childhood, what's digital versus what's real, something along those lines?" Everyone glances at Ben to gauge his reaction, and he erases the grimace from his face, replacing it with a neutral expression that's almost as good as mine. "I know my Ava was my best friend for years, and I'm sure other students have plenty of stories about theirs," Ms. Prisby continues, oblivious.

Someone finally offers a hesitant "That sounds good," and the theme is set.

After another hour of reading angsty poetry and simplistic stories, when it's time for dinner, Ms. Prisby asks me to stay behind for a moment. "How did you like the meeting?" she asks. Her voice is not as bright, but she still tries to smile at me.

I shrug. "Fine."

She nods slowly, watching me. "Well, I think this next issue will be great, and it will be wonderful to have you be a part of it."

"I don't know how much help I'll be," I say. I look right at her, my smile dripping with derision. "I was never so pathetic that I needed a digital doll to be my best friend."

I stroll out of the room before she can respond.

I follow Ben and the others to dinner, my head high and my eyes carefully bored. I've mostly avoided the dining hall so far, only going in to grab a piece of fruit or a cup of cereal before everyone else arrives. Outsiders don't eat with anyone in the dining hall, and I want to seem mysterious, so I usually hide in the lounge or my room with my stolen food. Now, though, I need to orient myself and study everyone when they are gathered in one place.

The room, with its three walls of dark carved wood and its one wall of windows, is a hotbed of student harmony and discord. The air is filled with bangs and shouts and laughter and the scents of rich sauces and spices. Everywhere, portraits of disgruntled men with white hair glower down at the people below. Over a dozen long rectangular tables cut up the space, and they're filled with students gossiping and eating and strategizing. I spot Arabella at the farthest table, seated in the middle with her male and female admirers clustered around her. If the

most popular kids sit at that table back by the windows, then the least popular must sit at the one closest to the entrance.

I grab a tray and covertly study the unpopular table from the food line. There are people sitting at its edges, not speaking to one another. Dark lipstick, ill-fitting clothes, and unwashed hair seem to confirm their exiled status. I let the serving lady fill my plate with fresh Greek salad and grilled chicken with rosemary—much more enticing than the slop at public school—and head for my target.

Claire intercepts me before I can get far at all. "Where are you going?" she asks. "I saved you a seat in case you showed today."

She gestures at the table next to Arabella's. The table of the not-quite-popular-but-upwardly-mobile students, I assume. A group I can't belong to.

"Thanks, but actually I'm just going to eat quickly and head for the library," I tell her, stepping around her. "This table's fine." I sink into a free seat before she can stop me.

Claire opens her mouth and then closes it. A girl next to me says "hey" to her, and she smiles back, still confused. "I'll see you later, then."

I nod and turn to my food.

"I'm Tory," the girl, the Claire-friend, says, holding out a hand tipped with dark purple nails. Her light brown hair frizzes out of her round head, and I almost long to take a brush to it.

"I'm busy," I say, turning back to my food. My goal is to be friendless, but not one of the unpopular masses. I can feel her recoil, and then she pointedly scoots her chair away from me. Good.

I pick at my salad quickly, glancing up only to find Ben. At Arabella's table, of course. He doesn't seem to have noticed me. Or, if he has, he's not preoccupied with my strange table selection. Instead, he's laughing at something the overgrown boy next to him has said. I can see his white teeth. He leans back in his chair and pounds the table, making all of the girls around him giggle.

A group of giant guys, probably athletes, huddle a few feet from the tray disposal, right near the popular table. I grab my tray and stand, trying to time it perfectly as I stride across the dining room. When one turns to leave, I walk right into him, balancing my tray against my hip so nothing spills.

I brace myself by placing an open palm on the chest of the boy, who looks down at it in bewilderment, then up at me. "Sorry," I say, keeping my hand there for just a touch too long before pulling it away.

"It's fine," the boy says quickly, but I'm already leaving. I feel his eyes on my back as I go. I don't spare Ben another glance. I know he watches me, too.

CHAPTER 6

I try to pay more attention in classes on Friday. But not to the teachers. Instead I'm focusing on the students around me, the boys and girls of British privilege who dream and struggle to define themselves and everyone else, all in one small space.

Something buzzes within me all morning, though. Something that threatens to break out of my skin. I don't know what it is until lunch period hits, and I can't bring myself to follow the crowd into the dining hall.

I have to escape.

I head out into the slanting rain before I can think twice about it, hurrying to get away from campus. I feel as if the school itself is watching me. I break into a run, clambering over the wall and dropping down onto the sovereign ground below. I will show up late to class, drenched and remorseful, and my legend will only grow. I'll say I got lost. Maybe I really am lost already.

But before I can get far, I nearly run into something. No, someone. Someone tall. I have to swerve out of his way and stop.

Arthur holds his hands out, inches from my shoulders, as if to brace me. But he drops them quickly enough. "What are you doing?" he growls.

I shouldn't do what I do next, but I can't help it. With the tip of my thumb on the tip of my middle finger, I hold out my left hand. Our old gesture that meant one of us wanted to escape. It meant I would cover for Arthur while he snuck up to my attic room, and then I would follow him. And we could be alone. Free.

His eyes flick from my fingers to my face, and then he turns so that we're shoulder to shoulder, looking out at the moors. He points, straight ahead and slightly to the north. "If you run in that direction about a mile, you'll find a cottage. You can be alone there."

I stare at him, but he doesn't look back at me. He just walks away.

I watch him for a moment, lost in memories of our tangled, painful history. Then one memory in particular snaps abruptly to the surface.

One day, when I was seven, I met a girl at the park. We played hide-and-seek among the trees, our giggles giving us away every time. Mother and the girl's mother watched over us, and when we'd worn ourselves out, the girl's mother invited me over for a playdate. I turned to Mother, my eyes filled with hope. She shook her head firmly and insisted we were busy, pulling me by the arm back to the car. I looked back to find the girl watching me, confusion and hurt stamped on her face.

When we got home, Mother pulled me inside and slapped me hard. "Friendship is a weakness!" she yelled. She let me go, and I scrambled to the wall, out of reach. "You cannot be friends with *anyone*. You cannot trust *anyone*. You make people believe they are your friends, and then you use them for your own purpose." I nodded furiously, but she still wasn't satisfied. So she called for Boy and Helper.

She pointed one long, narrow finger at me when they came into the den. "She has disobeyed me. She has to learn."

Everything about that moment is imprinted on my mind. The curtains were drawn, as they always were, so that only a few cracks of sunlight lit the room. The portrait of Mother's mother, a stern, haughty-looking woman wearing a diamond necklace that Mother had to sell off years ago, sneered down at us from above the fireplace. The rough, chipped-paint wall bore into my back, but still I pressed against it, trying to melt into it. Helper blocked the doorway with his sturdy frame, his face impassive. Mostly, I remember Arthur's expression as he stared at Mother: confused, angry, scared for me. But it wasn't me he should've been scared for, and I began to realize this just as Mother gestured at Helper's cane, the ornamental item he carried with him with the round black ball on top of it.

Without a word, Helper lifted the cane and swung it, hard. Right onto Arthur's back.

I screamed. Maybe I begged for her to stop. I don't know. I don't know if what I said was even coherent.

Mother grasped my chin in her hand, jerking my neck up. "Yes," she said, peering into my eyes with a satisfied smile. "It seems that will work. If you disobey me again, he will suffer the consequences."

I looked into Arthur's tear-filled eyes, and I knew that I would do whatever I could to make sure he never had to serve as my whipping boy again.

It didn't work. Every few months, at the slightest provocation, Mother would order Helper to beat his son while I watched. I close my eyes now and take a deep, shuddering breath as I remember the scars that cross Arthur's back, the scars that exist because of me.

Arthur is out of my sight now, and I look back out at the moors, hesitating. But only for a moment.

I break into a sprint, running in the direction he pointed to, breathing in the clean scent of the rain as the heather tries to cling to my bare legs. The land is one of hills and valleys and mud that threatens to pull me down. The sky is a dark mass of clouds, gray and swirling. The rain grows harder, pelting into me. I can't see. All I can hear is the deep roar of the rain and the growl of thunder. The day has turned dark, and everything is in confusion.

I run until I feel like something is stabbing my lungs, until my clothes feel ten pounds heavier, until I feel like I'm free from the school and everyone in it. I'm alone. I bend down, trying to catch my breath as the rain pours over me.

I look up to see something solid in front of me. I run to it and find a small, broken-down building of soaked wood, with one lopsided chimney stretching out of it. When I open the door and step inside, the rain can't find me.

It's something from another century, this one-room cottage. Someone's humble home, perhaps. There isn't any furniture, but there is a hearthside. The roof has caved in at the center, and the rain pours through to form a deep puddle underneath the gaping hole, so I step around the edges to reach the hearth. I sit before its slate stones and pretend there is a fire there to warm me. My shivering stops.

A flash of something white in the fireplace catches my eye. It sticks out of the soot, and I reach out to grab it.

After brushing the dirt and soot off, I realize what it is: part of an old photograph. I see a girl's body dressed in a faded

Madigan uniform. The other half of the picture and her head are torn away, but there's writing on the back. I have to trace my finger over the letters as if I'm writing them myself to figure out what it says. "Me and him." This photograph meant something to someone once. I prop it against the wall and promise to tape it up the next time I come. It feels like an appropriate way to honor this place's history, its story before me.

I stretch out, lying on the packed dirt of the floor, and finally let myself think the thought that has been clamoring for attention since I woke up: I'm eighteen today. When I was little, I learned that most girls celebrate birthdays with big parties and presents and cake. They create a day that's all about them. It's a strange custom, but still, I like the idea of it. I decide that this cottage is my birthday present.

The only presents Mother ever gave me were meant to make me more seductive: makeup, clothing, or jewelry—anything that would make me noticeable and irresistible. She once devoted an entire week to showing me how to put on eye makeup for every occasion and every outfit. The week after that, she taught me how to flutter my eyelashes, how to peer through them enticingly, how to use the expressiveness of my eyes to feign remorse or fear or any other emotion I would need. "Eyes are the most important tool you have," she told me. "You have to control them at all times, or they will give you away."

Like the mother of the Venetian courtesan and poet Veronica Franco, Mother taught me everything she knew about how to attract a man. Franco's mother was a courtesan as well, and she trained her daughter to be a captivating, powerful, eloquent woman. She was utterly irresistible, just as I am meant to be.

I fall asleep thinking of Veronica as the rain softens outside. When I wake, the day has grown even darker. It's dusk, and I don't know how to get back to campus, but my growling stomach urges me to try.

I leave the cottage behind and head in the most likely direction.

The sky is now deep blue with a netting of gray clouds covering the sliver of moon like a mantilla. The trees are ink drawings: gnarled lines beneath the dark sky. There are no identifying markers that I can recognize, but I stay calm. I can find my way. I'm sure of it.

I walk along the moors as the deep blue sky melts into blackness. The crescent moon offers almost nothing in the way of light, and the wind and the rain grow stronger, battling my every move, dragging down my soaked clothes. The only sound I can hear beyond the roar of the wind is the creaking of the trees, their branches reaching for me as I pass. The ground beneath me feels unsteady, as if it might give way and swallow me whole.

I take deep breaths and keep going. I will not let the immensity of the moors frighten me.

I must have been walking for an hour in the heavy downpour. My legs ache, and the grumbling in my stomach has grown into a roar. My teeth clack together, and though I wrap my arms around myself, I can't stop the shivers running through me.

I am lost in the shadows of the night.

And then, suddenly, a sound. I hurry to it, to the voice calling my name.

The person I find, however, is the last person I want to see.

"What happened?" Arthur asks when I practically stumble on him. He looks just as drenched as I am, as if he's been looking for me for hours. The rain slides down his cheekbones like a caress. His T-shirt sticks to his chest, where there are muscles I don't remember him having. "You're miles from the cottage. And the school."

I force myself to look up into his eyes, and I have to blink as the rain streams down my face. "I got lost." I mean to sound cold, matter-of-fact, like someone who doesn't need his help. The voice I answer him with, though, is small and shaky. Real.

He takes a deep breath, looking down at me. "We'll get you back. You need to get warm."

He glances at me again as we start moving. He curses under his breath, some harsh word I don't quite catch. "I shouldn't have sent you out here. You could have killed yourself. It's not forgiving land. But I wanted—" He stops himself. "I wanted you to have somewhere you could be alone. Be the Vivian I remember."

I shiver, though I don't know if it's from the cold or from his words. I don't say anything back. I can't.

We say nothing else for nearly an hour as the rain finally lets up and he leads me back to the school. It's only when campus is in sight that he stops and looks at me. "I'm not your friend anymore," he says, scowling. He means to sound gruff, but I can hear the faint waver of uncertainty in his voice.

"I know," I answer.

"I won't help you destroy Ben."

"I know that, too."

He sighs and looks as if he wants to say something else, but then he shakes his head. His hair has mostly dried out now, and it's the same mussed, black hair that I remember. He turns away, then turns back. "Happy birthday," he says quietly. Reluctantly.

I feel my eyes grow wider as I stare at him. Why would he say that? Why would he even remember my birthday?

Before I can think of what to say, he walks away, leaving me to face Madigan on my own. I watch him go, his tall form a black shadow in the dim moonlight. The one person in the world who knows and cares about my birthday. Even if he hates me, too.

I tell myself to focus as I trudge up the hill to the main building. Lightning flashes, lighting up the old gray stones, and I start to run.

I buzz in at the main gate. A teacher comes out, his eyebrows raised and his mouth a tight line of disapproval as he points me to the headmaster's office. I leave a trail of water along the marble floor as I march. I'm shivering constantly now, which will help me with Harriford.

I see him out front, talking to the secretary. His eyes grow wide when I enter, and I fill my own eyes with regret and fear and misery.

"Are you all right? We were worried." He steps forward, then looks back at the secretary. She glares at me.

"I'm so sorry," I wail. "I was feeling homesick, so I went outside, and I got lost. And it was raining so hard, and I didn't know where I was."

I hide my face in my hands and let my body shake as if I'm quietly sobbing.

The headmaster stays where he is, held by the force of the secretary's glare, but I can feel the sympathy radiating from him. "Don't cry," he says, helpless. "It's all right now."

"Shouldn't she be disciplined for going off school property?" the secretary asks, her voice cutting through Harriford's sympathy.

"Now then, I'm sure it was just a mistake."

I lift my eyes, watery with false tears, and nod. "I won't do it again, I promise!" It's a promise I'll break, of course, but I certainly won't be caught again.

He nods furiously at me. "There, see?" he tells the secretary. "No harm done. Now go warm up. If you feel feverish or anything, the school nurse will help you."

"Thank you, Headmaster Harriford." I attempt a smile through my tears, then glide out of the room.

Mrs. Hallie meets me at the entrance to Faraday, concern etched in every wrinkle of her face. "Are you all right, darling?" she asks, placing a hand on my shoulder.

I resist the urge to shake it off and nod. "I just need to warm up. I'm sorry for the trouble I've caused."

"No trouble, dear. I was just worried for you." She looks at me more closely, and I try to keep a remorseful expression on my face. "Hurry along and shower," she says finally. "And let me know if you need anything at all."

I force myself to smile at her. "Thank you so much, Mrs. Hallie."

I claim one of the empty shower stalls and stand under the hot water, letting it wash away the shivers.

It won't wash away my memories, though, which have been coming at me all day. Especially the one of my eighth birthday, when I realized that my world was much darker than I had imagined. That day, I found three stray kittens hiding in the bushes in the front yard. They were so tiny that they almost didn't seem real. I ran to fetch Arthur, sure that he would know what to do. He took one look at the kittens and hurried inside, sneaking a carton of milk out of the fridge and a couple of bowls from the cabinet. He set the bowls of milk in front of the kittens, softly coaxing them to drink. "You can't tell your mother," he warned me. "We'll take care of them together."

He helped me carry them up to my room, where we hid them in my closet. But Helper must have been watching us, because not nearly an hour had passed before he told Mother. She stormed into my room, pushing Arthur aside without a word. I clutched the mewling kittens as she towered over me. Slowly, she reached out a hand, and I only had the strength to hesitate for a second before handing her one of the helpless creatures. I remember she kept her eyes on mine as a knife flashed in her hand and she slit the kitten's throat. I remember the gurgling scream the kitten gave as its life flowed out of it. I think I'll remember that scream for the rest of my life.

By the time Mother had killed the last one, tears were streaming so thickly down my face that I couldn't see her gray eyes glaring into mine.

"Remember this, Vivian," Mother said, her voice calm and cold. "I will kill anything you love." Then the ice left her eyes and she reached out, cradling my chin in her hand. "I will not let love destroy you," she said softly.

After she left, Arthur hugged me close and let me cry until I had nothing left.

I knew even then that she did what she did to show me how painful love could be. I knew it was a lesson I needed to learn. A lesson I would never forget.

I shut my eyes tightly against the memory and step out of the shower. Back in my room, I curl up in a blanket on my bed and write a quick email to Mother, telling her that I got closer to Ben while implementing my desirable and intriguing outsider status. I recount the scenes from the literary magazine meeting and dinner the night before and hope that will be enough. I close the laptop before I can read her reply and take out a notebook.

Mother sent several notebooks along with my textbooks so that I could take notes, or at least pretend to, in class, but I'll appropriate one as a sketchbook. My fingers itch as soon as I touch the paper, and when I find a pencil, I let it fly across the page. I'm sketching my cottage, my new refuge, so that when I can't visit it, at least I can see it. I can see the rough wooden walls, the wide hearthside, the bit of remaining roof that shelters me from the rain. It's different from my usual drawings, the ones that show a harsh, cruel world—the world as it truly is.

I keep going, losing myself in these drawings, sketching one of the trees I have seen clinging to the land. And then I sketch Ben. I look for the arrogant features in his face, drawing the enemy as I need to see him. I want to draw Arthur. But I don't.

I can't quite capture him yet. He's too unfamiliar, too wild. Instead, I draw an abstract of him, a figure bearing down on the viewer, blocking the way. He's a force trying to stop me, and that's how I need to think of him.

The Arthur I used to know was the one person who knew about my art, and he would write poems to go along with my drawings. Ekphrasis, he called it, poetry to echo the beauty of visual art. His poems were like bursts of fresh air in the stillness. We would hide away and spend hours trading sketches and poems, making our own conversation, responding to each other's creativity. He made my art matter.

I'm so wrapped up in thinking about the way things used to be between us that I don't even notice when Claire comes in.

"Thank goodness you're all right!" she yells, startling the pencil from my grasp. "Where'd you go?"

She's standing over me, glancing down curiously at my sketchbook. I cover the drawing of Ben's conceited face with my hand, but I'm not quick enough. I see a flash of recognition in her eyes.

She looks up to meet my gaze, and I shake my head, silently begging her not to say anything. She doesn't. She just waits for an answer to her initial question.

I tell her what I told Harriford about my getting lost in the moors.

"Are you okay?" she asks, genuinely concerned. Her forehead wrinkles as she peers down at me.

I nod. "I'm fine. Just stupid, that's all."

She looks like she wants to keep lecturing me, but she keeps her mouth shut. Instead, she hands me a small package wrapped in napkins. "I thought you might be hungry."

She's made me a sandwich, sliced chicken breast and cheese on thick wheat bread. My stomach rumbles, and I look up at her with what I hope is a thankful expression. "This is perfect," I say before tearing into it, barely chewing before I swallow.

Claire looks pleased as she settles down at her desk. I don't understand this girl. But I begin to think that if I had been raised as a normal human being, if I wasn't a weapon constantly aimed at others, I would truly want her to be my friend.

CHAPTER 7

On Sundays we're allowed to go into town, and I'm the first one in line for the shuttle. Loworth, the nearest village, is a ten-minute drive, and as soon as I step off the bus onto a muddy sidewalk, I know there won't be much here for me.

The village is only a small collection of short stone buildings, little more than an intersection of two streets. There are a few generic shops, a pub, and a post office. All of the buildings are frighteningly close to the road, and as I walk past what must be a couple of apartment buildings, I can see right into the windows, where one family is gathered around a kitchen table and one man watches a soccer game in nothing but his underwear. A few elderly women sit outside on a bench, shaking their heads as their quiet town becomes overrun with Madigan students.

I head for the charity shop first, where they sell ratty old

clothing and broken pieces of pottery and other strange trea-
sures all jumbled together on rickety racks and wooden shelves.
I don't find any art supplies, but I do discover a blue and white
china teacup with the handle missing. If I fill it with water and
place some small flowers in it, it will brighten up my desk. Or, I
can break it into pieces and make a mosaic. That little teacup,
sold for only fifty pence, makes me hum with anticipation.

I also find a pair of beaten-up combat boots that will be perfect
for stomping around the moors. They fit well enough, and I put
them on as soon as I pay for them.

The drugstore has charcoal pencils, brushes, and adequate-
quality paints, and in the bookstore, I find a little journal hidden
away in the sales rack. It's made of worn brown leather and filled
with blank, rough-cut pages. Perfect for an impromptu sketchbook and much better than the lined notebook I've been using.
I'll just tell Mother these expenses were for seductive clothing or
some other necessary purchase.

Suddenly I hear the nasal twang of Arabella's voice before I see
her. I creep around the bookshelves until I spot her with several
of her hangers-on, laughing at the covers of cheesy romances.
Her friends all laugh the way she does: their hands covering their
mouths, the gleeful giggles escaping through the space between
their fingers.

I wait until they move toward the teen fiction section in the back before paying for my new sketchbook and slipping out of the store.

I explore for the next hour, wandering around the village in my new boots and peering into more windows. All the buildings are made of stone, built to last. The windows are tiny, some with warped glass panes that must have survived at least a century.

Before I even realize it, I wander into a cemetery. I survey the graves, covered with slate and rising crookedly above the ground, all jammed together under the watchful eye of the church clock tower. The day is gray and misty, and I shiver in the gloom as I shuffle through the plots, reading about infants and women and men who died all too young. My feet sink into the muddy ground, but I hardly notice. I'm too caught up in the depictions of angels and skulls and crossbones on the headstones around me. I have never been in a cemetery before, but I can't help but be enchanted by its bleakness. It reminds me of home.

And yet Loworth is nothing like the concrete-and-brick towns I'm used to back home. History seems to shimmer on the air here, and I wonder if I can capture that feeling in a drawing.

I meander out of the cemetery and behind the parsonage, where I come upon a house. It's a freestanding stone structure, narrow and tall. The gabled roof is pockmarked and missing several of its stone shingles. It rises high above me, and when I crane my neck, I see a flock of ravens shooting into the air, their caws sending shivers down my spine as their giant black wings flap wildly. The gardens surrounding the house are overgrown, their vines strangling a dying tree and climbing up the gray stone walls. The windows are shuttered and dark.

I stop for several moments, staring, as if I expect the house to shake off its stillness and reveal its secrets to me. Or maybe I'm expecting it to sink into the earth that seems to be trying so hard to claim it.

I hear a muffled sound behind me and whirl around. Two people are having a whispered conversation somewhere in the graveyard, and I head toward it. Because there's one voice I recognize. And it belongs to someone I need to talk to.

G-Man stands in a secluded corner of the cemetery, half-hidden by a straggly tree and a tall obelisk over a grave. He's handing something to a boy I faintly recognize from the halls, and the boy looks around. I duck behind a wide headstone, pressing my hands against its smooth, cold surface, before he can see me.

He leaves with whatever party favors he's acquired, and I stand up and walk toward G-Man.

I step on a pile of dead leaves. Their crunch gives me away, and G-Man turns around to face me. But he doesn't seem surprised to see me. Instead, his smile curves up in a knowing way. He has no idea how much he doesn't know about me.

"Come for more rainy-day supplies?" he asks, sliding a hand in his pocket and leaning against the gray stone wall surrounding the graveyard, one foot braced against it. He's trying to look cool, and I'm trying not to roll my eyes.

I step closer to him, a smile growing on my face. "Something like that," I murmur.

His eyes widen a bit as I move even closer to him, invading his personal space for a change. His foot slips off the wall.

I let my gaze fall to his lips, then drag my eyes back up to his. "How much for a few hits of Molly?"

He has to clear his throat before he speaks. "It depends."

"What do you mean?" I ask innocently.

He attempts a leer and leans into me. "Well, there's a friends-and-family discount." And a discount for popular kids, too, I assume, as long as they invite him to their parties.

I look up at him through my eyelashes. "And do I count as a friend?" I coo.

He nods slowly. "I think so."

I reward him with a dazzling smile and step back.

He takes a breath, clearing his head. "How much you want, then?"

"How much you got?"

He sells me several pills, enough for a few months, at least. Plenty of time to get Ben addicted to them and addicted to me. It costs me nearly all of the money Mother provided for this task, but not quite. She'll be pleased with that detail.

I put the packets in my purse and lean back toward G-Man

again. I give him a quick peck on the cheek and hurry away before he can ask for more, then manage to catch the last shuttle of the day.

I clutch my new sketchbook in my lap all the way back to school, but it's only when I'm alone in my room that I open the cover and let myself get lost in its pages for a few hours. I try to sketch the house I found beside the graveyard, but it won't spark to life under my fingers. I rip the wasted pages out and crumple them in frustration. I stick to sketching Ben's face, showing him as the cocky adversary I must control and destroy.

When I glance at the clock, it's almost nine. Mother will be waiting for my call.

I run to the hall, but there's another girl on the phone. She chats contentedly with someone, twirling her hair around her fingers as she laughs and says, "That's ridiculous," over and over again.

I hover over her, crowding her until she gives me an ugly glare. "Have to go, Ames. Some bitch wants the phone."

I simply raise my eyebrows at her until she finally hangs up and walks away, muttering more nasty names as she goes.

My fingers tremble as I dial, and I take a deep breath, forcing them to be still.

She answers on the first ring. "Late" is all she says.

"Sorry, Mom," I say, trying to sound happy and privileged and not sorry at all. "There was a line. How are you?"

"Have you drawn him in?" she asks.

"I think so. The literary magazine meeting went well," I hedge, looking around the hall to make sure I'm alone.

"Not good enough. Have you talked to him yet? Alone?"

"No," I admit, waiting for her wrath.

It comes swiftly. "What on earth are you doing there, then? Wasting time and my money? Don't think that just because you are off in England I can't get to you."

I hold the phone away from me as she continues shouting her rage through the line. When she stops, I press the phone back to my ear. "I did talk to a new friend, who gave me some not-too-expensive presents."

"Fine. But still not good enough."

"I am sorry," I whisper. I don't put emotion into my voice. She doesn't respond to emotion. "I will draw him in as soon as possible, I promise."

"You better," she says darkly. The line clicks, and she's gone. When I stumble back to my room, I have to put my head between my knees to stop the nausea rising in my stomach.

It's going to be okay. I can do this. It's what I was born for.

I wake the next morning determined to make contact with Ben. Alone. If I catch him when he has friends or admirers around, it'll be harder to establish a connection. If I get him alone, he'll be more malleable. More himself.

But I can't find an opportunity all day. Or for the next two weeks. He's always surrounded, even in our Thursday literary magazine meetings, and though he still glances at me and seems to study me when he thinks I'm not looking, I can't seem to find a way to capitalize on that interest. I email Mother every night, assuring her that I'm trying. I know I'm running out of time.

It's Arabella whom I encounter alone first. I've felt her eyeing me in the hallways ever since the night almost three weeks ago when we snuck out onto the moors. I know she doesn't know what to make of me.

I'm heading for the shower one morning when she's standing at the bathroom mirror, putting on one of her several layers of makeup. She pauses when I come in, pulling the mascara wand away from her eye. "Hi," she says, a bit coldly.

I have to play this carefully before I reveal how much of an enemy I'm going to be. Surprise attacks are always the most devastating.

So I put on my brightest smile and say, "Hi!" like I couldn't be more thrilled to see her. "Thanks so much for letting me come along the other night," I add. This will make her feel like she has power of approval over me, and I see her eyes light up as she looks at me.

"Sure thing. If you want to join in again, just let me know." She looks me up and down as she puts away her mascara, still trying to judge if I'm worthy, but she's giving me the benefit of the doubt. For now.

"Thanks," I simper. "Claire tells me you're the most popular girl at Madigan. I can see why."

It's much too sycophantic, but she eats it right up, her smile growing wider as she turns to the mirror again, fluffing her red hair.

"Claire also told me about your best friend, Emily," I say in my most innocent voice.

Arabella rolls her eyes in the mirror. "That slag was *not* my best friend."

"Sure she was," I say casually. "I've heard the stories about you. Where else would she have learned to be such a slut?"

She whirls on me, but she only opens then closes her mouth with shock.

I smirk and step into a shower stall. As I lock the door, I can almost feel her fuming on the other side of it.

CHAPTER 8

With Arabella as my new enemy, my life at Madigan changes considerably over the next week, just as Mother wanted. Girls I don't know glare at me. Boys look at me more curiously, trying to make sense of the girl whom the queen bee suddenly hates so much. They don't understand girl drama, but it intrigues them.

I hope it intrigues Ben, too. I get glimpses of him in the hallway, and he catches my eye once when I perfectly match my walk across the courtyard with his return from rugby practice with his friends. But it's still impossible to get him alone.

It'll be easiest to do on a weekend, when everyone is more scattered, with time and more room to roam. On the last Saturday of October, I wake up early and watch for him in the dining hall. I sit over my desiccated grapefruit half for two hours before he shows up, bleary-eyed and disheveled. He greets his friends with a rueful smile and a high five. A reference to some female conquest, maybe? Or simply a wild night?

I wait for him to finish breakfast, then I slip out of the dining hall before he can, making sure he doesn't notice me. I'm supposed to be the hunted, not the hunter.

There's a hint of chill in the air, and the morning mist has only just begun clearing. I position myself on a bench outside the boys' house and already have my copy of Tennyson in hand when he comes outside. I pretend to be absorbed in the pages, but I watch him. He stops when he sees me, considering me. Then he continues sauntering toward me.

"I thought you'd already read Tennyson's poetry," he says without preamble.

I look up, feigning confusion. As if he has plucked me out of the world I was immersed in and pulled me back into this one. "Sorry?"

He shifts his weight from one foot to the other before answering. "In class, you said, uh, that, you know, you'd read his poetry already." He was paying attention. Good.

"I have," I say. "But I reread it every chance I get. Because every time I do, it makes me mad all over again."

"You read a poem because it makes you *mad?*" he asks with his eyebrows raised and a hint of a smile.

"Yeah," I answer with a small smile of my own. I look back

down at my book. "It's just that the story it's based on, Elaine of Astolat, is so infuriating."

"I don't know. I think it's . . . romantic."

I snort, genuinely amused. "You would."

"Oh, yeah?" he asks. He takes my little jab as an invitation and settles down next to me, stretching his long legs into my personal space. I let him. It's the first time I've really allowed myself to examine his face, his expressions. His hazel eyes with flecks of green and brown glance at me warmly. His smile, which he turns to me now, is wide and inviting. "Why's that?"

I shift, turning to face him. He responds, leaning in a little closer. "Because you're the nice guy. The good guy. The type who likes damsels in distress."

His lips quirk up even more. "What makes you think that?" he asks.

I shrug. "Just a hunch."

"I like it because the girl can't help falling in love."

"Yeah, and it destroys her. She sacrifices her life for some guy who hardly has any idea she exists. Who's so wrapped up in his own drama that he can't be bothered with her. It's pathetic."

I stop, remembering suddenly why I read this poem and learned the story behind it so long ago. It was Arthur's recommendation. He loved Tennyson and spent hours trying to convince me to love his poetry, too. He thought I would be inspired by the intense imagery in it. And I was, but this poem unsettled me so much that I threw the book at the wall in disgust the first time I read it.

I grit my teeth, refocusing my attention back on Ben. "Have you seen the John William Waterhouse painting of 'The Lady of Shalott'?"

"No," he answers, shaking his head. But there's a look of fascination and curiosity on his face. He's hanging on my every word.

"It's insulting. It shows this stereotypical damsel in distress. She's in her boat, looking down toward Camelot, her mouth open in desperation. Waiting for some man to come rescue her. She just sits there, inviting the male gaze."

"The male gaze?" he asks.

"Yeah, you know, the film and art concept? That women in portraits aren't looking out at the viewer; they're there to be looked *at*. They're objects of beauty, put on display for the male viewer. Ridiculous."

Ben smiles, looking at me as if he's never seen me before. As if he doesn't know what to do with me. My cheeks are flushed from my vehemence, I know. My wide blue eyes are sparking, catching the fire from my cheeks. I'm beautiful, in my own strange way.

"Sorry," I say. "It's just that I don't like weak women who let men destroy them and don't even protest."

"Lancelot does destroy Elaine," Ben says finally. "But she's not, you know, she's not weak. She's in despair. To think that your true love is unrequited—it has to hurt."

"She should have hurt him the way he hurt her," I counter.

He shakes his head. "No, she loves him. She could never hurt him, no matter what he's done to her. You can never hurt someone you once loved." He's looking deep into my eyes, like he's searching for a sign that I understand him. Like he *needs* me to understand him.

I think of Mother and Ben's father, how her love for him turned into anger and hatred. What would Ben think of that? I stand up, suddenly unsettled.

"Look up Waterhouse's painting. You'll understand what I'm talking about."

Before he can say anything, I walk away, leaving him in the morning mist.

It's best to leave him wanting more, anyway, I tell myself. I'm not running away.

I never felt unsettled seducing Ethan, the public school boy Mother had designated as a practice target and the whole reason I went to school at all last year. Like Ben, he was the king of the class, with floppy hair and a braying laugh. But he was conceited, full of himself, obsessed with his image. He fell for the slightly edgy, confident girl gambit and sought me out, pulling me into janitor's closets and empty classrooms as if I was his to steal away. To make him feel more than lust for me, I began a complex maneuver of avoiding him and then drawing him in, showing him a vulnerable side. He vowed that we were meant to be together, that he loved me. When I laughed off his confession and told him that I'd only been playing a game, he mooned around my locker for months, trying to get me to talk to him. His status fell dramatically when people found out he was heartsick over a girl who thought she was too cool for him.

Ben isn't like Ethan, that much is clear. But my new persona will draw him in just the same. It will be easy.

I keep repeating that to myself as I hurry away from him.

No one seems to have heard about my strange conversation with Ben. I have no doubt that if they had, that bit of news about Arabella's new enemy cozying up to the golden boy would be flinging itself around the school. I refuse to look at anyone as I walk down the halls. I know they don't know what to think of me, and I'll have to do something further to ignite their curiosity. Keeping myself in their conversations will help keep me in Ben's thoughts, too.

At my old school, I let everyone assume I was into drugs, which gave me a certain helpful notoriety. But it wasn't enough, because there were plenty of druggies. And considering the number of pills, joints, and packets of powder I saw G-Man distributing during the nighttime escape, that wouldn't be enough here, either.

I become more inventive. On Monday evening, I use the footholds in the stone walls surrounding the campus and climb up to the top, nearly twice my height above the ground. The top of the wall is only about a foot wide, the surface of the stones smooth and slippery, but I saunter along it confidently, a book in my hand, seemingly too absorbed in it to notice the stares of all the students streaming out of the dining hall after dinner. Over the next two weeks, as October fades into November, I bring my sketchbook with me everywhere and for the first time start drawing in public. I draw in the dining hall, in the courtyard, in the student lounge. I even join the popular crowd in a few late-night sneak-outs, and after giving the barest of shy smiles to Ben, I slip away, climbing a nearby tree and sketching by flashlight until it's time to sneak back in.

All of what I do is intriguing and confident, with only the slightest show of a vulnerable side to Ben. I make no more moves to encounter him alone. He'll have to seek me out himself.

CHAPTER 9

One Friday afternoon, nearly two weeks since I spoke to Ben, I'm sneaking behind the residence halls to head off to my cottage as the late fall wind grows icier and angrier. Suddenly, there's a heavy footstep behind me. I whirl to find Arthur, covered in mud and dirt and holding a shovel, his eyes almost amused as he looks at me. It's a cold amusement, though. Everything about him now is cold.

"Where are you going?" he asks. "Are you running off to get caught in the rain again?"

"It's not going to rain today." I try to sound confident, but I look up at the sky. The clouds are white and unthreatening.

"Weather here is unpredictable. Don't expect me to come after you if you get lost again." He leans on the shovel, the corded muscles in his arms supporting his weight.

I flick my eyes back up to his and laugh, and the brittleness of it reminds me of Mother. "I wouldn't dream of it," I say dryly. "You've made it very clear that you hate me now." I move to step around him, longing to be safe in my cottage, hidden from this world. From him.

He puts a hand on my arm, stops me. "Do you remember?" he whispers.

I shiver at the pressure of his breath in my ear and close my eyes. I stay still. His hand still grazes my arm, I'm so close to him. I can smell him, his scent of grass and soil, a scent that calms me and electrifies me all in one thrilling moment. And I remember.

When I was fourteen and Arthur was seventeen, something changed between us. It was subtle at first: We would hold each other's gazes just a touch too long, or our hands would brush against one another and skitter away. Soon, though, the change became all-consuming, choking the air between us.

We spent more and more time together, seizing any moment that we could escape our parents. One day, Arthur pulled me to our spot, out of sight behind the little house he and his father shared. It was dusk, just before dinner, and the fading light left us in shadow as we hid between the brick walls of his house and the prickly hedge. He placed a gentle hand on my cheek, and I looked up at him with an emotion I still can't name.

Slowly, he bent toward me, his eyes locked on mine, making sure I was okay. I closed my eyes, and soon I felt his lips brush over mine, whisper-soft. It was my first kiss, and it felt like the sparks of a fire, setting me aflame. When I opened my eyes, I saw the stunned expression on his face, the one that must have mirrored my own.

He held my hand until we were back in sight of the main house, and I felt as if I was floating up with the clouds, even as I bid him goodbye. I looked up at the door of the house, dreading going inside. I tried my best to compose my features and get through dinner with Mother without revealing the excitement bubbling inside me. I could hardly look at her, but she didn't notice.

Arthur and I spent the next few weeks in a golden fog, secreting ourselves away in the spot behind his house whenever we could and kissing each other like we could make the whole world disappear.

One afternoon, instead of taking me into his arms and kissing me, he looked at me with the most serious and hopeful expression I had ever seen on anyone before. "I have to tell you," he began, looking down at the ground and then back up at me. "I have to tell that I love you."

I closed my eyes, absorbing his declaration. And then I opened them and smiled the most brilliant, shining smile. "I love you, too," I whispered, the truest words I'd ever spoken. I loved him. I stood there and offered him my entire heart.

I couldn't sleep at all that night, too afraid that the moment I closed my eyes, that afternoon would become nothing more than a dream. I replayed the scene over and over in my mind, committing to memory the look in his eyes as he gazed into mine. The way he brushed the dirt off his hands before he touched me. The press of his lips on mine.

That next morning I tripped down to breakfast, hoping to hurry through the meal with Mother so that I could find Arthur and kiss him again.

Mother was waiting for me in the breakfast room, buttering a piece of toast. "No prepared breakfast this morning," she told me. "Boy ran away. Helper says he packed up all his things and left in the middle of the night." Her voice didn't hold her usual amount of ice. It confused me so much that I had trouble processing her words.

"He's . . . gone?" I asked.

She nodded, still focused on her piece of toast.

"But, he can't—he can't be gone," I sputtered out before clamping down on my words. I wasn't supposed to care, I reminded myself. I was supposed to think of Boy as less than human, the way Mother treated him.

It was too late, though. Her gaze snapped to mine, and then

the strangest thing happened. Those gray eyes looked at me not with wrath, but with something more like pity, maybe even empathy. "You loved him, didn't you?"

I couldn't deny it. And I couldn't admit to it either. I said nothing, but I couldn't hide the misery on my face.

He had left me. He'd run away, just like he'd always planned, but he hadn't taken me with him. He didn't care about me at all.

"I told you what would happen if you let love overpower you," Mother said softly, rising from the table. "He didn't *care* about you. He ran away to escape you."

I didn't know if it was the softness of her tone or my lack of sleep, but suddenly I was crying. I hadn't cried in front of her in years, but now I couldn't stop.

Through the blur of my tears, I saw her step toward me, and then she enveloped me in her arms. "I am so sorry," she murmured. "I never wanted you to go through what I went through."

I clung to her for what felt like hours, until the very last tear had dried on my cheek. I could count on one hand the number of times Mother had hugged me, and all had been because we were in public. This time, though, she hugged me because she cared. Because she knew the blinding pain that I felt.

"Take your time," she cooed softly, pushing me back so she

could look in my eyes. "Get over this heartbreak. And when you're ready, I will teach you how to be strong."

I hid in my room and cried for days. How could he have left me? Had he been lying when he told me he loved me? He must have. It must have all been a joke to him. Or at least not enough to keep him here.

When I emerged, I promised myself I would never fall in love. I would never care about anyone ever again. Mother needed me to be a weapon, and I would not fail her.

Back on the moors, I pull myself out of that memory, realizing I've lingered too long. I'm standing too close to him. I open my eyes and step away, out of the reach of his arms. I face him and let fire fill my expression. "I hate you." I'm desperate for the words to be true, but their sharp edges cut my tongue as I spit them out.

"Stop acting," he orders, his voice low.

I blink, and he steps forward again, and suddenly we are engaged in a complicated dance.

"You don't hate me." He hesitates, then brings his hand to my face, smoothing a wisp of hair behind my ear. Steps closer again.

"What are you doing?" I ask, stiffening. The feel of his skin on mine makes me shiver. I don't know what he wants with me.

Something in my eyes makes him step back, and finally I can breathe again. "Why are you really here? At Madigan?" I ask.

"Because of you," he answers, his eyes still locked on mine. It's the same answer he gave before, but it feels different now. It means something different.

"To stop me?" I ask.

He shakes his head slowly. "Because of you," he repeats. He's opening his mouth to say something else when something catches his eye behind me, and before I can stop him and beg him to give me more answers, he turns and walks away.

I look over my shoulder and find Arabella spying on me from the back door of the boys' house. I'm too far away to read her expression, but I know it can't be good. My mind scrambles back over the last few minutes, trying to see them as she would. I was talking to the gardener. No, I was too close to be just talking. And that moment, when his hand brushed against my cheek . . . something flutters in my stomach.

She's still watching me as I lift my chin and head back toward Faraday as if it was my destination all along. I wait until the coast is clear before I climb the wall and disappear down the hill.

I spend the next several hours at the cottage drawing Ben's face and charcoal sketches of the house I saw in Loworth, trying not to think about what I have to do when I get back to campus. I need a strategy. But I can't think about that yet. Not here. This is a place of escape, not somewhere to sharpen my weapons.

Still, the dark thoughts creep in. I begin sketching a shadowy figure across a wide space of dead earth, imbuing the picture with the alarm and the shock I felt when I saw Arabella watching me. The figure stares out at the viewer. It's the viewer's enemy.

I throw my sketchbook and pencils into my bag and head back. Better to face the problem head-on, I decide. I can manage it easily enough. But I hate the thought of Arthur becoming a part of this. I want him to be separate. Untouched. Unbloodied.

Because he was right. I don't hate him, no matter how badly I want to.

I start running. Dinner will be over soon, and I have to gauge how dire the Arabella situation is before I respond to it.

I slow down to catch my breath as I approach the dining hall. I have to look confident and calm to *be* confident and calm.

When I open the heavy wooden doors, people look at me and then turn to their neighbors to whisper, and I know that my fears are confirmed. They think I'm dating the gardener. That I've been sleeping with him, too—that's how Arabella will spin it. I hunt the room for Ben, and when I see him, he meets my gaze with one of curiosity. He doesn't smile. He just looks back down at his food and chuckles half-heartedly at something a boy next to him says. Maybe he's laughing about me. In any case, he thinks he has a rival now.

I wait until Ben deposits his tray and leaves before I walk steadily toward Arabella's table. "Why, exactly, is everyone staring at me?" I ask her.

She looks up at me and smirks. "Because you're shagging the gardener, of course," she answers matter-of-factly.

I like the girls who are direct. They're easier to dismantle.

"I'm not shagging him, actually," I say nonchalantly. I step closer to her and lower my voice so that only she and the two curious girls next to her can hear me. "But it sounds like you want to be."

"What?" she scoffs. In the unforgiving light of the room, she looks pale, her blush two incongruous rosy spots on her cheeks. Her pink lipstick has smudged and strayed from the line of her lips. She's just a girl.

I laugh. "He was telling me how you left that pair of underwear with a note on his doorstep last week," I whisper. "A bit kinky, if you ask me. Sorry he wasn't interested."

She stares at me, her mouth open in shock, as I smile. I'm walking out of the dining hall before she can think of a response.

***

Ben finds me the next afternoon sitting at a study carrel in the library, far inside the stacks where no one can hear us. Most students study in the main reading room: a two-story cavern with bookcases lining the walls and paintings of Greek gods on the ceiling. It's a place covered with an awed hush, where the only sounds are the squeaks of chairs being dragged and the crisp flicks of pages being turned. Everyone is on display there, and even on Saturday afternoons like this one, it's always crowded. In the stacks, though, I'm surrounded by only clothbound history books, and the scent of worn pages permeates the air. When Ben turns a corner and spots me, I shove my sketchbook under a textbook so that he won't see the drawings I'm working on. I didn't expect anyone to discover me here.

"So what, you're a bitch now?" Ben asks, standing over me.

I widen my eyes as if I'm surprised, then widen them even more as if hurt. "Is that what they're calling me?"

He nods, his eyes serious as they examine me.

"Because Arabella told them I was shagging the gardener?" I ask, my tone incredulous.

"No, because you accused her to her face, and in front of the whole school, of, you know, trying to shove her knickers on him."

"What?" I say. "God, the rumor mill at this school is ridiculous. All I did was tell her that *I'm* not dating the gardener. And then I apologized, because it seemed like she was upset about it. I thought she had a crush on him or something."

His forehead wrinkles in confusion. "Why would everyone be spreading this other story, then?"

I shrug. "Maybe because they're not her biggest fans? I don't know."

He considers this for a moment. Then his forehead clears, and his easy smile is back. "So you're not dating the gardener?"

I look down at my desk, then back up at him. "No," I say. My softness wipes the smile from his face. "Did you find the portrait of the Lady of Shalott that I told you about?" I ask.

He relaxes again. "Yeah."

"And?"

He half smiles. "I don't know. I don't really 'get' art, you know? But I can see what you mean about the male gaze."

I nod with an encouraging smile.

"And I can see why you hate it," he continues.

"I don't hate it," I say quickly. "I mean, I *do*, but I always value paintings that produce such strong reactions. The paintings that I love or hate. Have you ever heard of the play *Art* by Yasmina Reza?"

He shakes his head, that half smile still on his face.

"It's about this guy who buys an expensive painting. To his friend who doesn't like modern art, the painting is just white paint on a white canvas. But the guy who bought it sees so much in the painting, and it changes their friendship. So the painting's powerful, even if it's just white on white, because the people react to it so strongly. That's the point, I think, of art. The reaction. So even though I hate it, I don't really hate Waterhouse's painting. If that makes sense."

He shakes his head slowly, his smile in full bloom now. "Not really," he says, "but you know who you should talk to? Ms. Elling."

"Who's she?"

"Art teacher. She gives private lessons to anyone who wants them. She's kind of mad, but she's all right. And you seem so, uh, so passionate about art." He pauses. "I see you all the time with that sketchbook."

I stand so that I face him, so that we're on an even playing field. "I'll think about it. Thanks."

He glances down at the red writing on my ballet flats. "What does that say?" he asks.

"It's a poem. By Catullus." I trap his gaze. "It means 'I hate and I love. You ask me why, perhaps, I do it. I don't know, but I feel it done, and it burns me.'"

There is a breathless pause between us. "You know Latin?" he asks.

"No. Someone translated it for me."

He steps forward, drawn in, and there is so little space between us now. Nothing but a thin sheet of air. I peer up through my eyelashes into his hazel eyes. Then, as if nervous, I step back, nearly tripping over the chair in my haste, and I can breathe again.

"I still like the story of Elaine and Lancelot." He's trying to joke, but his uneven voice gives his nervousness away. "Do you want to study together sometime?"

"I study better alone," I say quickly.

He raises his eyebrows. He's not used to rejection. "Maybe we can get together for something else, then."

I bite my lip, as if his words have affected me. "I don't think so," I say, letting my voice become breathless, uncertain.

He steps forward again, just as I wanted him to. I look at the floor. Before he can say anything, I sidestep him so that he no longer blocks my exit. "I have to go," I say over my shoulder as I leave him there.

Why do I always feel so strange leaving him? As if I have lost something, as if he has beaten me somehow? I'm playing a game, I tell myself. It's all just a game, and I'm in complete control.

CHAPTER 10

The Sunday morning I wake up to the next day is dark, the wind and rain banging against the window. Claire stays burrowed under her covers, hiding from the dreary world. She clattered in at three in the morning, smelling of sweat and alcohol and earth. And something else, too, that I can't quite name. I buried my head in my pillow as she stumbled onto her bed. She smelled dangerous.

I get dressed and tiptoe out of the room, as much as one can tiptoe in heavy combat boots.

The rain pelts my skin as I head outside, and the wind whistles harshly around me. I duck my head and run to Arthur's cabin, pounding on the door until he opens it.

He stares at me a second, taking in my soaked hair and clothes. I jerk my chin up, trying my best not to look pathetic.

"Let me in," I demand. I'm tired of dancing around the truth with him. It's time for answers.

He narrows his eyes at my tone but nods. "Come inside," he says with a deep sigh. "I'll make you some tea. We need to talk."

I should ignore him. I should keep him out of my life completely. But I have too many questions.

His shed is small, and he stoops to fit in the space, but he's made it his home. Sheets of paper marked with the long, easy scrawl of his handwriting clutter the table, and a cot rests in the corner. A healthy fire roars in the grate, keeping out the cold and the rain and the bleakness of the world outside. I reach my hands toward the flames.

"I forgot you wrote poetry," I lie. I haven't forgotten. I haven't forgotten anything about him.

"There's a lot of inspiration here. On the moors. My verses have gone wilder." I feel him look at me, but I keep my eyes on the fire. "Do you still draw? Or has your mother twisted that out of you yet?"

I ignore the barb in his words. "I draw all the time. I want to capture this world."

"It's impossible to capture," he says, but he's not mocking me.

"It's impossible not to try."

The crackling flickers of the fire fill the heavy silence of the room.

"I have questions," he says before I can say the same thing.

I wait.

"My father . . ." He stops. But I know the rest of his question.

"He's still with Mother. Still her spy. He goes away for longer periods of time, though." I glance at him, but his face gives nothing away, his jaw set in a firm line.

He just nods. "There's more going on now. He needs to make sure Collingsworth doesn't know what your mother is planning."

"And that takes weeks to find out?" I ask.

He shrugs. "He has other jobs, too. He works as a private investigator for wealthy clients from the city. Only the shady guys with shady connections know how to contact him."

I didn't know that, though I had always assumed it. I keep my mouth shut. I don't want to reveal how ignorant I am, how terrified I was of asking Mother any questions about the man who lived in the guesthouse.

He hands me a mug of tea, which I cradle in my hands. The mug is white and cracked and smells of cinnamon and what must be the scent of comfort. I take a sip, letting it warm me from the inside out.

I feel the heavy weight of his gaze, and I make sure my face is blank before I turn it to him.

He looks down at the sheets of paper on the table and shuffles through them, looking for something to do with his hands.

"Why didn't your father ever give you a name?" It's a question I've never had the courage to ask. No, that's not quite true. It was only that I used to care about not hurting him. Now—I shouldn't care. I know that much.

"I was never a son to him," Arthur says, his eyes still examining the paper under his hands in order to avoid meeting my gaze. He learned years ago that his mother was an addict, which was why she abandoned four-year-old Arthur and his father. If she had named him, he never remembered it. Or he had blocked it from his memory. He never talked about her, and he hardly ever talked about his father. It was all too painful.

I always thought that, despite her faults, Arthur's mother loved him. How else could he have turned into the boy who always knew how to show me light in the darkness?

"Why weren't you a son to him?" I ask.

Arthur snorts, still not looking at me. "Because he's incapable of love. You know him. Okay, so he didn't let me die. Maybe I should give him credit for that." His hands are forming into fists. I watch them, fascinated, as the knuckles turn white with the effort.

I drop all hope of not appearing ignorant. There are too many things I want to know. "Why does he help her? What kind of hold does she have on him?" Curiosity overcomes the guilt I feel about questioning Mother.

"It's not a hold. It's a partnership." He stops, and then a ghost of a smile appears on his lips, but it's a bitter smile. A smile that puts me on guard. "Sometimes you act so innocent. It makes me forget who you really are."

"Who am I?"

"A person designed to deceive. Don't you see what she's turned you into?"

I lower my head. "You don't trust me."

"I'll never trust you. I'd be a fool."

I nod. And then, without warning, tears spring into my eyes. Real tears. Tears from some unknown source buried deep inside me. I blink them away, try to hide them.

"Do you remember when I told you I loved you?" he asks softly.

I feel like I'm about to shatter. I shove my fists into my eyes, desperate to dry them. "Stop it," I growl. "Stop torturing me."

I hear him step forward. His hand tugs gently at my arm. He wants me to look at him. I can't look at him.

I break free from his grasp and rush to the door, out into the rain. The cool drops mingle with the tears on my cheeks as I sprint for the girls' house.

Why does he have to keep bringing up the time he broke my heart? Why has he turned so cruel?

Back in our room, Claire is still hiding from daylight under the covers. I reach down for the box under my bed, where I've hidden the pills I bought for Ben. It's where I keep everything secret, even though Mother isn't here to find it.

I take out the scrap of paper that I've guarded for years. It's a poem in Arthur's boyish handwriting, one of his responses to my sketch of my attic room. It's the only one I've kept, and it's been enough to sustain me all these years. It holds the memory of hushed laughter and friendship, all distilled into a few lines. I let my eyes drink in the familiar words one more time.

Secreted up in the eaves of the
World, away
Freedom of breath and thought
The walls widen
Open themselves to the power of her
Imagination
Fearless

I shove the box back under the bed and grab my textbooks.

CHAPTER 11

I can't stop spinning through my conversation with Arthur all day as I hide myself in the library and try to focus on homework. After a few hours of staring blankly at the book in front of me, I take out my sketchbook and let my fingers draw what they want. It's Arthur, the Arthur who wrote me that poem, the boy who was my friend and then so much more. His eyes are bright and warm as they look out at me, and he wears that half smile he used to show me when we were alone.

As it begins to grow dark outside, I shut my sketchbook and head to the student lounge. Dusk and its accompanying fog settle stealthily and silently around me as I walk through the courtyard to the main building. I breathe in the scent of wood fire, that smell of barely tamed wildness, which always seems to creep over campus as soon as the sun sets.

I peek my head into the student lounge, but see no sign of Ben, only Arabella and her court of sycophants on their phones, hanging out with their Avas. The tinny sound of digital laughter fills the room as the girls tell their programmed friends all the latest gossip. I turn on my heel and head back down the dim hallway to the staircase, but before I reach it, a plaque above one of the classroom doors catches my eye. "Ms. Elling, Fine Arts."

The light is on inside, and I see a woman standing over one of the tables. The classroom is filled with paintings and sculptures and faded posters of famous works of art.

I knock on Ms. Elling's open door to get her attention. She's bending over a lump of clay, patting it with her hands. There are smears of clay on her cheek and floral dress, even though she has a smock on. Her gray hair sits in a bun on top of her head, and wisps of it float around her face.

Ms. Elling looks up quickly, catches sight of me. She blinks.

I shift my weight from one foot to the other, not sure what to say. "Hi" is all I can come up with.

"Oh, hi, hi," she says hurriedly, waving me in. "Come in, please. Sorry. You just look . . ." She stares at me a few more seconds, not finishing her thought. "Sorry."

"Um, I'm Vivian Foster." I step in past the doorway but don't come much closer.

She raises her eyebrows. "Right, of course. Does this look like anything to you?" she asks, looking back at the piece of clay before her.

It's about the size of a human torso, and there are crevices and bumps scattered along its surface. It doesn't look like anything but clay to me, but I don't think it's socially acceptable to say so. "Is it supposed to look like something?"

She sighs. "It's a piece by one of my Introduction to Sculpture students. I know I shouldn't be touching it, but it just doesn't *look* like anything, and I'm trying to see if I can make it better somehow."

That doesn't sound like the most appropriate action for a teacher, but I don't let the judgment show in my eyes. "Maybe it's abstract."

She wrinkles her nose at it. "If it is, it's not a very *good* kind of abstract."

She turns to me, wiping her hands together in a vain attempt to get the clay off her fingers. "What can I help you with?"

"Someone told me you offer art tutorials," I say, my voice rising at the end to make it more of a question. I must have picked this habit up from Claire.

"Hmm? Oh, yes, of course! Are you an artist?"

I shake my head. "I do sketches sometimes."

"Have you brought any of them?" she asks. I clutch my sketchbook more closely to my chest, and the movement catches her eye. "May I see?" she says.

I try not to bite my lip as I hand it over to her.

"If you don't want me to look, I won't," she says, peering into my eyes.

I shake my head the tiniest bit. "No, it's okay. You can look."

She smiles and opens to the first page. I've ripped out the drawings of Ben and Arthur, leaving only my landscapes and scenes of Madigan life. She examines a sketch of the dining hall filled with shouting faces. "Interesting," she murmurs.

The next one is a study of the school under a cracked moon. The walls rise to terrifying heights, crowding the viewer. "Lots of emotion in this one," Ms. Elling says, glancing briefly at me.

The third one she turns to is a sketch of one of the trees out by the cottage. It's a recent one, in which I've been trying, not very successfully, to show the tree not as a barely there survivor but as a strong force to be reckoned with. She stares at it for a moment, her eyes widening, then looks up at me. It's as if she's searching my face for something familiar.

"Is it . . . not any good?" I ask, taking a step back.

"No, it's wonderful. Remarkable, actually. There's something about you—about your drawings—that reminds me so much of a former student of mine. Rose." She finally looks away from my face and back down at the drawing. "Here. You've drawn the tree as if it's almost . . . hopeful. It's not as dark as the others."

"I wanted to show its strength, not hope," I say, staring at that curved tree between us.

"There is a lot of strength in hope," she says softly, and I can still feel her eyes on my face. I can't look up.

"You should enter these sketches in the Yorkshire Young Artist Festival, the year-end contest," she says. "The judges are local artists and art teachers, and they accept submissions from students all over Yorkshire. They look for the most engaging portfolio, and if you round these pieces out with a few portraits, I know you could be a strong contender. I'd certainly be happy to tutor you."

"You would?" I ask, looking back up at her in surprise.

She nods with a quick smile. "Of course. You've got rare talent, Vivian."

I blink, and only then do I realize that I'm holding back tears. I look down at the floor and clear my throat, horrified. "Thank you."

"I hold open hours after dinner most nights. Come whenever you feel like it, and we'll see what we can accomplish together."

I thank her quietly and leave her to the unsatisfying sculpture, which has already claimed her attention again.

I wake in the morning after a restless night, determined to make Arthur answer my questions. But when I sneak over to his shed and knock, he doesn't answer. I stand in front of the rough wooden door, the wind whipping past me like a live animal. The air is growing colder, and I hug my arms around myself as I peer into the dark windows. I should have worn a coat, one of the slim, fashionable ones Mother sent with me. My thin leggings and long-sleeve cotton tee do nothing to hold off the damp chill, but still, I search the grounds of the school, wandering down the hilltop through the back gate into the mist-covered soccer fields below, the dew of the grass seeping into my sneakers. He's nowhere.

When I climb back up the hill and search behind the gray stones of Canton Library, I feel a prickle on the back of my neck. Like someone is watching me. I turn on my heel quickly, but there's no one there. Maybe someone simply caught sight of me from a window. I examine the building, but there are no faces peering out from behind the glass panes. I must be imagining things.

I sigh and head back to Faraday Hall to get ready for class.

I spot Ben walking among a group of friends as I pass through the courtyard. I run a hand over my hair as he spots me. I should've taken more care of my appearance before stepping out where he might find me. But he smiles at me, a small smile, a secret smile, and turns back to his pack.

Claire is up when I reach my room. Her eyes are bloodshot,

and for a moment she looks at me like she doesn't recognize me. "I had such a crazy night last night. My head's killing me." She pauses, as if she's waiting for me to ask a question. I stay silent. "Is a shower free?" she asks finally, rubbing a hand over her forehead.

"I don't know," I say, grabbing my towel. "I'm going to take one now."

She says nothing as I slip out of the room again.

She's been spending more and more time out on the moors at night, waking up with deep bruised circles under her eyes and moaning about headaches. It keeps her out of my way, anyway. She hasn't been studying me as closely as she used to.

I'm still mulling over Claire's new behavior on the way to history class later that morning, though I don't know why I'm so interested.

As I enter the classroom, it takes me a moment to realize how *wrong* it feels. How cold. *He* is there. Like a spider, waiting in his silken web to capture me. It rattles me to encounter him in this context. I'm used to him in the corner of Mother's den, whispering secrets into her ear. I stand staring at him, half-sure I'm hallucinating.

"Vivian," Helper says, with a deep nod. All of my classmates watch me carefully. He's truly here. He's not a tall man, but he stands with his feet planted apart and his head held high, and somehow he looks massive. His shaggy gray hair hangs to his shoulders, but his carefully trimmed mustache and beard give him a more dignified appearance. He wears a dark suit with a black shirt and no tie, and he carries the same cane as always. That cane with its round black stone at the top that used to make deep purple bruises in almost perfect circles on Arthur's back.

I say nothing. I don't know what to do. I've never spoken to this man, not without Mother there.

"Mr. Smith is here with a message from your mother," Dr. Thompson tells me, looking at me curiously. It's clear that I know him, but I'm sure Helper didn't explain our relationship. "You're excused from class today."

I give a bare nod and follow the man—whose name is surely not Smith—out into the hallway.

"We need to go someplace private," he says, his voice low.

I could offer my room, but I don't want to. I don't want him to see the broken teacup filled with wildflowers or my sketchbook or anything to do with the life I've secretly allowed myself to make here. So I search through the halls until I find an empty classroom. I close the door behind us and face him, subtly wiping my sweating palms on my plaid skirt.

He looks older in the fluorescent light. As I've done so many times before, I search for Arthur in his face, but I find nothing similar. In that moment, I realize I'm glad Arthur looks nothing like him.

"I'm here to check on your progress with the Collingsworth boy." He rests against the teacher's desk, his black eyes staring out at me from his cavernous face.

I swallow. I feel like a mouse staring into the yawning mouth of a snake. My heart skitters in my chest, and the air has grown thin around me. I breathe in short, stuttering gasps. "I have told Mother about my progress."

"And she has told me it's not enough." His voice is flat, as always. Unvarying, unemotional. "You've had a month and a half now, and nothing much has happened. You've attracted him, but it needs to go deeper than that."

"You've been spying on me." I remember that strange prickling feeling from earlier, as if someone was watching me. Of course Helper was hiding in the shadows. I'm suddenly thankful that I didn't find Arthur. If Helper had discovered us together, we would both be in danger.

"I saw you in the courtyard this morning," he says, confirming my suspicions. "You did not look your best, and he barely acknowledged you."

"But he looked at me and smiled. He is clearly interested in me."

"You're failing."

"I'm not," I say, my voice trembling. "I just need a bit more time."

"You don't have much time left. You have to get him addicted to the drugs you bought so that he'll become addicted to you. You must get him to the point where he will settle for nothing less than running away from Madigan with you. And you have to do it right after he turns eighteen, on March seventh, so he'll be free of his father's custody. You have four months."

I jerk my head up at him, trying to read his expression. For a moment, I think I've heard him wrong. Mother never mentioned making Ben run away from school. I thought I was just supposed to break his heart, make him feel what Mother felt all those years ago. I didn't think I would have to destroy his entire life.

I know better than to ask questions, though. I learned that lesson a long time ago. Because whenever I asked Mother an unwanted question or said anything that could be construed as backtalk, she would have Helper hold me down while she drew a shallow cut down my tongue with a kitchen knife, something that made eating or drinking or even just being conscious painful for days.

"I'm sorry," Mother would say when she was done, when the salty tang of my own blood hit the back of my throat. "But you need to learn."

I would do my best to hold back my tears until I could escape to my room with the bottle of mouthwash she gave me so that the cuts wouldn't become infected.

I close my eyes against that memory now, swaying slightly on my feet. Helper turns for the door, then stops with his hand on the knob. He doesn't look back at me as he says, "I'll be keeping an eye on you. If you don't start turning him, I'll tell your mother. And you'll have to answer to her."

I shiver as I watch him leave the room. I wonder what torture she'll devise for me if I fail. I try to press from my mind the images of a dark locked closet, of marks on Arthur's back, of the slick blood pouring from a kitten's throat.

CHAPTER 12

I don't have a plan, but the panic rising within me demands that I act now. I have to get Ben alone as soon as possible.

He gets to English class just before the bell, leaving me no time to pull him aside. And though I catch his eye at the end of class, one of his friends pulls him by the arm to the dining hall before I can signal him over.

It's not until after dinner that I find him sitting alone on the wrought-iron bench outside Rawlings. As if he's been waiting for me, too.

I walk slowly toward him, trying to come up with something enticing to say. How can I move him past initial attraction to full-blown enthrallment in one conversation?

He looks up from his book. He wears a forest green scarf around his neck, which brings out the deep flecks of green in his hazel eyes, and the wind ruffles through his golden hair. I look down at him, my face impassive, and for a few moments, we are caught there. Looking at each other, trying to figure each other out.

Then he stands and looks down at me, his expression still serious. "I heard your father came to visit."

"He's not my father," I say quickly. "He's . . . my mother's lackey."

"What does that mean?" he asks carefully, sincerely. He wants to understand me.

"It means he's not my father." That's all I can give him.

Ben's forehead wrinkles as he looks at me. I need to divert his attention.

I look down, then look up at him through my lashes. I step forward. Once. Then again. I'm close to him now, so close that I can smell the mint on his breath. Did he go inside and brush his teeth before coming back out here? Maybe he really has been waiting for me.

He seems surprised for a moment, then a slow smile starts on his lips. He's used to this kind of behavior from other girls. I'm messing everything up.

"Sorry," I say quietly. "I don't like talking about him." I look down, as if the weight of some unspeakable sadness is burdening my body.

I'm not looking at Ben's face any longer, but I know his smile has disappeared. He thought I was hitting on him. Now it seems as if I'm confiding in him, sharing some secret pain.

"I'm sorry," he says. He reaches a hand under my chin and gently lifts my face so that my eyes meet his. I pretend to catch my breath and hold it as I watch him. My lips part ever so slowly.

His breath hitches in his throat, and before he can lean in toward me, I step back. "I—I should get back," I say, as if confused. I open my mouth, look at him, then close it.

I know I've done well by his eyes, which are filled with longing, pleading with me to step forward again.

I hate what I'm about to do. I have to sacrifice the one thing that has come to mean something to me at this school. But I need to get Ben alone to make him truly mine. "Do you want to go somewhere with me tonight?" I say finally.

He nods, his longing eyes still on mine. "Yeah." His throat is dry, and his voice rattles as it comes out.

"Meet me here at lights-out," I tell him.

"Okay," he says. He trusts me. I see it in his eyes, hear it in his voice. He doesn't even know me, will never know me, but he trusts me.

I turn, nearly tripping in my haste, and hurry back to Faraday.

CHAPTER 13

It's an eternity until lights-out. I try to focus on my history reading about Louis XIV and Versailles, but none of the words stick in my head. So what if he built a magnificent palace? His descendant, Louis XVI, married Marie Antoinette, one of the most ridiculous, weak women in history. The French Revolution occurred when she was queen, and the revolutionaries were only too happy to cut off her head. Mother taught me through Marie Antoinette's example that when you have power, you shouldn't waste it.

I finally shove the textbook aside and try to calm myself by sketching. I sketch Marie Antoinette as I think she might have looked: a decorative woman obsessed with fashion and frivolous things. Her hair is piled high on top of her head, so high that it must droop over and bring her whole body with it.

I call Mother once the hallway clears out, certain she will be eager to talk to me about Helper's visit.

She answers with "He told you that you must get Ben to run away with you?"

A part of me was hoping Helper was wrong and she would tell me to stick to the original plan of just breaking his heart. I stifle a sigh. "Yes."

"Do you think you are capable of that?"

I give her the only acceptable answer. "Yes."

"And you have to do it right after March seventh, as soon as he turns eighteen, so he won't be able to graduate. Make it happen, Vivian, or there will be consequences."

"Yes, Mother," I say.

I hang up and walk back to my room, where I fling myself on my bed and stare up at the ceiling. Four months. That's how long I have to make a boy so obsessed with me that he leaves his entire life behind.

I rub my temples as I remember what Mother told me about Collingsworth. She met a boy and fell instantly in love with him, but he didn't notice her. So she threw herself in his path, training herself in the art of coy glances and flirtatious conversation that she would later teach me. And he paid attention to her, for a while. "But I had no sense of how to keep a boy," she told me, her eyes gazing out the den window as she remembered, her voice cracking with pain. "I did not know how to keep his love. So he rejected me. He threw me off like I was nothing."

She learned later how to correct her mistake. Making a boy fall in love with you is infinitely harder than attracting him, she taught me. But by drawing him in and pushing him away, pulling him away from his friends, and slowly building a connection, I can do it. I have to do it. And then, maybe, I can convince him to run away with me.

Finally, Claire returns from the library, and it's almost time for lights-out. She watches me as I hurry into my coat. I have to get outside before they flash the lights and order everyone back to their rooms. "Cover for me if anyone asks, would you?" I ask Claire as I fan my long hair down the back of my coat.

She nods. She has snuck out so often this week that she shouldn't question my own rebellion, but she still tilts her head, looking at me curiously. That's something I'll have to deal with later.

I rush out into the darkness, staying away from the gas lamps that light the yard, their circles of hazy gold threatening to reveal me. It's much riskier to sneak out now instead of waiting for Jenkins's smoke break, but if we leave when everyone else does, it would be too obvious that we're going off together. We have to take the risk.

Ben is waiting for me, his broad form covered with shadows. He smiles at me, but his eyes are uncertain.

I don't smile back. I look back over my shoulder, as if I'm afraid of being pursued, and catch hold of his wrist, pulling him along with me over the worn footholds of the wall and down the hill.

"Where are we going?" he asks, his voice a whisper in the whistling dark.

"You'll see," I answer, shooting him a mysterious smile. The wind pushes us along as we sprint, and I hear the measured in-and-out of his breath beside me.

The moors are transformed under the night sky. The land is black and murky, but the sky above us shimmers with stars. A few clouds drift between us and them, but they can't overwhelm the brightness. The wind is perfumed with the smell of earth and rain, and I drink it in.

I don't slow down, even when we're out of sight of the school. There's something comforting about my sneakers thudding against the earth, as if I'm pounding out all of my uncertainty and frustration and fear. Ben seems content to keep up, flying over the hills with me. There are moments when he comes so close that he almost runs into me, but he swerves out of the way just in time, laughing. I pretend to laugh, too.

We are wild things.

It doesn't take long to reach the cottage, though I wish it would. Cold dread twists through me when I think of what I have to do when we get there. But the cottage comes into sight much too soon, its wooden slats gleaming in the light from the half moon above. We slow to a walk, both of us breathing hard, our breath creating slight puffs of steam that shimmer around our heads.

"What is this?" Ben asks. He runs his hand over the rough wood panels, as if he can't believe this is here until he touches it.

I watch him, try to reconcile this boy with the hidden part of my life. I slip past the door, and he follows. "I found it a few days after I came here. I needed someplace—someplace to be alone."

I light the candles, and he looks around the room, taking in the collapsed roof and my sketches taped to the walls. There is one of him, my first attempt at capturing the enemy as I need to see him, and I rip it down when he's looking the other way. "You really are an artist," he says, giving the word serious weight.

I say nothing. I stare at one of my drawings, one depicting the strange trees around here, and try to see it as the work of an artist. But it's too personal, too much a part of me, to be considered that way.

I've never shown my work to anyone besides Ms. Elling. And

Arthur. He knew about all the hours I spent up in my room, pouring my emotions out into images only he and I could read. I feel cut open, exposed, as Ben stares at the inner workings of my mind.

For a moment he fingers the ripped photo of the headless girl, the one I found on my first visit to the cottage, and then comes to stand behind me to look at my sketch of the tree. He's so close that I can almost *feel* the small distance between us. As if we're magnets. I lean into him. He's solid at my back, and my head fits into the groove of his shoulder.

"What made you draw this one?" he asks. I can feel the rumble of his voice all along my spine.

I try to focus. "I wanted to show how strong it is. How willful. It shouldn't be there. It's bent over like it's about to be ripped out of the earth. But it isn't. It stays." The sketch still doesn't show the power of the tree, though. Instead, it seems as if the tree is on the verge of collapse. As if the tree is weak. I haven't been able to capture that strength yet.

One of Ben's large hands comes up to rest on my hip. I know something will happen, if I let it.

I step away, digging in my pocket, and turn to him. I pull out two pills, which lie small and white in the palm of my hand. "Do you want one?"

His eyes narrow as he takes one. "I've never tried Molly before."

I shrug, as if it's no big deal. "It makes you feel light. Incredibly, almost unbearably happy." So happy that you don't feel real anymore, I almost add, but I stop myself.

He smiles. "That doesn't sound so bad." He looks at me, then pops the pill in his mouth when I do.

I hold mine under my tongue and silently spit it out when he looks the other way. I can't lose control around him.

It will take almost an hour for him to feel the effects of the drug. I sit on the ground with my legs crossed. He follows my example, sitting so close that our knees brush together. I've brought my sketchbook, and I flip it open to a blank page. "I want to draw you," I tell him. "But I don't know which *you* I want to capture."

"I didn't know there were, you know, different versions of me," he says with a short laugh.

I smile as I pick up one of my charcoal pencils. "There's the you in class. The boy who raises his hand with the right answer. There's the boy in the dining hall, laughing with his friends. And then there's the boy I like best."

I begin drawing lines on the page, capturing his strong jaw first.

"What boy do you like best?" he asks when I don't say it.

"The boy who debates Tennyson with me. The boy with the warm hazel eyes. The boy who sees me. The real you."

He stares at me intently, and I know I've done well. "Capture that one," he says, his voice soft and deep.

I nod, my head bent over the paper already. It takes only a few strokes to get his face on the page, but his eyes take much longer. I want to show them as they are now, filled with softness and new understanding and want. When I'm done, I'm looking at a sketch of a boy who's anything but arrogant. It's a truer likeness than any of those drawings where I tried to see the enemy in him, and that realization startles me. I show it to him, and he studies it carefully.

"Can I keep it?"

I nod.

He looks up at me, his eyes big and serious. "Draw yourself now."

I blink. I've never drawn myself before.

"Which me should I draw?" I ask finally.

He answers without hesitation. "The girl who leads a bloke to a rundown cottage in the moors in the middle of the night. The one who seems like she belongs to another world. The one who can't help but be noticed."

I let my eyes rest on him for a moment. I feel a blush rising up to my cheeks, which surprises me. I like the way he sees me. Even though all of it is fake, even though I'm supposed to be a heartless weapon, I like the way he sees me.

I sketch out something quickly, trying to follow his instructions. A girl emerges on the page. Her hair is thick and glossy. Her mouth is a bow. Her eyes are wide, trusting, true.

I look nothing like this girl. But the image pleases him. "Can I keep this one, too?"

I nod, and he takes it reverently. As if it is a promise.

And then the drug begins to rear its head inside his body. I can see it when he starts drumming his fingers on his leg, and a careless smile spreads across his face. "This feels . . . brilliant."

"Mmmm," I murmur, closing my eyes and letting a slight smile show. When his hand covers mine and begins rubbing up and down my arm, my eyes snap open. I stand, pulling him with me. "Come on," I whisper with a giggle in my voice. "There's something I want to do."

His eyes widen as I pull him outside. I let go of his hand and run up a hill, stretching my arms out to the sky. And then I scream, let out a howl of glory at the moon, my voice rising up over the hills and into the night.

It's all an act, a bit of wild abandon to make me even more irresistible. But part of me feels a sense of release, like all of the tension of the day is escaping with my cry.

He collapses in laughter behind me. "What . . . are you . . . doing?" he asks, gasping for breath.

I grin wildly at him. "Try it!" I yell. "Just scream at the moon." I do it again. I am the embodiment of a free spirit.

Behind me, a low but joyous howl echoes mine. And then he's running, bounding over the hills, splashing mud onto his jeans in his frenzy. We run and yell and terrify the night with our joy.

He runs up to me as I fling my arms up to the moon, tackling me onto the mud. It knocks the wind out of me, and it takes a few moments before I can laugh and reassure him that I'm all right. He's lying on top of me, his body pressing down fully on mine. He looks into my eyes, his smile fading into something more serious. Into a look of resolution.

And then his lips are on mine, and for a moment, I almost lose myself to them. It shocks me. I taste the urgency on his lips, feel the soft flicker of his tongue, and something in me wants to surrender to it. As if I'm just a girl. A normal, guileless girl tangled up with a boy on the moors.

I kiss back, answering his urgency with some of my own. We are dark and desperate.

He seems content to kiss me in his drug-induced state, and soon he slows, his kisses becoming more deliberate and more devouring. We lie there for hours, sinking into the mud, kissing each other as if there's nothing else in this world but our connection.

He falls asleep next to me after taking off his warm coat and folding it over the two of us to guard against the chill of the night. I count his breaths, tracing the contours of his face with my eyes. He almost looks innocent as he sleeps, younger, more vulnerable. I want to paint him like this, the spatters of mud on his face, the trusting stillness. The boy who is letting me ruin his life, though he doesn't know it yet.

CHAPTER 14

I watch the rise and fall of Ben's chest until the sun begins flickering on the horizon and shake him awake when it has bathed us in a golden light.

He wakes with a start, sitting up and looking around in confusion. We lie on the damp earth on top of a hill, the land stretching out around us. We are startlingly alone. It's a gold-and-brown morning, and the wind is kinder than usual as it brushes over us. He doesn't know what to make of this new world I've led him into.

I wait, silent, until he turns to me. Some of the confusion fades from his eyes, and he leans into me, claiming my mouth again with his. My lips are almost rubbed raw from last night, but I let him kiss me now, sweet and gentle.

I pull away softly. "We should get back," I say, letting regret seep into my voice.

He nods, cupping my chin in his hand and leaning his forehead against mine. "Only if you promise we can come here again."

I brush against his cheek softly, a flutter of a kiss. "I promise," I say, though the thought of another night like this one sends a shiver up my spine that I can't define.

We walk back to school hand in hand, his long fingers wrapped securely around mine. I want to pull my hand back, reclaim it as my own, but I swallow that feeling and keep it in his. It seems to make him happy.

At the wall, we separate with a deep kiss. He looks into my eyes and seems to like what he thinks he finds, because a bright smile lights up his face. We part without a word.

I scale the wall behind Faraday, and just as my head clears the top of it, I spot Jenkins lumbering out the back door. I duck down, my feet scraping off the footholds, and I have to clench my fingers on the top of the wall to hold on. By the time I find my footing again and peek my head back up, Jenkins is gone.

I clear the wall and creep into the dorm, hoping no one is up early. It would help my strange reputation if someone saw me sneaking in, but I don't want to deal with anyone else looking at me right now, judging me, forcing me to acknowledge her presence. I want to lock myself away somewhere, alone. The halls are thankfully empty in the early morning stillness, and I get through them without any hassle.

But when I get to our room, Claire isn't nestled up in her blankets, sleeping off another hangover, as I expected her to be. Instead, she is sitting at her desk, typing furiously. She doesn't even look up. "Forgot a biology lab write-up due today," she mutters. "Where have you been?"

"Nowhere," I murmur. I try to sound nonchalant, but something in my voice catches her attention. She looks over her shoulder at me, confused, and then her mouth drops.

"What on earth . . . ?" She looks me over like she doesn't quite believe I'm real.

I look down. My clothes are covered in mud, practically caked with it. I know I probably have smudges on my face, too, and when I brush a hand over my hair, I feel how matted and dirty it is. I must look like a wild animal.

I smile sheepishly, which I know Claire will find endearing. "I should probably take a shower," I say, grabbing my towel before she can ask what I've been doing.

Mud swirls down the drain as I wash last night off of my body. I can't wash off the feel of Ben's lips on my skin, though. I wonder if I even want to. I close my eyes, replaying the night before. I was acting, wasn't I?

I can't remember what I was thinking when we kissed. Or

even if I was thinking anything at all. I know I started kissing him because I was supposed to, but then . . .

I'm traveling down a dangerous road, I tell myself, stepping out of the shower and twisting my hair up in a towel. I can't give my heart to a boy who will most certainly break it. Not again.

CHAPTER 15

Claire says nothing about my frenzied sunrise appearance. But all throughout the day I catch her glancing at me with her head tilted to the side, considering me, everywhere: in English class, in the dining hall, when we pass each other in the hallways. It sets my teeth on edge. I feel as if she's on the hunt for me, as if she's about to uncover my true identity and warn Ben about me. She's adding up all the details that have puzzled her, and it's only a matter of time before she comes to the correct conclusion.

Claire isn't the only one watching me in the hallways over the next two weeks as November wears on. Ben and Arabella seem to appear wherever I am, one of them smiling sweetly at me, the other one practically growling.

I can't find Arthur anywhere. His shed is always shuttered and dark, and there's no trace of him on campus. Did he see Helper and get away in time? Has he left me here? Or did Helper find *him*?

I can't think about that. I won't think about it. He's fine, and I have to focus.

It's never difficult to convince Ben to run away to the cottage. We disappear into the night, and he takes Molly whenever I give it to him, kissing me until we fall asleep.

One night, after two weeks of sneaking around together, we sit on the small hearth in front of a fire that I built, and his kisses become more insistent, more passionate. He eases me down to the floor, his body covering mine with its heavy warmth, and for a moment, I let him. I pull him close to me, but when he slips his hand up my shirt, I push at him gently. "I—I don't want to sleep with you yet," I say, biting my lip as if I'm flustered. I keep my hand on his chest and my eyes on his, a hint of uncertainty in my expression.

He watches me, his eyes dark, and for a moment, the only sound in the room is our deep breathing and the crackle of the fire.

"I want to wait until we're in love," I continue.

This is part of Mother's "playing hard to get" lesson, something that she swore would make him more obsessed with me. Anne Boleyn used the same tactic when she was trying to steal King Henry VIII from his first wife, and it certainly worked for her.

Ben gives a thoughtful nod and a reassuring smile, lifting me back up so that we're seated once more, shoulder to shoulder. "I can wait," he agrees before wrapping me back up in his arms, my side pressed to his. "For you, I can wait."

I bury my head in his chest to hide the surprise on my face.

It's getting harder to control him at school, however.

The next afternoon, I spot him with his usual crew between classes, when the halls are filled with the clattering of lockers and overexcited conversation. His friends, Liam and Colin, are laughing and slapping each other's backs as they watch a girl shoot what she must think are seductive glances at them. It's the girl who kissed Ben that first night out on the moors, I realize, and my eyes snap back to him, worried. Ben, though, leans back against his locker and seems bored by it all. Until he spots me, and then his face lights up, a broad smile stretching across it. The girl simpers, thinking it's meant for her.

He steps toward me, like he's coming to embrace me right there in the hallway. In front of his friends, his admirers, the world. He must have forgotten who I am, how people see me in this school.

I spin on my heel and hurry away.

"So should we, uh, tell people about us?" he asks a few nights later at the cottage before I can offer him anything to alter his mind and hook him to me.

I've been coaxing a small flame to life in the hearth, and at his words, I stand and face him. "What?" I ask, feigning surprise. As if I didn't notice his acknowledgment of me in the hallway.

"I just—I'd like you to be my girlfriend, and I . . . I want to tell everyone."

He looks not at me but at a spot on the ground. Which means he can't see the sudden flash of horror that I know travels across my face.

I have to think quickly. Mother would recommend that I push him away. She would want me to tell him I can't be his girlfriend, then leave the cottage and refuse to look at him for a week. Tormenting him and playing hard to get would make him want me even more.

A girl like the kind he's used to would gasp and swoon and say yes immediately.

But I can't do either. I can only stare at him. The wind howls outside, as if it, too, is impatient for my answer.

Finally, he looks up, meeting my gaze. "Well?" he asks with an uncertain smile.

Mother is wrong. Pushing him away, running away from him, not talking to him—that will only hurt him. It will be harder to get him back if I've hurt him like that. There's something in him that reminds me of a kicked puppy. It's hard for him to trust. There are moments when I recognize myself in him.

So I head for the middle ground. "I want to be your girl-friend," I tell him, earning a relieved smile. "But—"

"What?" he interrupts, encircling me in his arms. "No buts. Buts aren't allowed."

He pulls me in for a kiss, and it takes me a moment to end it and look back up in his eyes. "*But,*" I continue. "I don't want people talking about us all the time. I feel like it could ruin us." A secret relationship, when done right, can be a powerful aphrodisiac.

"Who cares what they say?" he asks.

"I just—I want to keep us a secret for a while. I don't want to attract too much attention."

"Too late," he teases. "You're much too beautiful not to attract attention."

I put a hand on his chest, pushing him back. "Ben," I say, as if exasperated.

"All right, all right," he says, putting his hands up in mock surrender. "I won't say anything to anyone. As long as you agree to be my girlfriend."

"Done," I say, nodding my head solemnly before rewarding him with a glittering smile. The smile hides the panic rising within me. I've disobeyed Mother, and if this tactic doesn't work, I can't bear to think what my punishment might be.

CHAPTER 16

When Arabella hip-checks me in the hall the next morning on my way to class, I know I have to respond. My books scatter across the floor, and my palms slap the cold marble ground to break my fall.

There's a hush, and then some laughter. "Watch where you're going, slag," Arabella singsongs.

I pick myself up, gather my books, and stand slowly. Arabella has already retreated out of sight, but I smirk, showing the others that I'm not cowed by her bullying. I even roll my eyes, as if her antics do nothing but bore me. And then I saunter down the hall to the chorus of whispers and speculation.

"Are you okay?" Claire asks as soon as I enter our room after dinner. "I heard about what happened." She looks at me with such genuine concern, and it hits me that she truly considers me a friend. She worries about me. She has no idea what I am.

"I'm fine," I say, waving my hand in the air like I could wave the memory away. "Just Arabella being Arabella."

Claire purses her lips. "She's a hard enemy to have," she says quietly. "It might be best to stay out of her way for a little while?"

"I'm never in her way. She just makes it her business to attack me."

"You did start that rumor about her giving her knickers to the gardener," Claire points out dryly, an amused smile playing on her face.

I shrug. "Fine," I say. "I'll stay out of her way."

"Good. I'd hate for Arabella to run you out of here." She wrinkles her nose, as if the very idea has disgusted her.

I laugh. "That won't happen, trust me. I'm tougher than I look."

Claire studies me for a moment, like I've revealed something important. "It should be a wild night on the moors, if you want to join?" she offers finally.

"No, thanks," I answer quickly.

"Why not? Are you going out tonight to roll around in the mud or whatever?"

I sit at my desk, facing away from her. "No," I answer.

"I don't mean to be insensitive. I just—I mean, what are you really doing when you go out there?"

I consider how to answer and finally decide that some approximation of the truth wouldn't be bad. She'll figure it out soon enough, anyway.

"I'm meeting Ben," I say, watching her face carefully. Waiting for the disbelief.

It comes swiftly. She laughs, her mouth opening to reveal her straight, wide teeth. "Very clever," she comments.

When my expression doesn't change its intensity, the smile falters on her face, then falls. "Wait, you're not serious?"

I purse my lips and nod. "He and I have a thing going," I say with a shrug, like it wouldn't create a tidal wave through the social structure of this school.

"A *thing*?" she repeats, like the word is unfamiliar to her. Did I use the wrong phrasing? I can't tell.

"It's a secret, so don't spread it around, okay?"

She juts her lips out, a word about to form on the ends of them, but she holds it in.

I wait for her to gather her thoughts. To decide what question she wants to ask first. "Why is it a secret?" wins.

"Because I want it to be," I answer, stacking my textbooks on my desk in the order I need them. "I don't want the whole school talking about us like we're public property. I don't really know what he and I are yet, but I know I don't want the scrutiny."

She nods slowly. It's actually a reasonable argument. "How did it happen?" she asks next. There's a smile forming on her face, and she sits on her fluffy pink bed, getting comfortable. This is the point where I'm supposed to dish, and we'll giggle, like all those teenage romance movies Mother made me watch as research.

The idea tires me, but I oblige. "We got to talking about a Tennyson poem once, because we're in English class together, you know? And he's . . . he's smarter than I thought. He was easy to talk to. And it became something more." I stop, hoping that's enough.

She's watching me with her mouth open in wonder. Like I'm telling her a love story. "So where do you sneak off to?"

I smile, as if the thought of it gives me butterflies. "Just somewhere."

She doesn't pry; that's not the interesting part anyway. "So when you came home that morning covered in mud . . ." Her voice trails off in a question.

I nod and hide my cheeks in my hands. I feel a blush rise there—a real blush. It confuses me. "He's different when he's with me," I say. Maybe I shouldn't be revealing so much, but her curious, happy expression opens up something inside me.

"He's so warm and sweet. I never expected him to be like that, because he's so cocky with his friends. He keeps surprising me." I stop myself, pursing my lips. Am I beginning to care for him? I can't be. It would ruin Mother's plan. It would ruin me.

"It sounds serious," she says with a teasing smile. "You sure you know what you're getting into?"

"No idea," I admit.

CHAPTER 17

I make my move against Arabella the next day by targeting her two best friends, Lily and Anna. I find them talking in the hallway by their lockers that Wednesday morning, clustered around Arabella. The hallway is filled with chattering people, all of them happy and mindless. The perfect spot to make a scene. I approach Arabella and her friends with a smirk firmly in place. They watch me coming, confusion marring their faces. "What do you want?" Arabella asks, cocking her hip and placing her hand on it.

I ignore her for a moment, looking around to make sure we have everyone's attention. Everyone around us has stopped, waiting for the girl drama to erupt. I focus on Lily and Anna. "Careful she doesn't do to you what she did to Emily," I say in a loud conspiratorial whisper. "I heard they were both having an affair with Mr. Park, but she turned Emily in so she wouldn't get caught herself."

"That's ridiculous," Arabella scoffs.

I raise my eyebrows. "Then why did you get such a good grade in the course? A bit suspicious, don't you think?"

It's not at all suspicious, considering Arabella is a fairly good student, but Lily and Anna look at their friend with uncertainty.

"You two know about her slutty sister, right?" I ask. "Looks like it runs in the family."

As Arabella fumes, I laugh and move on down the hall. Everyone watches me as I go, some of them smiling, most of them whispering to their friends, covering their mouths with their hands as their awe-struck, ridiculing words slip out.

I allow myself a small private smile as I walk away from the scene. Mother told me to keep provoking her, and I've certainly done that. Arabella will have to fight back now, and as soon as she does, she'll reveal to Ben how shallow his group of friends really is.

After the last class a few days later, I finally find Arthur, and the knot in my chest that I've been trying so hard to ignore for the past three weeks loosens. He's trimming the tall hedges at the front gate of the school, and I hurry over to him, looking back over my shoulder to make sure no one's watching me. There are a few students wandering about in the rare sunshine beaming down on us, so I'll have to be discreet.

"I have to talk to you," I hiss at him.

He looks up, surprised, holding his shears in the air as he watches me rush past him. I don't stop until I've reached his shed, and he's right behind me to let me inside. He brushes against me as he pushes his key into the lock, and instead of moving, I look up at him. I reach just to his shoulder, so when I look up at his face, I see the cut of his jawbone and the smooth planes of his cheeks. It makes my breath catch in my chest.

He opens the door and gestures me inside.

"What's going on?" he asks, his expression now impassive as he crosses his arms and looks at me.

"Where have you been?" I ask, crossing my own arms. I want to put as much distance between us as possible, but the minuscule shed, all of it cluttered with books and papers, makes it difficult. My arms almost touch his, even though I have my back pressed against the wall. "Your father was here."

"I know," he says with a sigh. "I saw him creeping around the edges of the school, so I got off campus as quickly as I could and told the administration that I had a death in the family so

I could stay away until I was sure he was gone. I had an errand to run in London anyway."

"What errand?" I ask.

"Nothing you need to worry about." There's something he's not telling me, but I don't press. "What was he doing here?" he asks.

"What do you think? He was spying on me."

"Did you talk to him? Did he mention me?" He's watching me intently, and I notice the dark circles under his eyes, like he hasn't slept at all the past three weeks. He must have been so terrified to see his father wandering around the school, so close to this new life he created for himself.

I surprise both of us when I reach out and touch his arm. I'm trying to calm him, but it only startles him, and he jumps back from my touch, nearly crashing into the wall. I pull my hand back, and a strange feeling courses through me. Embarrassment, I realize, as I feel my cheeks begin to flush. Why on earth had I thought to touch him? That's never been my reaction before.

I cross my arms again and try to regain some semblance of composure. "I talked to him, but he said nothing about you. He'd been spying on me that morning, but you were gone. Then he showed up in my history class."

"What did he say?"

For a moment, I don't know what to tell him. "He didn't say anything about you," I repeat, and then I close my mouth determinedly.

He stares at me with those intense brown eyes, trying to work something out in his mind. His cheekbones seem even sharper as he frowns. I keep my expression carefully blank, not sure what he's looking for.

One of the skills Mother taught me is how to stay silent when you sense someone wants to tell you a secret. Making them speak first makes them nervous, and they're more likely to tell more than they meant to.

Arthur's too smart for that trick, though. "If you see him again, tell me as soon as possible. If he finds me here, everything will be ruined."

"*What* will be ruined?" I ask, exasperated.

He shakes his head. "Just trust me." He smiles a little, something small and sad, as if he realizes how impossible his request is.

I nod and head for the door. There's nothing more to be learned here. But just as I get my hand on the latch, Arthur steps up behind me. I freeze. I can feel his warm breath on my neck, the heat radiating from his body. "You and Ben have been sneaking out," he whispers.

I don't turn around. I don't trust myself to move. "How did

you hear that?" We ran away to the cottage last night, where Ben accepted another white pill and kissed me under the stars.

"Are you sure you know what you're doing?" he asks, his voice so sharp it cuts into my skin.

I turn the latch and rush out into the fresh air. No one is around to see, but I run back to Faraday like I'm escaping a wildfire.

CHAPTER 18

A couple of days later, after the last literary magazine meeting of November, in which we vote on whether swear words will be allowed in the final publication (they pass unanimously), I come back to my room to find a girl I don't know sitting on Claire's bed, alone.

Surprised, I stare at her dumbly for a moment. I haven't seen her in the halls before. Suddenly, I realize who she must be.

"Hi!" she says brightly, springing up and holding her hand out to me. "I'm Emily, Claire's friend."

She's tall and willowy, with cropped brown hair that accentuates the angles of her face. Her light brown eyes have an almost almond shape to them, and her smile reveals a small but perfect row of white teeth. She's much more naturally beautiful than I am, and almost as striking. I try to smile. "You're the girl who used to live here," I say, shaking her hand quickly.

"So she's told you about me," Emily says, settling back down on Claire's fluffy pink bed and watching me carefully.

"She said you were great," I hedge.

"And?" Emily prompts with an embarrassed smile.

"And that you got kicked out for sleeping with your chemistry teacher for a good grade." I make sure to leave any sense of judgment out of my tone.

"The story that never dies," she says ruefully.

"Did you?" I ask, though I know the answer.

She raises an eyebrow at my bluntness, but laughs. "Please," she answers, rolling her eyes. "Mr. Park is, like, in his thirties. Disgusting. Someone forged those letters to make it look like my handwriting and sent them to the headmaster. I just don't know who would have done it."

Claire walks through the door I've left open, nearly tripping over her own feet when she sees the girl I'm talking to.

"Emily!" she cries out. Emily jumps up again from the bed and pulls my much-shorter roommate into a hug.

"I snuck in to see you," Emily announces, holding up a back-pack. "I brought sandwiches, so you have to skip dinner and catch up with me."

I grab my own backpack so that I can escape to the library.

"I'll leave you two to it." I walk out the door as the squeals and exclamations of "It's been *sooo* long" continue.

I wait until two hours after dinner before I head back to the dorm, ducking my head and running as rain sputters down from the sky. I want Emily to be gone, to have my sanctuary back.

But when I enter the room, she's still there, and Claire is even bubblier than usual. They sit on the floor, a mound of bright foil candy wrappers between them. Their laughter fills up the room, pushing off the gloom of the evening outside.

"Vivian!" Claire cries out, as if it's been years since she's seen me. "We're breaking into my candy bar stash. Do you want any?"

They both beam up at me. I shift my weight from one foot to the other, wondering if I should head back to the library. But the prospect of going back into the cold, spitting rain holds even less appeal than submitting to a night of girl bonding.

"Sure," I say finally, settling down on my bed.

"One for you," Claire declares, handing me a chocolate bar with a flourish. "And one for you." She hands another to Emily. "Don't worry. There aren't any peanuts in it," she says with a smile.

Emily laughs, tucking her long legs underneath her, completely at home in this room that used to be hers. "I have a severe peanut allergy," she explains, looking up at me. "If I have a peanut, the doctors say I might die, so I have to have an EpiPen with me at all times."

I nod, trying to seem concerned.

"Hey, did you ever find your EpiPen?" Claire asks, tearing open a new candy bar for herself.

"Nope. Had to get a new one," Emily answers. She looks back at me, and I meet her eyes. "I lost it a few weeks before they kicked me out."

Her words have set off a subtle alarm in my head, quiet but insistent.

Claire asks Emily about her new school, and I pretend like I'm fascinated, but really my mind is racing.

Is it strange that Emily lost her EpiPen around the same time Mother was targeting her and trying to get her out the way so I could enroll in Madigan? Could there have been some plan to kill Emily and make it look like an accident? Would Mother and Helper have gone that far to ensure that I got a spot? The thought makes bile rise in the back of my throat, and I take a shaky breath.

When the lights flicker for lights-out, we all hurry to find our pajamas and get ready for bed.

"Aren't you going to say goodnight to Victoria?" Emily asks Claire as she pulls a toothbrush out of her bag. I have no idea who she's talking about until Claire, biting her lip, glances at her laptop. Only then do I remember that Claire's Ava is named Victoria. It's been at least a month since I've seen her interacting with it.

"I think I've outgrown her," Claire says with a weak attempt at rolling her eyes. "I don't need some digital doll telling me how cool and posh I am anymore."

Emily frowns but says nothing, studying her former roommate with curious eyes.

She sleeps on the floor that night, her breathing slow and untroubled, and I spend the long, dark hours staring up at the ceiling and trying not to think.

Emily sneaks off campus the next morning, and life returns to normal.

But "normal" is beginning to feel claustrophobic. All of my free time must be spent doing homework or kissing Ben or kissing Ben while doing homework. And we're all crowded together on this hill, living on top of each other. I can't avoid Arabella's glowering looks in the hall, though the cautious looks her friends show me are definitely amusing. I've even had to give up my cottage, the one place I thought I could be alone. And I'm suffocating.

I drag Ben out to the cottage more and more over the next

two weeks as December falls over us, pulling him away from school on weeknights and weekends, any time we can get away. Even if I have to act around him, at least there's only one person in the space around me.

"What's your family like?" he asks one night when the wind is howling so loudly outside the cottage that we almost have to shout to hear each other. We're standing next to the fire he's just built, rubbing our hands together and trying desperately to warm up. The world outside has grown colder and more unpredictable, the wind and rain heavier, wilder.

Mother has prepared me for this question. "I never knew my father. He abandoned my mother when he found out she was pregnant. He didn't want anything to do with me, so I didn't want anything to do with him."

"I'm sorry," he says.

I shrug, a little gesture to suggest that I'm trying to act like it's not a big deal, even though on the inside it *is* a big deal. I stare unblinking into the flames.

"So your mum raised you?"

I bite the inside of my lip. "She brought me up in her image. She controls every little thing I do. Everything. That's why I was homeschooled for so long. She wanted to mold me herself. I'm not allowed to make any of my own decisions. And if I disobey her . . ." I stop and shudder delicately.

I can feel him watching me, and he shifts closer now. "What did she do to you?"

This isn't part of the story Mother devised, but for some reason I can't stop myself from telling him. "One time," I say slowly, "she got so mad at me that she took the fireplace poker and branded me. Here," I say, lifting up my shirt and showing him the inch-long burn mark on my hipbone. "She said I was hers." I had walked in on her yelling at the portrait of her mother over the fireplace, and I can still see the wild roll of her eyes and feel the poker singeing into my skin.

He breathes out one long, sad sigh. He reaches his hand out, trailing the back of a finger along the raised skin, and I shiver. "I'm sorry," he says. "I'm so, so sorry."

I resist the urge to shift uncomfortably. I don't know what to say to that.

Luckily, he speaks first. "My father's not as bad, not nearly," he tells me. "But he's still an asshole."

I hold my breath, waiting for him to continue.

"He's planned out my whole future for me. I'm going here, just like he did."

My eyebrows knit together. "Your father went to Madigan?"

He nods. "Both my parents did. It's where they met."

Mother never mentioned this, and that makes it feel even more significant. I shouldn't be surprised, because I've always known she and Collingsworth met at a school in Britain, but she always made it seem as if she'd researched Madigan from afar. I try to mask the confusion tumbling through me and focus on Ben.

"After I graduate," he continues, "I'm supposed to go to Oxford, because it's so prestigious. Never mind that he didn't, you know, even bother to apply to university. Then I'll work at his company and, when he thinks I'm ready, take over the business. He started a major tech company a year after high school, even though he knows absolutely *nothing* about computers. You know Avas?"

"Of course," I say, my eyes growing wide as I feign surprise, even though Claire told me about Collingsworth and Ava my first night here. "That's his company?"

Ben nods glumly. "It's all he bloody cares about. Money and power. He's about to start a line of girlfriend Avas. He says they're for boys who want more practice talking to girls, but it's basically porn. He's turning everyone's childhood best friend into a digital porn doll because that's where the profits are. He always says, 'All's fair in love and war.' He's too lazy to even come up with his own damn catchphrase." I press my lips together and try not to show my surprise. That's the phrase Mother always spat out at me, as if the taste of the words was too bitter. Of course. They'd been bitter because she'd been repeating *his* favorite saying.

Ben takes a deep breath. "He certainly never gave a flying fuck about me." He stops, blinking hard.

There's nothing I can say. He doesn't want my pity, I know that much. He just wants me there. So I move closer to him, wrapping my arms around his middle and resting my head in the crook of his shoulder, where it fits so well. He wraps his arms around me and touches his lips to the top of my head, a strong seal of a kiss. It's not like our other kisses, which are born out of desire and need. This one is more powerful.

I interrupt the moment to ask the question Mother instructed me to in her last email. "What about your mother?"

"She died when I was eleven," he says, almost in a whisper. "My dad shoved me off to boarding school not long after. He couldn't deal with me."

"I'm so sorry. What was she like?"

Ben thinks a long moment before answering. "She was . . . soft. Gentle. She had this way of sort of, um, sort of floating around the house and making everything brighter. She was very light, so light that she often didn't make any noise while she walked. Dad used to call her the ghost of the house, because she would always appear out of nowhere." He pauses, stepping out of my hug and looking down at his hands. "My dad killed her."

The statement hangs in the air, and it takes my breath away. "What do you mean?" I croak out finally.

"She had the biggest heart, and he broke it. She hardly had any family, just an aunt who sent her to boarding school when she was eight. When she got pregnant with me, she was about to start university, and he made her withdraw. He was all she had, besides me. And he cheated on her constantly, with women who could never hope to be as beautiful as she was." His voice grows sharper, and I know when he looks into the fire that he's picturing all of the things he'd like to do to his father to punish him. "He didn't even notice when she got sick. He didn't even care when she was too weak to come down for dinner or get out of bed in the morning. By the time she finally got to a doctor, the cancer had spread too far to be treated."

He presses his hands against the wall, pushing it with all his strength. "I promised my mum before she died that when I fell in love with a girl, I'd treat her right. She didn't want me to be afraid of marriage, so I promised her that when I found the girl I loved so much that I couldn't stand to be without her, I'd marry her. And that I'd, you know, I'd keep loving her." He stops pushing the wall, his arms falling to his sides and his chin dropping to his chest, but he doesn't turn back to me.

I step toward him cautiously and put my hand on his arm. "We can't rely on our parents," I tell him, making my voice soft and wistful. "We have to make our own destinies."

He looks at me for one long, hard moment, and then sweeps

me into his arms. That night he takes two pills and clings to me as if I'm the only thing keeping him attached to this earth.

I've been going to art tutorials more and more, drawn in by the silent space Ms. Elling and the other students offer in the studio. The next day after dinner, I'm trying to sketch the tree near my cottage, the one so bent over that its branches bump along the ground. But I still can't translate the feeling of it onto the page.

Ms. Elling peers over my shoulder. "Still interested in the trees, I see," she murmurs.

I toss my charcoal down. "It's not working."

She purses her lips off to one side, thinking. "I wish I had one of her drawings to show you. But it was so long ago."

"Whose drawings?" I ask.

"Hmm? Oh, Rose. Rose Travers. Or Rose Hampden, as she was back then. The student I told you about before, the one you remind me of. She did the most exquisitely emotional drawing of a tree a bit like this one here. But that was so long ago."

"How did she do it?" I ask.

Ms. Elling shakes her head. "Honestly, I don't know if I can describe it. She said the moors inspired her, and she would spend hours crossing them. Sometimes even getting into trouble for it. But she knew she had an ally in me." Her eyes drop down to the table, and I see the glint of tears gathering at the edges of them.

"What's wrong?" I ask, since the question seems to hang in the air between us.

Ms. Elling sighs. "Just talking about Rose . . . I'm reminded of what happened to her. It was tragic, actually. The year after graduation, her house was robbed. The burglars killed her husband when he tried to stop them. Shot him point-blank in the head. And then not one month afterward—well, she's had a few horrible experiences, let's just say that. I've tried to visit her since then, but she doesn't see people anymore. She stays locked up in that old house." Ms. Elling looks out the classroom window, caught in some memory.

I stay silent and wait for her to remember that I'm here, turning back to my paper and picking up my charcoal.

Ms. Elling snaps her fingers in my ear, and the charcoal nearly falls back out of my hand. "The yearbooks!" she exclaims.

"What?"

"Rose won an art prize in her final year. What was that, twenty years ago? Let's see, when did I go to that awards ceremony?" She looks down at her fingers, the pad of her thumb traversing from pinky to index finger as she counts.

"Rose's drawing is in the yearbook?" I ask when the silence has stretched on too long.

"Yes! You can see it for yourself. There have to be old year-books around this campus somewhere."

"The student lounge," I offer, remembering seeing the row of them there my first day at Madigan.

"Brilliant," she says, brushing me up from my chair. "Go look. See if you find inspiration, and come back tomorrow to show me."

I gather up my things as quickly as possible before she shoos me out of the room.

The yearbooks stand proud and neglected on the bottom shelf of the bookcase in the lounge, just as I remembered. I settle down on the floor in front of them, ignoring the curious stares of the three girls at a table behind me.

I start with the book from twenty years ago, riffling through it until I find the extracurricular section. Nothing. I go through a couple more, until, finally, I turn a page to find a charcoal study of a tree.

Half the page is taken up by a photograph of a girl clutching a trophy in front of a large oil painting of a tree on the moors. Her hair is thick and dark, and her eyes are big and thoughtful. I can tell even from the grainy photograph that Rose Hampden, as the caption identifies her, has much more talent than I do. She's captured the tree so particular to this land as I've been trying to capture it; its tenacity dominates the canvas.

I study the drawing for a couple of minutes, trying to find the inspiration Ms. Elling told me to look for. I trace my fingers along the rendered curve of the trunk, its intricately detailed scattering of bumps and knots along the bark. The image is technically perfect, but it's so much more than that, too. I just have no idea how to infuse my work with that much emotional power.

I put the yearbook back in its long, steady line and sigh. But I don't get up. I stay staring at those big leather-bound volumes. Those capsules of history. History, I realize, that might have something to do with me.

The books focus on year-thirteen students only, the year I'm in. I don't know how old Mother is, so I flip through several of the books, looking for Collingsworth's name and picture. Finally, I discover him in the same yearbook as Rose. He's a slightly warped version of Ben, with the same cocky smile and glinting eyes. But his nose is bigger, and his hair doesn't curl at the ends.

This is the man who broke Mother's heart. He's the one who set everything in motion, who ensured that I would grow up as a weapon to take him down. He's evil and manipulative and everything I hate. I don't want his smile and his eyes to look like Ben's.

The thought unsettles me. I'm supposed to hate Ben, too, I remind myself.

I have to focus. I hurry through the rest of the pages, looking for Mother. I nearly pass her picture by, because she's changed so much from the hesitant-looking girl with the drapes of brown hair nearly covering her face. She peers out at the camera as if she were a deer examining the barrel of a gun, unsure if it's going to hurt her.

But there's that heart-shaped mole on her cheek. And the night-dark eyes and thin lips. Her hair seems to be light brown in this black-and-white photo, but if I imagine it as prematurely gray, I can see Mother.

Morgana Whitfield. That's her name.

Names have power, Mother taught me. They can shape a person, or reveal things they don't wish to be revealed. I know she didn't tell me she went to Madigan because she didn't want me to know her name, and I can't believe my discovery.

The name fits her. Morgana is another Arthurian name, King Arthur's sister and, by some accounts, his rival. Sometimes known as Morgan le Fay, she was an enchantress. Another Vivian.

I don't know what to do with this information, but having it makes me feel somehow powerful. I shove the yearbook into my bag and sneak it out of the lounge.

CHAPTER 19

I spend days trying to figure out all the questions that the yearbook has raised, and I know Ben can tell that I'm distracted. But he's preoccupied as well. We run away to the cottage just as often, and he kisses me just as passionately, but I catch him looking at me out of the corner of his eye a lot. Especially when he sees Arabella glaring at me in the hallways.

We're walking back to the dorms one dark morning when Ben finally broaches the subject that I know he's been mulling over.

"Why does Arabella hate you so much?" The clouds above cloak the stars and the moon, so I can barely make out the outline of his face in the gloom, but I can feel his eyes on me.

I shrug. "I don't like to pretend to be nice to fake people."

"She's not fake," Ben protests, stopping to turn and face me.

"I mean, sometimes she talks behind people's backs, but she's really not a bad person."

I have to laugh at that. "Come on! Nothing about that girl is genuine. How can you stand to be around people like that?"

He shifts from one foot to the other. "My mates are good guys," he says, trying to make his tone light. He doesn't want to argue.

I can only push this so far. So I shrug and point my eyes away, as if I don't believe him. "If you say so."

An uncomfortable silence rests heavily between us for a moment, and I rush to think of something to break it. I can't let him leave with such a bitter taste of me.

"So what was your avatar's name?" I ask, striving for a light tone.

Ben raises his eyebrows, but he doesn't look at me. "My Adam? I named him Bob."

"Bob?" I ask with a laugh. "You couldn't think of a name more creative than Bob?"

"Bob is a good name. It's strong," he says, his tone still cautious, but I think I can hear a hint of amusement behind it. "He was my best friend until I was, like, ten. He was awesome."

"I bet he loved Tennyson and damsels in distress," I tease.

That draws a ghost of a smile onto his lips. "No, I think he was more into, you know, superheroes and bathroom humor. Completely juvenile. Don't know where he got it."

As I'm beginning to smile back at him, I find myself trapped in a slash of light. The sun hasn't risen yet, and I know that we've been caught. I shield my face with my hand and squint to see Mrs. Hallie shining a flashlight at us, a worried look on her face.

Ben lets go of my hand, and we both wait to see how Mrs. Hallie will react. My mind begins to race, trying to come up with excuses. Should I cry? I blink my eyes, trying to draw tears to them, just in case.

"What's going on?" she asks.

I study her face. I can see in her uncertain frown that she knows she should punish us for sneaking around during the night, but she doesn't want to. She's too soft and loving to punish anyone.

"I'm so sorry, Mrs. Hallie," I say, stepping forward so I can look her in the eye. "Ben and I needed to study for an English literature exam, because we're both so unprepared. I know we shouldn't be out, but I can't get a bad grade on this test. It won't happen again."

Mrs. Hallie bites her lip, and then her familiar smile is back. "Of course, dear. It will be our little secret, all right?"

I nod, beaming at her. "Thank you so much, Mrs. Hallie." I give a friendly nod to Ben, who looks at me curiously, and then walk past them both back to Faraday Hall.

I observe Ben carefully for the next few days. He still laughs with his friends like always, but there's something new in his eyes when he looks at them. It's as if he's weighing all of their actions and words and trying to classify them as good or bad. When I tell Mother this on our weekly phone call, she crows with delight.

"When you isolate him from his friends, all he will have is you. He will be yours completely, to do with as you will." She cackles like one of the witches in *Macbeth*, and I shiver. I pull the sleeves of my long-sleeve tee down over my knuckles and wrap one arm around my stomach, but I still can't get warm. It feels like such a responsibility, to hold Ben's fate in my hands. Even though I know exactly what I have to do with it.

What if I wasn't meant to destroy him? I wonder. *What would I do with him if he was just a boy, and I was just a normal girl?*

I can't imagine it.

"Is he still taking the pills?"

I tell her in a whisper that he is, and my stomach flutters at the lie. Because he does take Molly occasionally, and sometimes smokes up, but more and more, he wants to just be with me without any chemical enhancement. I tell her that I think he's already addicted to Molly, though. It's as if I want to keep those nights close to me alone. I don't want to give them up to Mother, who will twist their significance into something sinister. But isn't that what they are? They are nights of destruction.

She congratulates me. "You have got him hooked, definitely. And you have handled pulling him away from his friends well. But don't pull him too hard." I nod distractedly into the phone as if she can see me.

Claire appears at the end of the hall, heading for our room. "All right, Mom," I say quickly. "Talk to you next week."

Mother takes the hint. "Make sure you do," she says before she clicks off.

I hang up the phone and smile at Claire, who's studying me. "What?" I ask.

"You didn't tell your mum you loved her," she says.

Damn it. "We're not really expressive people," I say with a shrug as we both walk to our room. It's all these little details that will hurt me in the end. I need to distract her. "You going out again tonight?"

"Why?" she asks, suddenly defensive.

Apparently that was a bad subject to broach, though I can't think why. I look at Claire more closely as she gets settled at her desk, trying to see what I've done wrong. Maybe she's hiding a secret of her own. And I'm fairly certain it has to do with all those mornings she wakes up with a headache and bloodshot eyes.

It's not something I need to get involved with, so I mutter, "Just making conversation," and turn to my own laptop, shutting Claire out.

We spend the night in frozen silence, studiously ignoring each other. I don't need her friendship anymore anyway, I tell myself. I have Ben right where I want him. Still, there's something in me that wants to take back my words, apologize to Claire for whatever I've done to offend her.

I bury that feeling and focus on homework, keeping my lips pressed firmly shut for the rest of the night.

CHAPTER 20

The next morning before history class, G-Man appears at my locker. I haven't spoken to him since he sold me Molly two months ago, though I've sent him a few sultry smiles when we've passed in the halls, just in case I need something more from him.

His dark brown hair looks even messier than usual, and there is a look of deep concern in his eyes, which erases the wannabe cocky schoolboy mask he usually wears. He's actually much more attractive for it.

"What's going on with Claire?" he asks, without saying hello first.

I close my locker and lean against it. "What do you mean?" I ask, all bewildered innocence.

"She's out of control. She took way too much Oxy last night. Nearly passed out. I stopped selling it to her a while ago, but she must have begged a few pills off somebody."

G-Man looks at me like he's expecting me to say something, to take responsibility and promise to fix it. I shift from one foot to the other, then shrug, pulling my book bag strap over my shoulder. "Claire's old enough to make her own decisions, don't you think?" I ask, my tone bored.

"I think she's got a problem. Like I said, I'm not selling to her anymore, but she needs—I don't know, someone to watch out for her." He opens his hands palm up, gesturing at me.

I stare at his hands and then at him, watching the concern in his eyes morph into exasperation. "I'm late for class," I say, pushing past him. I leave him gaping at me.

When I walk into English class later that morning, Ben smiles up at me, then turns to his friends and listens to whatever lame joke they've come up with today.

"Ms. Foster?" Ms. Prisby asks, her lips in a thin line. "If it's not too much trouble, could I have your attention, please?"

There are a few giggles and snorts of laughter behind me. I cock one eyebrow at Ms. Prisby and nod tightly. I'm sure she hates that I write such flawless papers and ace all of the tests; she's so very tempted to fail me. I can see it in her eyes every time she looks at me. Even my work on the literary magazine isn't enough to make her ignore my dismissive attitude.

I finally understand why Mother wanted me to build such animosity between us, though, when Ben catches me by the arm after class and pulls me into a supply closet. His lips are on mine as soon as the door has closed securely behind us, and I can't see anything in this dark room. My only point of reference is the feel of his hands on my hips, his tongue searching into my mouth. It anchors me, and I feel myself relax into him. Almost as if I missed this.

He pulls away for a moment, running his fingers through my hair. "I've wanted to do that all day," he whispers. "Sorry Ms. Prisby was in such a strop."

"She hates me," I say, nuzzling into his neck. "I don't know why."

He keeps his hands tangled in my hair and kisses my forehead. Like I really am a girlfriend. Like I really deserve his love and have permission to love him back.

"No one's allowed to hate you," he declares, his voice making the disinfectant-scented air swirl with anger. "I won't let them."

I laugh a little, and then fake-simper, "What would I ever do without you?"

He pulls me in for another deep kiss. "Sometimes I wish we could just, you know, run away," he murmurs, leaning his forehead against mine.

I hold my breath. I can tell from his tone, though, that in reality, it's an impossible thought to him. Something he wishes, not something he thinks will actually happen. I still have a long way to go.

"How about we just stay in here all day?" he asks, only half joking.

"Let the world outside disappear," I agree.

We let ourselves forget the world outside for a few more minutes, but if he doesn't show up for lunch, people will talk. By silent agreement, we push the door open, make sure there's no one in the hall, and head out. He goes to lunch, and I hide in the library until next period.

A smile threatens to bloom on my lips the entire time.

It's clear Claire has had enough of our mutual silence when she spots me in the hall that afternoon. She grabs me by the arm before I can walk past her. "I'm sorry about being such a bloody idiot," she tells me, locking her sorrowful eyes on mine.

I look at her, really look at her, trying to reconcile this little blonde ringleted thing with a drug problem. It doesn't make sense. Though her face does seem a little thinner, and there are purplish circles under her eyes. "It's all right," I shrug. "I was being a 'bloody idiot,' too."

She smiles widely and links her arm through mine, pulling me down the hall. "So," she asks, "how's lit mag going?"

"It's fine," I answer, though I can tell from her tone that it's not really lit mag that's she interested in hearing about, and I roll my eyes for her benefit.

"Oh, come on," she says, nudging me. "Are you two starcrossed secret lovers exchanging love poems under the table? You are, aren't you?"

I shake my head at her, but my smile falters a bit. There's only one boy who's ever written poetry for me.

"Sorry," Claire says, her eyes wide. "I didn't mean to pry. I thought—is everything okay?"

I muster up a bigger smile and show it to her. "Of course! Sorry. He did tell me that he's writing a short story inspired by me." Though he still hasn't let me read it, no matter how much I beg.

"Aw, that's so sweet! He must really like you."

"He doesn't really know me," I murmur, but only when she's already moved beyond me down the hall.

CHAPTER 21

The first snow falls in mid-December, covering the moors with a thin white powder. Each day is grayer than the last, and everyone seems to feel the gloom resting more heavily on their shoulders as we struggle through classes.

Ben and I spend more time tucked away in the stacks enveloped by the warmth of musty library books than we do in the cottage, since the prospect of walking a mile in the snow and bitingly cold wind has grown less appealing. But he knows I long for the privacy and the peace of the cottage, and every once in a while, we put on our heaviest coats and escape into the cold-hearted night.

"What are you doing for Christmas break?" he asks one night as we sit under one of the warm blankets we snuck out here and watch the golden blaze of the fire. He didn't take the Molly I offered him, but he lit a joint, and he seems even more affectionate than usual. His arms wrap around me securely, like nothing can touch me.

Mother's voice enters my mind before I can stop it, though. She's made very specific plans for my Christmas break, and I have to make them happen.

"I'm not going anywhere," I tell him, filling my voice with sadness.

"You're not going home?" he asks, surprised. His arms tighten around me.

"No. I—I told my mom I had to stay for the break to get some studying done."

"Why?" he asks softly.

"Because I can't go back there. I've only just escaped her." I let my body start to shake, and tears spring up into my eyes.

"Hey," Ben says, his voice even softer than before. He scoots back and tugs at my shoulder until I turn to face him. My face is a crumpled mess of fear and pain, and I even think some of it is real. It's not hard to pretend, in any case.

"I'm sorry," he murmurs, hugging me to him. I let him comfort me, let myself hold on to him, and the tears dry up on their own.

"I'm sorry," I say finally, my voice still heavy with sorrow. "I didn't mean to freak out on you like that."

"You don't have to apologize," Ben says. "I know how screwed up families can be. Mine's not much of a family either."

I nod, cuddling into him to offer him comfort.

And then he says exactly what I want him to. "What if I stayed with you over Christmas break? I don't want to go home anyway. We'd have the school to ourselves. Just you and me, you know, snowed in."

I pull back to face him, my eyes shining with enthusiasm. "Really? You really want to?"

He smiles back, catching my excitement. His hazel eyes grow brighter. "Yeah. I can't think of anything better than being alone with you for two weeks."

I hug him tightly. "That would be perfect."

Claire and almost all of the other students leave a few days before Christmas. Even Mrs. Hallie leaves, giving us all suffocating hugs before she goes.

Claire grumbles the whole time she's packing about how lucky I am that I get to stay here, without any real supervision for two weeks.

"Whereas my parents are going to make me study for A-levels the whole bloody holiday," she mutters, shoving books into her suitcase. "Because if I don't get perfect scores, I'll be even *more* of a disappointment."

I cluck sympathetically and swing my legs off the edge of my bed. I must look like a little kid waiting impatiently for something exciting to happen. "The break will be over before you know it. And then you get to be back *here* studying for your A-levels."

She stops and looks at me, surprised. "Did you just make a joke?"

I smile brightly. "I think I did."

She laughs and shakes her head. "So lucky."

Once she and the others have left, I trudge out into the wet and mushy snow. The day is warmer than average, with a hint of sun peeking behind the gray clouds, and the air is filled with the sound of melting snow dripping from the benches and the trees. I head toward the dining hall. I don't have to live on fruit and cereal anymore. I can actually eat a real meal and not worry about looking like too much of an insider.

There are about a dozen other students scattered around the dark wood tables. They're mostly sixth formers using the break to study, books and papers exploding around them, and other assorted people who don't celebrate Christmas or international scholarship students who can't afford the airfare to travel home.

Ben is waiting for me at an empty table, and his entire face lights up when he sees me. He catches me in a hug despite the other students' prying eyes. He wraps his arms around me, our bulky layers of clothes scrunched between us, and I have to stand on my tiptoes to rest my head on his shoulder. "We can stop being a secret now, can't we?" he asks.

I guess I don't have much choice in the matter, since everyone, including the kitchen staff, is staring at us. I shrug and kiss him lightly on the lips. The buzzing gossip starts immediately.

We're kissing in the yard Christmas morning, a rare bolt of sunshine lighting up the remnants of snow in a thousand blinding sparkles, when I feel Arthur's eyes on us. My stomach flips over, and a strange sort of heat spreads over my body, a heat that has nothing to do with Ben's kiss. I break my lips from Ben's and turn to see Arthur, his mouth in a tight line. He wears a heavy black coat that emphasizes how broad his shoulders have grown, and he crosses his arms over his chest to look even more imposing. I don't know what he sees in my face, but it only makes his eyes flash more. I feel flushed and deathly pale all at once, and my lips part slightly as I watch him, my eyes locked on his intense stare. My legs want to move, want to carry me to him, want to brush that disapproving look off his face. It's all I can do to stay in Ben's arms.

"It's just the gardener," Ben says with a laugh, loud enough for Arthur to hear him.

I glance at Ben, studying his face. Anger rises up through my body, but I keep it in check and don't let it show through my eyes. "Let's get out of here," I say, my voice only a touch cooler than it should be.

CHAPTER 22

That night at dinner, I'm trying to pay attention to Ben's soliloquy about how unfair A-levels are and how he's never going to get into Oxford when I see a flash of movement by the dining hall door. I look over to see Arthur standing there, watching me. He jerks his head, then disappears.

I should ignore him. I need to focus on Ben right now. But I can't.

I excuse myself, saying I'll be back in a moment. I hurry out into the hall, but Arthur isn't there. When I push open the outside door, I see him on the other side of it. It has begun to snow again, and a few flakes land softly on his shoulder and in his hair. "What are you doing?" I hiss.

He beckons for me to follow him, and we rush to his shed. "I have to get back," I tell him as he opens the door.

"No you don't," he says simply. I shut the door behind me, cutting off the cold. He has a roaring fire in his hearth, and I move closer to it. The warm light makes the room seem even more like a home, illuminating the piles of papers on his desk and the rumpled blanket on his bed.

"You want some tea?" Arthur asks, already moving toward the stove with a teapot.

"No," I snap. "I need to get back."

He glances up at me. "Disappear for a little while. Keep him guessing. Isn't that one of your mother's lessons?"

I open my mouth but shut it without saying anything. He's right.

I throw myself down on Arthur's red plaid armchair and hold out my hands to the fire. "Fine," I say. "Have you only kidnapped me to force me to drink tea?" I ask.

He laughs, as if I've made a joke. "Let's pretend I was bored and that I wanted some company for Christmas."

"Get a dog," I grumble, earning another infuriating laugh.

"I guess I should congratulate you," he says, watching me from across the room. He picks out two chipped white ceramic mugs from a kitchen cabinet.

I wait.

"You got him to stay here with you. You've already got him wrapped around your finger."

I stare at him, trying to read his face. "Why don't you tell him to stay away from me?" I ask finally.

He stops moving. "What?"

"Why don't you warn Ben that I'm wrapping him around my finger for revenge? That I'm going to break his heart? It's a simple solution. You could destroy everything for me if you wanted." I begin to pick at the worn fabric of the chair, trying to seem unconcerned.

He sets the mugs down carefully, his eyes falling from mine. "It's too dangerous," he mutters.

"How? All that would happen is he would start to hate me, and everything would go back to normal in Madigan society."

"Not dangerous for *him*," Arthur says through pursed lips. "Dangerous for *you*."

I stand up and step forward, so close that I can see the long eyelashes framing his deep brown eyes. "What do you mean? Because Mother will be mad at me?" I try to sound nonchalant, but my voice is strained, tinny in my ears.

"Because she will have no use for you anymore."

His words make me shiver, like cold fingers tracing down my spine. And when he finally raises his eyes to meet mine, there's a strange mixture of pity and fear in them.

The next moment he's smiling that infuriatingly wry smile at me.

"So what are you going to do with Ben now?"

I shouldn't tell him. He's the enemy. But before I can stop myself, I answer, "Run away with him."

Arthur drops the teakettle on the floor, where it lands with a bang. He doesn't seem to notice it, though. His face has gone pale, and he stares at me as if I've just confessed to murder.

Why on earth did I tell him that? I can't decipher my own intentions, and that scares me more than anything. "Don't look at me like that," I tell Arthur, burying my head in my hands. I have to get myself under control, and I can't do it when he's looking at me like that.

"Why? Why do you have to run away with him?" he asks, his voice rasping as it comes out of his dry throat. "Do you even know?"

I look up at him, pulling my hands away from my face. "What do you mean?"

"What do you think will happen to the two of you after you run away?" he asks, his voice now deadly calm.

It's not my place to ask questions like that. Mother will tell me what to do when the time comes. But the way he's looking at me, like he knows everything I don't . . .

Every question that's been building up in my mind threatens to come spilling out. If he has the answers I need, why is he keeping them from me? All of a sudden, I can't take it anymore.

"What aren't you telling me?" I ask, nearly shouting now. "What do you know?"

Arthur looks at me. No, he studies me. I should turn away, hide myself from him, but I can't. All I can do is watch him, my eyes locked on his. We're caught there for a few heavy, silent moments.

"Ask your mother," Arthur says finally, his expression full of disdain. "Make her explain what will happen after you've ruined an innocent boy's life. If you even care."

Ben's face flashes across my mind. I see his hazel eyes filled with warmth, feel the insistent press of his lips on mine.

"You really won't tell me?" I gasp.

"You're your mother's pet," he says, grabbing the teakettle off the floor. "You don't care."

He's lying. I know he saw how much I care in that horrible moment I lost control. He knows how desperate I am to know what he knows. But he doesn't trust me.

He sets the kettle on the counter and grips the edges of the small wooden kitchen chair that separates him from me. I watch his knuckles go white with the effort, and suddenly, the air between us shifts. And I want to—have to—be closer to him. His eyes grow darker as they watch mine, and I feel as if a flash fire is burning over my skin.

I shouldn't. I shouldn't, shouldn't, shouldn't.

I step forward, keeping my gaze on his chest. I don't have the strength to meet his eyes anymore. The magnetic field between us pulls him forward, too, and he sidesteps the chair so it's no longer between us. There's nothing between us. All I have to do is lift my face, and my lips will be right next to his. Breathing the air he breathes.

I feel my breath coming faster, tearing through my chest. I can't lift my face to his.

I have to.

He takes a sudden, shuddering breath and steps back.

"You should go," he says, his voice uneven. Unsettled.

I don't even look at him before I fling myself out of the room, letting the door slam behind me as I run into the cold.

CHAPTER 23

That Sunday night, I call Mother and give my weekly perfunctory report, finally able to be more specific since all the girls from my floor have gone home. I tell her that Ben and I continue to meet at the cottage, and he seems more and more devoted to me.

She offers no words of praise. Instead, she sounds more agitated than I have ever heard her be, her words traveling furiously across the Atlantic. "Remember, the most important thing you have to do is get him to run away with you. Nothing else matters. And you need to do it soon after his eighteenth birthday, before his father begins to suspect anything."

"Yes, Mother," I say. *What am I supposed to do with him after that?* I wonder, remembering Arthur's look of fear and pity, but I bite my lip and keep quiet.

"If you fail, there will be consequences."

Arthur's insistence that I'm in danger flashes into my mind again before I can stop it. I hear a click, signaling that Mother has hung up, and I let the phone fall from my hands. I watch it swing by its cord for a few seconds, my eyes wide.

I hurry down the hall, my whole body itching for action. I need to reassure myself that I'm able to do this. I have to see Ben.

There's something else pulling me to his room, too. It's like he's become the one safe haven in my life. Like I *need* him.

I don't see Jenkins guarding the halls, but I still tiptoe as I leave Faraday and head across the newly fallen snow to the boys' house. The cold bites into me, the wind stinging my cheeks. The tied-down trees seem to point the way to Rawlings Hall, their branches thin and bare like the brittle fingers of a crone. There's a light burning on the fourth floor, and I count the number of windows to make sure I can find it once I'm inside.

I knock quietly on his door, and there's a rustling noise within. As soon as Ben opens the door, I fling myself into his surprised arms. I need his warmth, and he obliges, pressing me closer to him.

"What are you doing here?" he asks. I can hear the delight shining in his tone, and it calms me.

"I needed to see you," I explain as I stand on my tiptoes for a kiss. He smiles into my lips and then gets caught in my frenzy. His arms pull me against him. I pull the heavy sweater he's wearing up over his broad chest, and he pushes off my coat before spinning me around and laying me on his bed.

Before I can speak, he's lying on top of me, and his hands are exploring regions he's previously been so careful to avoid. I make no move to stop him. Instead, I slip my hands under his thin cotton shirt, feeling the hard planes of his back and pulling him even closer to me. I can't get him close enough to stop the chill that has shaken my whole body. But I can try.

I pull his shirt off, and he pulls mine off for me. When I reach for the waist of his pants, he pulls back, straightening his arms so that his chest is no longer pressed against mine.

"Are you sure?" he asks, his voice so much lower than usual. He holds himself above me, and for a moment, I let my eyes take him in: his firm jaw, his crooked nose, his golden eyelashes.

I nod, not trusting myself to speak. His hazel eyes examine me for a moment, and then his lips are back on mine, open and warm and everything I need right now.

For once, I'm not numb. I'm not experiencing this with a blank mind, the way I have all those nights before. Tonight, I feel everything. The touch of his hands, the press of his lips, the weight of him bearing down on me. And, even more powerful, the ache in my heart that reaches out for him, straining to escape my chest.

We fall asleep in a tangle of limbs.

Every night for the rest of the break, I sneak into Ben's room at night, and we sleep on his narrow twin bed. I'm surprised to find that I sleep deeper now when I share the air he breathes. I almost believe myself when I tell him that I'm happy.

CHAPTER 24

It all crashes down on us, though, when the boys' house guard catches me sneaking out of Ben's room the last morning before the end of break.

I'm closing the door when I feel a presence behind me, and I whirl around to find a very unfriendly face scowling at me with narrowed eyes. The guard is barely taller than I am, but the way he glowers at me, he seems almost monstrous.

"I was just borrowing a book," I say, for once unable to think of a better excuse. I can see that it wouldn't have mattered, though. This man is not Mrs. Hallie; I can't manipulate him so easily.

The guard steps around me and knocks on the door briefly before pushing it open, revealing a surprised and still half-asleep Ben. "Come on, both of you," he says shortly. "We're going to the headmaster's office."

Ben shuffles along beside me, shivering in the sudden cold as we hurry through the yard to the main building. He only had time to throw on a shirt and jeans, and the muscles of his arms tense up in the bitter morning wind.

We reach the office with its imposing gold seal just as I decide what to do. The secretary isn't sitting at her desk yet. Her animosity toward me would have been helpful, but I focus on the headmaster, straightening my shoulders.

Ben takes my hand and squeezes it before we walk into the office together.

Harriford looks up from the sheaf of papers he's examining, and I wonder if we've interrupted him writing his novel. He doesn't look all that pleased to see us, in any case. "What's this?" he asks, looking to the guard for answers.

"I caught this one"—he shoots a thumb at me—"sneaking out of this one's"—thumb at Ben—"room."

Harriford widens his eyes as he looks at me, then purses his lips as he glares at Ben. He has cast me as the unwitting victim somehow and Ben as the calculating seducer, and I have to bite my lip to keep from smiling at the irony.

"Do you have anything to say for yourself, Mr. Collingsworth?" Harriford asks, clasping his hands together on top of his papers. Even the bronze bust of Nabokov sitting on the corner of his desk looks at us with disapproval.

Ben glances at me, then answers. "She came to borrow something, that's all."

Harriford smiles, clearly not buying it. Then he leans forward, searching Ben's face. "Are you on drugs, Mr. Collingsworth?"

I look at Ben, whose bloodshot eyes must have given him away. Harriford may be more observant than I give him credit for.

"No, sir," Ben lies, shaking his head. For a long, breathless moment, Harriford keeps his little narrow eyes on Ben's face. If he thinks Ben is using, he'll expel him. Which should be what I want. But even after all that we've shared these past few nights, I don't know if Ben is addicted to me enough to run away with me. I can see it now: He'll go back to his father, who will transfer him to some other prep school. And I'll never be with him again. I will fail. Mother will be angrier than I've ever seen her before, and I'll have no way to escape her.

My breath comes faster and faster as I watch Harriford examine Ben.

Then he harrumphs and leans back in his chair, and I stifle a sigh of relief. "We don't condone girls in the boys' house. This is a hard and fast rule, even during Christmas holiday. I'm afraid I have to give both of you detention for a month."

"That's not fair," I say now that there's no threat of expulsion.

My voice is loud in the chilled space of the office. "The guard just caught me *outside* of his room. I mean, it wasn't that bad. You can't punish us like this."

Harriford raises an eyebrow at me.

"She's right," Ben chimes in, just as I wanted him to. "We didn't do anything *really* wrong."

"Enough," Harriford says, directing his anger at Ben. "Unless you want suspensions, which will be put on your permanent record, I suggest you leave this office. And don't ever let it happen again."

Ben storms out, and I follow. He's furious, his breath coming in angry gasps, as we head out into the yard. "This is ridiculous," he fumes. "You're my girlfriend, and it's Christmas break, and who bloody cares?"

"I know," I say quietly. I don't have to add anything. He's angry enough with Harriford as it is.

"It's just not fair," he mutters.

His rebellion has already started.

CHAPTER 25

The other students return to campus much too quickly. Our safe haven is shattered, and we brace ourselves for the inevitable gossip and questions that will come when everyone finds out we're together. If that news hasn't already spread around the country.

Claire bangs into our room with her huge suitcase and an even bigger smile on her face. She's certainly glad to be back.

"Did you have a good holiday?" I ask as she throws her clothes into the drawers and glances every few seconds at the clock.

"It was awful," she says absentmindedly. "I snuck off with some friends one night, and my parents went mental. They grounded me. Told me they were *disappointed* in me. Like they're ever anything *but* disappointed in me. I was dying to get back here."

I watch her carefully. She looks even more ragged than she did before break. There are deeper, darker circles under her eyes, and her skin seems more yellow than pale.

She turns to me with her usual wide, bright smile, however. "I did hear some interesting news, though," she says.

I groan. "Who told you?"

"Only about twelve different people. Everyone wanted to know if I had any idea my roommate and the school god were shagging."

I roll my eyes. "What'd you say?"

"I told them to mind their own bloody business. But you're going to have some fun days in the hallways, I bet. Absolutely *everyone* knows."

She's right, of course. Everyone stops what they're doing and stares whenever I walk down a hallway or enter the dining hall, their intense curiosity and naked disapproval making goose bumps rise on my skin. And when Ben comes up to me the first day of class and leans me against my locker to kiss me, there are actual audible gasps.

As Ben's lips claim mine, I can't help opening my eyes and watching the faces of the people around us. Ben's friends look horrified, and even some teachers raise their eyebrows in surprise. No one is smiling. I have no allies here.

Ben seems to take it in stride, grabbing my hand and walking me to class. But once we reach English, I can feel his grip tighten.

His friends Liam and Colin are sitting in their usual spots in the back, waiting for us.

Ben gives them a slight nod and pulls me to a chair in the second row, sitting beside me. I sneak a glance back at his friends to find that they're staring at us in utter confusion.

After class, Liam and Colin corner Ben before he can leave the room. "What's going on, mate?" Colin asks, giving me a not-so-subtle once-over. "Is *this* the reason you didn't go to London with us over holiday? Is she worth it?"

Before I can even pretend to look offended, Ben shoves Colin against the wall and pins him there. Ms. Prisby squeaks and hurries over to break up the fight, but not before Ben tells Colin, "You ever talk about her like that again, and I'll break your face, you got it?"

Colin holds his hands up in surrender as Prisby pulls Ben off of him. She glares at me, but I ignore her. "Ben and Colin, to the headmaster's office, both of you," she orders.

Ben rolls his eyes and follows her out into the hall, where everyone has gathered to watch two of the most popular guys in school fight over me.

As I stroll to my locker, I pretend not to notice everyone's sudden fascination. Arabella stops cold when she spots me, glowering at me until I walk past her. Her eyes are like two frozen blue flames burning into me, and I swallow, holding my head up high.

Suddenly, I'm shoved from the side, crashing into the solid wood of the lockers. I spin around to find Arabella smiling frigidly at me and turning to walk away. Before I can react, a teacher I don't know comes barreling down the hallway. "What on earth are you doing?" she asks, her bluntly cut brown hair almost shaking with rage as she stares at Arabella. "Both of you to the headmaster's office at once!"

She marches us to Harriford's office. The hallway has gone silent, the only sound our heavy footfalls as wide-eyed students watch us pass. Arabella keeps trying to send me dirty looks, her mouth twisting in ridiculous grimaces, but I'm too busy figuring out how to control this situation.

The secretary looks up when we walk in, her eyes slipping over Arabella and landing on me in a scowl.

"This one shoved the other one," the teacher tells her, and I can see it takes the secretary a few moments to understand that I'm the victim in this situation. Her mouth curls in distaste. This is not the story she was hoping for.

The headmaster's door opens, and Ben and Colin come out, looking at me curiously. Ben's gaze flicks from me to Arabella, and his confusion intensifies. Before I can talk to him, the secretary orders me into the office, her sour face so hostile that it's almost amusing.

Once again, Harriford doesn't look pleased to see me. I'm still not off the hook for sneaking out of Ben's room. But his disapproval quickly shifts to Arabella when the teacher tells him what happened.

"What's going on?" he asks me after he gestures for Arabella and me to sit down on the chairs facing his desk.

"She's been bullying me for a while," I murmur, staring down at my clasped hands. "I don't know why she hates me. But this isn't the first time she's shoved me."

I can nearly feel the fury simmering off of Arabella, but I keep my head down. "She spread rumors about me shagging the gardener!" she bursts out. "And she told my friends that I had something to do with Emily getting expelled. And she's a manipulative little slag!"

It hits me then that, besides Arthur, Arabella might have the truest grasp on my character of anyone at this school.

"Even if these stories are true," Harriford says with a long glance at me, "that's no reason to shove someone, Arabella. I'm going to have to give you an in-house suspension for the week. You'll be doing your homework in an empty classroom all day, and you won't be allowed to eat with your friends."

"But that'll put a mark on my permanent record!" Arabella protests. "Universities will see that."

"You should have thought about that before you shoved her, then," Headmaster Harriford says in a tone that lets us know we're dismissed.

Arabella must be biting her tongue to stay silent as she rises to leave.

"Ms. Foster?" Harriford asks. "A moment, please."

I sit back down and ignore Arabella's powerful glare as she walks out the door.

"I gave you detention three days ago. I just saw your boyfriend about a fight. And now you come in having been involved in another one. I'm concerned, Ms. Foster." His forehead crinkles, making his face even smaller and his bald head even more grotesque.

"I know it looks bad, Headmaster Harriford," I say calmly. "But Ben was provoked into that fight because they insulted me. And Arabella—she just attacked me out of nowhere."

He gives me a hardened look, and I realize that I'm not as secure at this school as I thought. I try to look as helpless as I can, shrugging my shoulders and biting my lip.

"Try to stay out of trouble from now on, all right?"

I nod quickly. "Yes, sir."

I walk out and pass the secretary without a look. She's not who I need to worry about now.

I know it's only a matter of time before Arabella attacks me again. And this time she won't be content with just a shove.

I wait in the shadows of the stacks during lunch, where Ben will know to find me. After almost half an hour, he finally comes, his face flushed and angry. "Arabella shoved you?" he asks.

I nod. "Harriford suspended her for a week."

"She deserves it," he says bitterly.

I have to hide the flicker of triumph in my eyes. "What did Harriford do to you?" I ask.

"Suspension," he spits out. "Even though it was Colin's fault. I told Harriford what he said about you, and he just gave some, you know, bullshit 'fighting's not the answer' speech. I'm out for two days, and it'll go on my record."

"I'm so sorry," I murmur, clasping him in a hug. He presses against me, and a metal shelf behind me digs into my back. "It's like the whole stupid school is out to get us," I add, ignoring the discomfort.

He nods into my neck. "We won't let them."

"Of course not," I say, burying my smile in his shoulder.

CHAPTER 26

It takes me a few days after Ben's suspension to realize that Arabella must be thinking up a plan to destroy me now that I've gotten her suspended. Her glares have become pregnant with self-satisfaction and suppressed excitement, and one dark mid-January afternoon when I pass her in the yard, she actually smiles at me, her eyes filled with cunning, and I grit my teeth. She has a secret, and I have to get ready for its fallout.

I doubt she can shake Ben's faith in me, though, if that's what she's hoping for. The first night in February, to celebrate the end of our month-long detention, he and I slip off to the cottage to spend the night reading the anonymous student submissions for the literary magazine and sleeping in each other's arms until we have to sneak back in.

Around midnight, I'm staring into the flames, trying to figure out what Arabella has planned for me, when Ben looks up from the story he's reading.

"What's the matter?" He brushes a rough hand over my cheek, catching my attention. His hazel eyes flicker like liquid gold in the firelight.

I straighten my shoulders and roll my eyes with a small smile on my face, like I'm making fun of myself. "Nothing. I'm just thinking too much, that's all."

"Less thinking, more reading," he says with an echoing smile, tapping the pile of pages in my hand.

I wrinkle my nose.

"Which one are you reading now?" he asks, noticing my expression.

I riffle through the pages in my hand, staring down at them. "It's this sappy short story about two watches."

"Sappy?" he asks.

I sigh. "One's a digital watch and one's an analog, and they're not supposed to be together, but they fall in love. Rip-off of *Romeo and Juliet*, basically."

I look back up to see that his expression is carefully guarded, and my mouth falls open. "Oh, God, this is your story, isn't it? The one you wrote about me?"

He nods, but I breathe out in relief when I see a smile playing on the edges of his mouth. "You're the digital watch. Because, you know, you're new and uh, revolutionary, I guess. To me, at least."

"It's not bad writing at all," I scramble. "The writing's really *good*. It's just that I've never liked *Romeo and Juliet*."

"Why not?" he asks, surprised. "I thought, you know, *all* girls loved *Romeo and Juliet*."

"Haven't you learned by now that I'm not like all girls?" I tease. "But really, it's horrible. It's a tragedy—that's even in its title. And Romeo is a fickle hero. In the beginning he's all swoony and pining for Rosaline, and then he sees a pretty girl at a party, and—poof—suddenly Rosaline is nothing to him. Then he and Juliet kill themselves for no good reason. They're not in control of their emotions, and those emotions destroy them."

I realize that I'm ranting and stop myself. My cheeks are flushed, and I've been throwing my hands all over the place. Juliet isn't the only girl not in control of her emotions.

I take a deep breath as Ben laughs at me. "Is that all?" he asks.

I nudge his shoulder, putting on a reluctant smile. "It just annoys me, that's all."

"But it's about the power of young love," he protests.

"The power of young love to destroy," I say. When I look up at him, I find him studying me, his hazel eyes dark, his mouth in a serious line. I spoke without thinking, and now I hold my breath, waiting for him to realize that I'm right.

Instead, he cups my face in his hands and pulls me close to him. I lean in, expecting a kiss. But he keeps looking at me, drinking me in. I try to look enchanted instead of nervous.

"I love you," he says. His voice is clear, strong.

It takes me several moments to absorb his words. And what they mean.

I did it. I made him fall in love with me.

But I don't feel the way I thought I'd feel. I'm not excited, not anywhere near it. What I feel is something more like cold dread.

I'm supposed to smile a delighted smile and declare that I love him, too.

I can't.

I pull away from him, standing up and backing into a corner of the room. "I don't want to hurt you," I whimper before I can stop myself.

The air between us becomes something heavy and terrible.

Ben rises slowly and approaches me. He holds up his hands, showing me he means no harm. "Vivian," he says. And he fills that word with such . . . devotion. Almost like it's a prayer. He says my name again, and I start to cry.

He rushes to me now, enfolding me in his arms. Hiding me away from the rest of the world.

I sob onto his shoulder. I'm terrified, and it takes me a moment to realize what I'm terrified of. I'm terrified of myself. Of what I can do to this boy. Of what I'm supposed to do.

Yet even as I realize this, I'm trying to come up with a way to spin this sudden panic attack to my advantage. And something within me hates myself for that.

My tears slow and then dry up completely, but Ben still holds me. He won't let me go until I tell him to, and I have no desire to do that. I stay buried in his shoulder for several minutes, trying desperately to control myself.

"I love you," he murmurs in my ear. "I won't let anything hurt you."

I blow out a breath between my teeth and finally lean back, looking him in the eyes. I say the only thing I can say. "I love you, too." It tastes like a lie coming out of my mouth. Like poison. Because I don't mean it. I don't love him. But hurting him—it's starting to hurt *me*.

He beams at me, his smile suddenly stretching wide across his face, and then we're kissing, and I can't take my poisonous words back.

I don't offer him any Molly, and he doesn't request any. He's already addicted to me.

CHAPTER 27

The day after Ben tells me he loves me, I head to the nurse's office. I've taken care not to go there, since Mother told them I have some kind of heart condition that I barely understand to get me out of the sports requirement. I don't want an interrogation.

But there's something I have to know. Something that has been plucking at the back of my mind since I met Emily and learned that her EpiPen had gone missing around the time Mother was trying to get rid of her. And now, with the memory of Ben's confession and the feel of his kiss on my lips, I can't stop this one doubt from breaking through.

The nurse, a thin woman with a brisk smile, looks up when I walk in. "Can I help you?" Her dark blouse and pants stand out against the sterile whiteness of the room.

I smile broadly, though my stomach feels like it's flipping over on itself. "I'm doing a research project on allergies, and I was wondering if you had an EpiPen I could look at? Just so I have a better sense of what it does."

"Well, we do," the nurse says, standing from her chair and rummaging through her shelves of supplies.

"You do!" I say, a little too enthusiastically.

She hands me a plastic case with a needle inside that I pretend to find fascinating.

I can feel her watching me, and I wonder how long I need to examine this needle to make my story convincing. "You're lucky," she says finally. "We ran out of these a few months ago. Had to get a new shipment in November."

My throat grows dry, and I clear it. "You ran out?"

"Yes. The computer system said we had three left, so we didn't check. Can't trust computers."

I shake my head. "No," I say, my heart pounding so loudly that I can hardly hear myself. I hand the case back, my hands trembling. "Thanks so much. That should do it."

I escape before she has a chance to stop me.

I'm running to Arthur's shed before I even realize it. I need to make sense of all this, and he's the only one I can talk to. He's the only one who can help sort out all the questions that are screaming in my head.

I slam my fist on the rough wood of his door until he opens

it. His eyes, full of confusion, sweep the landscape behind me as he pulls me inside. "What the hell is wrong with you?" he asks once we're out of sight.

"Was she going to kill Emily?" I ask. My voice is high-pitched and panicked, and I try to take a deep breath, but it gets caught in my chest.

The anger in his eyes fades into uncertainty, but only for a moment. "Sit down," he growls. "Breathe."

I shake my head, crossing my arms over my chest. "Was she?"

"Are you telling me you really didn't know?" he asks. He hasn't moved away, and there's less than a foot of space between us. He's close enough to see every emotion flashing across my face, emotions I can't stop.

I shake my head. "I didn't think—I didn't think she would do something like that." I finally get a good deep breath and breathe out slowly. I need control.

"Of course she would. Revenge is the only thing that matters to her. I would have helped Emily deny those rumors about her and the teacher, somehow, but I knew if I interfered, my father would kill her. I had to watch her get expelled, knowing that you would come soon to take her place." He steps closer to me, his tall frame filling my field of vision. "I didn't want you to come here. I was naïve enough to think I could spare you from all of this." His voice is low and raw.

"It's what I was raised to do," I remind him. "Nothing could spare me from it."

"Your mother was ready to kill an innocent girl just to get you a spot at this school. How can you act like you don't care?" He reaches his hand out and nearly brushes my shoulder before he draws it back.

Another deep breath. "She won't kill me." I say it with as much conviction as I can muster, but I can't look up to meet his eyes.

"You really think that?"

I nod firmly, trying to clear my face of all emotion. "She's my mother. She needs me."

He steps forward. "Don't you know what she did to her own mother?"

I freeze, not even daring to breathe, my eyes fixed on a knot on the wooden wall, not on him. I don't want to hear this.

"She had my father cut the brakes on her car. Her mother kicked her out of the house for having you, so she got my father to make her murder look like an accident."

I force myself to look at him, searching for any sign of deception, any flicker of untruth. But in his dark stare, all I see is the boy I've always known.

"Why would he agree to do that?" I ask, grasping for anything that might make this story fall apart. "Why would he kill someone for her?"

"Because he's in love with her. Because she manipulates him just like she trained you to manipulate everyone."

"But it really could've just been an accident."

He sighs, shoving a hand through his hair. "It wasn't. I overheard your mother once. She was ranting at the portrait of her mother, you know, the one over the fireplace? She was muttering, 'What mother kicks her own daughter out?' Over and over, until she threw her drink at the painting. And on top of that, my father once showed me how to cut the brakes in a car."

"So?" I ask, brightening. "That's it? It's just a coincidence. Just because your father knows how to cut someone's brakes doesn't mean he killed Mother's mother."

"You know I'm right, Viv." His words are soft and regretful and more hurtful than if he had shouted them. He thinks he's telling me the truth.

I picture the portrait of Mother's mother that hangs over the fireplace in the den back in upstate New York. That woman with her diamond necklace and haughty expression. "No, it's not true. It can't be true. She always, always told me that family is the most important thing. She loved her mother, even if she disowned her. The car wreck was just an accident." I try to find comfort in the words, but the room is spinning. I close my eyes.

Suddenly, Arthur's hands are firebrands on my shoulders, and my eyes fly open. His dark stare flashes with anger. "Do you still not see what she's turned you into? You can't keep playing her game."

"She needs me," I repeat. "She won't kill me."

"And what happens if Ben doesn't want to run away with you? Do you think she'll just let you go back to New York? Or that she'll set you free?" He steps even closer to me, just a fraction, as if trying to read my eyes.

"The plan *will* work," I say fiercely, my eyebrows contracting as I stare him down. "And I'll be fine."

The anger finally slips from his eyes, and all that is left there is pity. And it nearly breaks me.

I turn away and set my shoulders as I open the door and walk away from him. I don't need his pity. I *will* be fine.

It's March fifth, two days before Ben's eighteenth birthday. I spend most of the evening in the art room, filling reams of paper with black lines of desperation. I draw a woman's back, hunched in grief. She's staring into a dying fire, a portrait of her disapproving mother above her. Then I draw that same woman, a black shadow overtaking the viewer, undefined except for her eyes, which are wide with rage and revenge. I sketch a boy with eyes full of trust and love. Then a boy—a man—reaching his hand out to me, trying to save me.

I hide the last two sketches from Ms. Elling when she walks by. She rests a hand on my shoulder, trying to be reassuring. She can see the shadows enveloping me.

When I head back to the dorm, the gas lamps lining the courtyard are straining against the darkness. I'm staring blankly at my
feet, lost in my head, when a gust of wind blows through and rips
away some sheets of loose paper sticking out of my bag. They're
the sheets I tore out, the portraits of Ben and Arthur that I didn't
want Ms. Elling to see, and they scatter across the yard.

I mutter a curse under my breath and hurry to gather them.

He's too quick for me, though. Before I can stop him, Arthur
snatches one of the sketches and holds it up to the light.

I run to his side. "It's not what you think!" I cry, sure he has
found the portrait of himself.

When I look down at the paper in his hands, though, I see
Ben. One where I was trying to capture the way he looked at
me when he told me he loved me. I wanted to show the hope in
his eyes, the mixture of certainty and uncertainty as he poured
his heart out to me.

"You've drawn him like you're in love with him," Arthur says
softly. He brings his eyes up to mine, and my breath stutters in
my throat.

I rip the sheet from his hands. I can't think of anything to say,
so I hurry off without a word. I can feel his eyes on my back as I
march resolutely to Faraday Hall.

CHAPTER 28

By the time I reach my room, I'm shaking, and it takes a great deal of effort for me not to slam the door. I'm angry, though at whom I don't know. Claire must see it in my face, because she looks up from the book she's reading and then looks quickly back down again.

I take a deep breath and try to clear my face of emotion.

I go to the dresser in search of a hair tie so that I can pull my hair back. Really, I'm just looking for something to occupy my hands.

But when I open up the top drawer, I notice something's off. I usually keep everything in neat, ordered rows: my make-up brushes, my nail polish, my hair clips. But now everything is jumbled. Maybe I pulled the drawer open too hard and bounced everything around?

I check the next drawer down to find my sweaters and jeans crumpled and mixed together, and my heart starts beating faster.

"Did you go through my drawers?" I ask Claire.

She looks up. "No. Why?"

I examine her face. Her brow is scrunched in genuine confusion, and I know she's not a good enough liar to fake it. "They look disorganized, that's all. Like someone messed with them."

"The door was locked all day. Only Mrs. Hallie has the key."

I nod. "I must have just messed them up myself this morning and forgotten about it," I murmur.

I think of Mrs. Hallie being in the room and nearly start to panic. As soon as Claire leaves for the library, I lunge for the box under my bed where I've stashed the yearbook I took from the student lounge and my meager mementos from childhood. The packet of Molly that I bought from G-Man is still there, still half-full since Ben has been using less and less.

Nothing else in the room could have gotten me in trouble. But the box looked a little askew when I first reached for it, like it had been shoved back under my bed hastily. Had I done that? I've always been so careful.

A shiver runs through me. Something has happened—*is* happening. I just have no idea what it is.

When Claire comes back from the library two hours later, I'm sitting on my bed staring at the wall. I'm scouring my mind for clues, trying to figure out why someone would search my room but take nothing. Someone might have been looking for the pills, but if they found them, they left them there on purpose. Why?

"You have to come out with us tonight!" Claire says as soon as she walks in. "Everyone's going out on the moors, and you haven't been in ages. I mean, with someone other than Ben."

"It's not really my crowd, Claire," I say with a grimace. "It doesn't sound fun."

"It's going to be brilliant," she says, ignoring me. "Someone's scored a stash of pills that are supposed to blow your mind. I probably shouldn't keep going, honestly, but this stuff is going to be really good. You have to come try it."

"Sorry." I turn back to my textbook.

She shrugs, but I know I've hurt her. She feels like I'm judging her. She doesn't know about the packet of pills beneath my bed, the pills I have to get rid of immediately.

As soon as Claire and the others sneak out at midnight, I grab the bag of pills and head for the bathroom, where I flush everything down the toilet.

That night, I can't fall asleep. I wait in my bed, watching the fingers of moonlight play across the ceiling, trying to sort out what I know and what I speculate.

And right now there's only one name jumping out at me: Arabella. She might be a more vicious enemy than I'd anticipated.

CHAPTER 29

After a few hours of staring up at the ceiling, I hear the girls tiptoeing up the stairs. There are only a few of them tonight, probably just Claire, Arabella, and her two minions. One is murmuring, but it's not the usual giggling type of murmuring. It's softer, lower, like something's wrong. I wait for Claire to scurry into the room, but she doesn't come. The murmuring dies off, and the door to my room remains closed. I hear a quick knock, and someone scampering away. Claire? Arabella?

I throw off my covers and open the door as softly as possible, peering down the shadowy hall. No one in sight. I pull on jeans and a black sweater, then patter down the hall and the stairs. It's so dark that I have to feel my way, gliding my hand along the wall and hoping that no one has left anything out for me to stumble over. Jenkins must still be outside on her smoke break.

As soon as I push open the back door, I see her.

Claire lies, limbs strewn out, on the bottom of the cold steps, as if someone has dumped her there. She's on her back with one arm crossed over her chest and the other flung over her head. Her eyes are closed, and her face looks like the pale surface of a pearl in the moonlight.

I stand frozen for a moment, blinking and unsure, and then run down to her. "Claire!" I yell, shaking her. "Claire, wake up!" Her head rolls, and I stop shaking her, worried I'll make her hit it against the stone steps.

I bend down. She's breathing, but it's so shallow I almost miss it.

I have to do something. But what? If I take her to the nurse, they'll think I was the one who gave her whatever she's overdosed on, and I'll be expelled. Or worse, the administration will look too closely at me and start to unravel all of Mother's carefully constructed lies. No. I just need to get her better. If I could get her to the hospital, if I could just get her fixed and back to Madigan without anyone noticing . . .

I run straight through the courtyard past Rawlings Hall to the light shining through the fog. Arthur. I sprint to his shed and bang on the door until he opens it. "It's Claire, please!" I say, not knowing if I'm making any sense. "We have to get her to the hospital."

"Where is she?" he asks, scanning the darkness.

I run back to Faraday, and he follows. "She's overdosed on something," I explain. "She won't wake up."

Arthur kneels down and cradles her in his arms, picking her up and moving swiftly across the yard and around his shed. He places Claire carefully in the back of a tiny black car parked there, and I jump into the backseat with her. He's roaring down the hill before I can get my seatbelt on.

I hold Claire's head in my hands and beg her over and over to wake up. She answers me with nothing but her shallow, slow breathing.

The nearest hospital is miles away, in a village even farther than Loworth. Arthur goes as fast as he can, speeding in this tiny car with its cracked leather seats through the heavy fog encasing us. But it still doesn't seem fast enough.

I stare down at Claire's pale face. I knew she was going out tonight. I knew she was going to take some kind of pill. I knew she had been out on the moors more nights than I could count. I knew G-Man was worried about her, that if I had been a real friend, I would've worried about her, too. I knew everything I needed to know to stop this from happening, but

I'd done nothing. Because I didn't think it was my business. Because keeping Claire alive was not part of Mother's plan.

I feel as if all the blood is draining from my face, leaving me as pale as she is. *I* did this. My inattention, my refusal to acknowledge that Claire had a problem, has led to this night. It's all my fault.

We pull into the emergency entrance of the tiny hospital, and I jump out of the car. Arthur gathers Claire in his arms as I run into the building.

A distraught mother and three children sit in the white blankness of the waiting room, and they stare at me with wide, hollowed eyes as I run in. I turn to the nurses at the reception desk. "My sister—I think she's OD'd," I say with the best British accent I can muster, as Arthur brings Claire in behind me.

The nurses bustle around the desk, calling for a gurney. An orderly takes Claire, her head lolling as she's transferred from Arthur's arms.

"Is she going to be okay?" I ask, my messily accented voice a wail in the cold space.

They wheel her away, leaving us alone with a stocky nurse who reaches a hand out to pat my shoulder, her eyes kind and comforting. "They'll do their best. Now what did she take?"

"I don't know. Some kind of pill, I think. I overheard her talking about it on the phone. I wasn't supposed to hear, she hates me eavesdropping." I try to look beyond the nurse to see if I can get a glimpse of Claire.

"You didn't hear what kind?" she asks.

I shake my head, focusing back on her. "No. All she said was that her friends had scored some pills, and she was going to try them."

"Okay, that's fine, dear. We'll sort it out. Now what about your parents?"

"Business trip," I say quickly. "I've been calling, but I can't reach them."

She pats my shoulder again. "How about you take a seat here," she says, gesturing to the waiting room, "and we'll start getting your sister better."

"Thank you," I murmur. I settle into a seat as far away from the distraught family as possible. I can't let their worry and stress melt into my own.

Arthur sits beside me as the seconds drip by, his face tense and motionless. The fluorescent light buzzes above, nearly drowning out the howl of the wind outside. The nurses refuse to look at me. No one is telling me anything. I try not to picture Claire's pale face, the lifeless weight of her body, but I can think of nothing else.

A doctor comes out, and I straighten up in my chair, but he heads for the family. He says something to them, and then they're crying.

I reach for Arthur's hand on the armrest beside me, needing something to hold on to.

For a moment, he freezes and lets my fingers intertwine with his, lets my palm graze against the calluses of his much bigger palm. His thumb brushes a half circle on the back of my hand, but instead of calming me, it feels like sparks burning into my skin. And then he takes a sharp breath in, pulls his hand away, and stands. I drop my hand back in my lap.

"I'll go get some tea," he says without looking at me.

I don't know what's come over me. I bury my head in my hands. I'm alone with the crying family, and the seconds seem to move backward now. I wish Ben were here. He would hold my hand as long as I needed him to.

But his hand would never feel like sparks against mine.

Another doctor enters the waiting room, and she heads right toward me. "You're Claire's sister?" she asks.

I nod.

"We've eliminated the oxycodone from her system. She's sedated, unconscious, and we won't know anything until she wakes up."

I can hardly breathe, but I force my voice out. "Can I see her?"

She nods with a sad smile. "Yes, but only for a few minutes. She needs to rest."

I nod, thoroughly obedient as always. The doctor leads me down the hall and points to a room. I take a deep breath, staring at the door for a second before I twist the handle and push it open.

At first all I see is her hair. Everything else is covered in wires and tubes. I look away quickly. One of the machines beeps a monotonous rhythm, but the room feels still and silent. Like a tomb. I am underground with the dead, and I don't know if I will ever be able to get out.

I shake my head, trying to get the strange thoughts out. Claire is right here on the bed, and she is going to be fine. I know it. She's too happy, too precious and pretty a thing to be destroyed by something like this. This kind of thing doesn't happen to good people. It happens to people like me.

For a moment, I wish I were the one lying on that bed instead. I wish it so hard that my knees nearly collapse under the weight of my wishing. I stare at her a few more minutes, not daring to move closer.

My fault. All my fault.

I need air. I leave without another glance at Claire.

I close the door behind me and lean back against it, my knees still threatening to buckle underneath me. I close my eyes and take a few deep breaths, desperate to loosen the tightness in my chest.

When I open them, I realize I'm not alone in this hallway. And someone—a much too familiar someone—is staring at me.

Arabella.

She stands outside the room huddled with Headmaster Harriford and a couple of policemen, and I'm so tired that it takes a moment to realize that there is a shiver running down my spine. This tableau in front of me signals nothing but danger.

The cops barely glance at me, until Arabella raises her finger. "That's her," she says.

I look to Harriford, my ally. Only now he's staring at me not with the care and devotion that he used to show me, but with something more like revulsion.

"What? What is it?" I ask. "Whatever she's told you, it's not the truth. She's lying. She hates me!"

The cops look at each other as I protest, and then one of them approaches. He spins me around and traps my wrists in handcuffs, snapping them shut so quickly that one of them scratches my skin.

"Vivian Foster, you are under arrest for the possession and sale of illegal narcotics."

"What?" I ask. "I didn't do anything! I just found her!"

He continues to talk over me. "You do not have to say anything. But it may harm your defense if you do not mention when questioned something which you later rely on in court. Anything you do say may be given in evidence."

Arthur comes running toward me. He takes in the scene, then tells me urgently, "Viv, don't say anything. We'll get you out of this, just don't say anything."

I keep my mouth shut as the cop pulls me down the hall and out into the waiting car.

CHAPTER 30

They've put me in an interrogation room, a box of concrete and harsh fluorescent light. They leave me in here alone for what feels like hours, though it may be only minutes. It's long enough for me to curse Arabella and picture all the ways I can exact my revenge on her.

I don't think she's cruel enough to make Claire overdose. I'm sure Claire did that all on her own. But Arabella took advantage of the situation and told them that I provided the pills. And she must have convinced the others to leave Claire on the steps and knock on my door so I would be the one to discover her and implicate myself in her overdose. *She* left her on those steps. To die.

I want to scream, take the shiny metal chair I'm sitting on and throw it against the wall, beat my fists against the concrete.

Instead, I let my head sink into my hands and try to regulate my breathing.

A cop I haven't seen before walks in. He isn't in uniform, but his straight posture and cold smile give him away. "We usually don't have this much trouble with Madigan students, even the American ones," he says by way of introduction. He's letting me know that he knows everything about me. Or at least he thinks he does.

"Let's make this easy, yeah?" he says, settling down in a chair across the table from me. "You tell me everything, and we can call it a day."

I stare at him, my face blank. He will get nothing from me.

His cold smile fades, and he looks down at the folder in his hands. "You've been accused of possessing illegal drugs and selling them to your roommate, Claire Templeton. You gave her so much that she overdosed, and you brought her to the hospital for medical attention." He pauses, looking at me. "At least you did the right thing, in the end," he sniffs.

I stare into his icy blue eyes and show absolutely no emotion.

It seems to unsettle him, as it should. I know I look less than human with this blank stare in my eyes.

"You're facing several years in jail, Vivian. And if your friend doesn't wake up, you could be charged with manslaughter. You're eighteen, so you'll be tried as an adult." He's becoming more frantic in his quest to elicit emotion from me. "She might not make it through the night, and then you'll have to live with her death on your conscience for the rest of your life. How does that make you feel?"

When I say nothing, he slumps in his chair. "Do you have any questions?"

"Am I allowed a phone call?" I ask. My voice is dead, frozen, desolate.

He nods, slamming the folder down and standing up. "Come with me."

I follow him into the next room, the main room of the station. There are only three desks, each one piled with messy stacks of paper. No one else seems to be here.

He points me to a phone on the wall. "You get only one call," he says.

I nod, close my eyes, and take a deep breath. My fingers fly across the familiar numbers before I can think any more about it.

"What?" Mother answers, that brittle voice resounding in my ear.

"I've been arrested," I say. The cop crosses his arms and watches me, showing he has no intention of giving me any privacy.

"For what?" Her voice is low. A deadly calm.

"They're accusing me of possessing and selling drugs. My roommate overdosed, and Arabella's framed me."

The cop raises his eyebrows and then grins, telling me clearly that he doesn't believe me.

"He is in London," Mother says, meaning Helper. "Tell me where the jail is, and he will come get you out."

I shiver as I tell her, though I try not to let the cop see.

"Vivian?" Mother adds. "You know what happens when I am disappointed in you."

There's a bang as she slams the phone down, and the line goes dead.

The cop puts me in a cell by myself. It has a cot, a toilet I have no intention of using, and metal bars that are supposed to intimidate me.

I should want to stay in here forever. I know what's waiting for me as soon as I step outside the security of these bars.

As the hours melt on, I realize I have no concept of time. I can't tell if the world outside is sunny or dark. It doesn't matter, I tell myself. But I want a window. I want something that will assure me that I'm not back in the closet at home, locked away for days, that Mother's cold gray eyes won't be waiting for me on the other side of this cell.

I close my eyes and take a few deep breaths, trying to brush off the claustrophobia. I'm fine. I'm going to be fine. This is all just a misunderstanding, and Mother will come to see that. It won't harm my chances with Ben, which I know is what she's afraid of. It may even help them.

I hear footsteps approaching, and I open my eyes and hold my breath.

Helper and the cop who questioned me stand before my cell, wearing twin looks of disapproval, though for very different reasons. Helper grips his cane so tightly that he looks pained, his mouth in a deep frown.

The cop unlocks the cell. "Come on," he tells me. I follow him and Helper down the hall and back into the interrogation room.

"We don't have enough evidence to hold you," the cop says. "You're released."

I swallow as I look up into Helper's flashing eyes. I've never seen him look so emotional—I've never seen him not looking cold and calm—and I know it doesn't bode well for me.

I hope with everything that I am that Arthur stays away from the police station.

"I'll go get the release paperwork," the cop says. "You two stay in here."

Helper continues to stare at me as the cop closes the door, sealing the two of us off. "Do you realize what you've done?" he asks, his voice low and deadly.

I swallow and look up at the corners of the room. "Don't they have cameras in here?"

He shakes his head slowly. "Not in a middle-of-nowhere station like this. And how about you let me do the talking?"

I bow my head.

"Why didn't you call your mother if you had suspicions about this girl?"

"I thought I could handle it on my own," I say, refusing to meet his gaze. "I didn't think she would go to such lengths."

"Well, she did, didn't she?" he says, his voice quiet but brutal. It's the kind of quiet that fills up the room, and I wish he would just yell instead. My knees go weak. "You're ruining *everything*." He steps forward, grabbing me by the shoulders and shaking me. "You can't marry him if you're expelled before you've even convinced him to run away."

"*Marry* him?" I ask before I can stop myself. Helper finally stops shaking me.

"Yes, marry him. It's what your mother needs. Otherwise this is all for nothing. You convince him to run away, and then you get him to marry you."

Marry me? That's been her goal all along? The money. She wants the Collingsworth money, which I can access through Ben, but that's only guaranteed if I marry him. Of course. But what teenage guy wants to get married?

"Your mother is on her way," he says, "to take matters into her own hands. And you are going to pay for your incompetence."

I feel myself go slack as he digs his fingers into my shoulders. She will kill me.

I can see it in his face, the way his eyes fill with rage as he watches me. If I fail, she will kill me, just as Arthur said. Just as she would have killed Emily, if her plan to get her expelled hadn't worked.

I didn't want to see it before. I thought that she was too weak for that, that those nights she spent weeping in her room meant she would never really hurt me. I thought that she needed me. She was my mother, and she relied on me. But now I see that she doesn't care about me. If I don't do the one thing I was born to do, she won't need me anymore. She will have to kill me to make sure her secrets stay secret. And she won't care. Just like she didn't care when she had her own mother killed. I can't ignore the truth, not when it's screaming at me like a banshee trapped in my head. She had her mother killed, and she will kill me.

There is a rustle at the door that draws Helper's attention away. I turn and see Ben standing in the doorway, fury etched onto his face. But it's not directed at me. It's all for my tormentor.

"She didn't do it," Ben snaps. "I don't know who the hell you think you are, but you can't talk to her like that."

Helper seems to have been struck speechless as he watches

Ben come to my defense so strongly. His grip on my shoulder loosens, and I step out of his grasp.

His emotionless face is back. "I'll go see about those release papers," he says.

"What are you doing here?" I ask Ben as soon as Helper leaves.

He crosses the room and enfolds me in his arms. I'm still trembling from the realization of how precarious my situation really is, and he hugs me tighter.

"It's all around school," he explains, rubbing slow circles on my back.

"I didn't do it," I say.

He stops me before I can keep defending myself. "I know. I know you wouldn't do that to Claire."

I breathe a sigh of relief. Even though he knows I have ample access to drugs, he doesn't believe I could be that twisted or careless. Nothing will make him doubt me. He doesn't know how dangerous I am.

I bite my lip.

"People are saying you've been expelled," he says softly.

I shake my head and nestle it back on his shoulder. "I don't know, but it wouldn't surprise me. Headmaster Harriford seemed furious. He'll probably send me back on the first plane to America."

"You can't go home with him!" Ben shouts, stepping out of

the hug and gesturing at the door to show he's referring to Helper. "You can't go back to your mother and let her rule your life."

"What am I supposed to do? If they expel me, I have nowhere else to go."

He takes a deep breath, looking at the floor for a moment before looking back up at me. "Run away with me."

There it is. I've done it. For a moment, that's all I can think. He's mine, completely. He is mine to ruin.

I'm so relieved that I want to sink down onto the floor and weep, but then there's another part of me. . . . I look into those hazel eyes and see complete trust and love and care. And I wish that I had actually earned those things.

I nod and let him pull me close. I can't speak.

"We'll get out of here, okay? We'll go where my father and your mother can't find us. Everything's going to be okay."

The door opens, and the grim cop stands there with the papers in his hands. "You're free to go," he says. "For now. You'll need to stay close in case we charge you."

I catch Helper's eye over the cop's shoulder. I try to stop shaking, to look confident and in control. "I just need a moment alone with Ben," I tell him. Helper nods.

I let Ben walk me out of the room, out of the station. I know Helper is watching us, even though I can't see him. He never misses anything.

"I'll withdraw as much money as I can out of my bank account before my father notices," Ben says as soon as we reach the bright sunlight of the world outside. "And we can go to Oxford—I have a mate there who can put us up for a while. We'll be safe, okay?"

He cups my head in his hands, and I know I have to look at him. I have to reassure him that this is what I want. That he is what I want.

But before I can look at him, I realize something that I've been trying to deny for months: I don't want this boy to ruin his life for me. I want him to run far away from me, to the ends of the earth, where I can't reach him. I care about him too much.

I care about him.

The shock of that thought nearly undoes me.

Everything is so confusing and happening so fast. I can't catch my breath. I feel it growing shallower and shallower in my chest, and then I'm falling, actually falling to the ground, my knees hitting the hard cobblestones of the sidewalk.

Ben has a strong hand on my back. "Breathe," he tells me. "Just breathe."

He draws in a long breath, encouraging me to do the same. I try, but it catches. Finally, I get a good one, and I expel it just as slowly. I close my eyes, feeling my heart rate slow. I wipe away the tears that have escaped.

If I let this opportunity slip away, she will kill me. That thought comes to me again with startling clarity. She will have no more use for me, and I know too many of her secrets to be allowed to escape.

Arthur's face flashes across my mind. He escaped. Helper has never been able to find him, though I know he's tried. He could help me.

But he won't. He doesn't trust me, doesn't care about me. He's made that clear.

What I need to do is get Ben to run away with me and marry me. And then what? Will Mother feel content with her revenge? Will she let me let him go? Or will something happen to him? Will something happen to him if I don't marry him?

Arthur was right all along. I don't know what I've gotten myself into. I don't know where it will all end.

I shiver, looking into Ben's trusting hazel eyes. I have to make a decision about who I can trust: Arthur or Mother. I remember what Helper said, that Mother is coming to take matters into her own hands. I know who I have to trust. There's no other way.

Ben must see my face brightening, because he lets out a sigh of relief and steps back. "Are you okay?" he asks.

I nod. "Let's go. Let's run away."

CHAPTER 31

I stand up, and he pulls me in for a kiss. And while his lips brush over mine, I scramble to think of what to say next.

"We can go somewhere, some small town, and get jobs," he says, his words somersaulting over one another. "You can draw and I can write, or something. Anything, as long as we're together."

It all clicks together, and I stifle a sigh of relief, biting my lip as I look up at him. "I'm on a student visa, though," I say, looking back into the police station as if I'm afraid they'll come out and arrest me again for even thinking of violating the terms of my visa. "If I'm not in school, I have to go back to the States."

"We'll hide from them," he says, taking my hand. "You'll be safe, I promise."

I beam at him like he's my salvation, my eyes filled with love and admiration. "I trust you," I whisper, tightening my hand around his.

He looks down in wonder at the worshipful expression on my face, a surprised smile playing across his lips. And then his eyes widen as he lands on the idea I hoped he would. "We could get married."

I blink in feigned surprise. "What?"

"We could get married," he repeats, his eyes still locked on mine. "Then you'd have your visa, and we can stay here."

I part my lips slowly, like I don't know what to say.

He pulls me closer, his hands burning into my shoulders. "My mom wanted me to find the girl that I loved and never let her go," he says softly. "I can't let you go back to the States. I want to be with you, Vivian. Forever." He pauses, then lets a smile stretch wide across his face. "Marry me."

"Yes," I say quickly. "Yes." I wrap my arms around him and hug him as hard as I can. I feel like I might start sobbing.

He pulls back and looks into my eyes again, searching them as he cradles my head in his hands. I do my best to look back at him with every ounce of excitement and joy I can muster, but that almost breaks when he tells me, "I love you."

I swallow, hard. "I love you, too."

He glances back over his shoulder at the police station, and I close my eyes, still dizzy and shaking from everything that's just happened. "We have to hurry," he says, his voice now urgent.

He takes my hand and pulls me toward a dark and dangerous future.

We call a cab and hurry back to Madigan. Ben needs to find his friend's address, and I need to set the other details of my plan in motion.

As he runs to his room, I hurry to Arthur's cabin and, pretending to stop and readjust a shoe, slip a note under the door, trying to do it quickly in case Helper is watching.

And then, in a matter of hours, Ben and I are on a bus to Oxford. We ditched our cell phones so we can't be traced, and we've told no one where we are or where we're going. Helper will have seen us running away, but I haven't caught sight of him since the police station. I'm hoping that we've escaped him for now, at least. I just need to buy some time.

"Tell me why we can trust this friend of yours again," I demand.

Ben sighs. He's told me three times already, but something in me needs to make absolutely sure. My entire plan hinges on some guy I've never met.

"Mike's American, like you. He came to Madigan as a fifth former, and he was a year older than I was. He was quiet—didn't make many friends, kept to himself, you know? But he and I got to know each other pretty well on the rugby team. We both hated our dads and wanted them to shove off, I guess. So he told me when he graduated that if I ever needed to get away, I could stay with him."

We sit in the back of the bus, huddled together in a corner with no one around us. Still, we speak in low voices. Our lives have become a series of whispers.

Ben didn't even call Mike from the hall phone back at Rawlings, afraid someone would overhear. "And he won't care that we're just showing up?" I ask.

"He won't mind, I promise," Ben says.

I bite my lip and watch the landscape fade from the harsh wildness of the moors into a soft green idyll, filled with tall trees and grassy hills. Most of the trees have lost their leaves, but soft green smudges are beginning to cover their dark, naked branches. We speed past farm fields and clusters of lumbering cows in between small villages with gabled roofs and the occasional grafittied urban sprawl. The only thing that doesn't change is the sky: The clouds above are the same gray and threatening ones, hanging low over the ground. I've left my sketchbook behind with everything else, but my fingers itch to fly across a page, capturing this transition.

Ben sits silently beside me, his eyes wide open and fixed out the window, his hand still grasping mine. He has hardly let it go since his desperate proposal. Neither of us has slept in hours, but there's too much adrenaline coursing through us to allow for any rest.

It takes almost four hours traveling due south to reach Oxford. But as the bus rolls through the town toward its stop, I feel as if we've traveled back in time. It's a world of gray, brown, and dark green, and everything breathes history. The university's various colleges tower above us, their Gothic spires reaching into a sky fading into a sea of rose and gold as the sun sets. Students amble along narrow cobblestone paths, disappearing from view. I can hear their loud conversations and shouts of laughter through the thin plastic window. They wear heavy sweaters and bright smiles.

I glance at Ben. If he followed the path his father had chosen for him—if I had not come into his life—this is where he would end up. He would be one of these bustling students, trekking from important class to important class, discussing literature and politics with his classmates, maybe even punting on the narrow green river we ride over. I am looking at everything I've taken away from him.

We get off on a more commercial street, with pharmacies and clothes shops and streams of people crowding the sidewalks. As I step down from the bus, swiveling my head to take it all in,

Ben offers me his hand. I take it, and he wraps his hand securely around mine, quirking the corner of his lips into a hint of a smile. We can do this.

Mike lives in a flat not too far from the bus stop. We wend our way over a few blocks, past impressive stone walls and gates that lead to the colleges, bells pealing from their towers as the hour turns. We pass several restaurants, the smell of cooking food wafting through the air and making our stomachs rumble, and finally come to a street of brightly colored row houses.

A short but muscular boy with dark skin, deep brown eyes, and a quick smile answers the door on the second floor of a light pink building. "Ben? What the hell are you doing here, man?"

He looks curiously at me. I'm still wearing the rumpled jeans and thin black sweater that I threw on just before finding Claire. My eyes must be blank from lack of sleep, and my hair feels limp and flat against my head. I am not as enchanting as I usually am.

It doesn't matter. All Mike has to think of me is that I'm sweet and innocent. I smile warmly at him and let Ben do the talking.

He introduces me.

"Hey," Mike says, beckoning us into the living room.

There is a lone couch and a giant flat-screen TV and piles of clothes and trash everywhere. And a smell, like dirty feet. Mike is clearly not concerned with tidiness.

"So?" Mike asks. "Are you going to tell me what's going on, or do you want me to guess?"

"We've run away, and we need your help," Ben tells him.

Mike's smile fades, and he nods, sitting down on his bed. "Start talking."

Ben tells him that he and I have fallen in love, but he knows his father won't approve. He says nothing about the drug charges or the fact that I'm probably expelled from Madigan, but he makes our case sound desperate anyway. "I can't follow my dad's plans anymore," he says with vehemence. "I need to take charge of my own life, and my life is with Vivian."

"So why did you need to leave school to be with her?" Mike asks, his voice measured and even. He's a rational thinker. He'll be harder for me to convince than I thought. But he looks at Ben seriously, waiting to hear what he has to say.

"Because we want to, you know, start our lives together, and we want to start now. It's my eighteenth birthday tomorrow, and we want to get married."

Mike's eyebrows shoot up.

Ben turns to me, asking for help with his eyes. "I know you don't know me," I say softly to Mike. "I know that getting married must seem like the most ridiculous move for people our age. But the way I feel about Ben, and the way I know he feels about me . . ." I look up at Ben, filling my eyes with admiration and love. As if I can't believe that someone this amazing is by my side.

When I look back at Mike, he looks a touch more understanding, his eyes crinkling with concern.

"I can't imagine living without her," Ben continues, turning to me. I put on my best radiant smile as I meet his eyes. "I don't want to ever let her go."

"Can you help us?" I ask, my dreamy gaze skittering away from Ben's earnest one.

Mike looks from me to him and back again. "Of course. You can stay here."

"And you won't tell anyone else we're here?" Ben looks at him closely.

"No," Mike replies. "Your secret's safe with me."

"Thanks, mate," Ben says with a wide, easy smile.

"No problem," Mike answers. "I'm more than happy to put up Romeo and Juliet."

Ben catches my eye, and we share a small, private smile. But my stomach twists over on itself. I can only hope we don't end up like Romeo and Juliet.

We spend the night at Mike's flat. I fret over my plan and keep refreshing my email on Mike's laptop to see if Mother's written to me while Ben and Mike play some sort of explosive video game and slap each other's backs like everything's normal.

That night, we refuse Mike's offer of his bed and settle on the couch instead. It's large and soft and covered in crumbs, but Ben and I don't mind. We cuddle together under a blanket, and I fall asleep almost as soon as my head hits the pillow, his arms strong and comforting around me.

We are safe. For now.

CHAPTER 32

I wake up twisted in Ben's arms, my limbs heavy with sleep, and he wakes as I stir. I watch as he struggles to remember where he is, as he remembers everything I've led him to. His confusion melts into a sleepy smile. "Good morning," he says softly, brushing a kiss onto my lips, covering me with his body so that I sink further into the lumpy couch.

"Happy birthday," I answer, kissing him again, looping my arms around his neck. "What are you going to do today?"

He yawns. "I think I'll follow Mike around. See what this Oxford life is like."

I feel a twinge of regret again as I see the excitement in his eyes. He doesn't understand the urgency, but I can't tell him to keep hiding out. But with luck, Helper doesn't know where we are yet.

"That sounds great. While you do that, I'm going to make arrangements for the wedding," I say, trying to match Ben's excitement.

He pulls me closer. "Are you sure you don't want me to go with you?"

I nod, kissing his cheek and snuggling into him. "I'm sure. I want it all to be a surprise."

Later that morning, Mike tears Ben away from me to take him out and show him what Oxford life is like. He slings an arm around Ben's shoulders and pulls him down the cobblestone path, and Ben glances back, meeting my eyes with a smile. I watch them until they round a corner, out of sight, and then I run for the bus station.

There won't be any wedding planning today. Instead, I get on the bus to London. It's time for the real plan to begin.

I wrote what I was preparing to do in the note I slipped under Arthur's door, and I asked him to meet me in London once I got off the ten o'clock bus. Now I can only hope that he decides to show up.

As the bus pulls into the London station, I see him.

Arthur stands on the platform, his muscular arms crossed over his chest. His tall frame and jet-black hair, so different from the traits of the golden boy I left behind in Oxford, make him difficult to miss. As the tires squeal to a halt, his dark eyes study the windows, and when I step off he walks toward me, his hands in the pockets of his black coat.

There's an awkward pause. "So let's go find Collingsworth's house, then," Arthur says finally. I nod and follow him silently through the bus station to the Underground stop.

My palms are sweating as we pass through the crowds, and I try to take deep breaths in the stale, polluted air. But everything looks so strange and different to me now. The world has tipped over on its axis, and nothing is the same. I am not the same.

I know I can't trust Mother. Not when I know she could kill both Ben and me with barely a thought. She's not who I thought she was. She's not the poor, damaged woman crying in front of the fire, someone to be pitied and protected. She's the woman who planned to kill an innocent girl to get me into Madigan. The woman who had her own mother murdered. The woman who used my best friend as my whipping boy and slit the throats of kittens in front of my eyes and kept me imprisoned in that cold and terrifying house.

I owe her nothing. At least I try to tell myself that, though some strange tendril of guilt still twists through me. She was the woman who taught me everything I know, who put a roof over my head, who made sure I had everything I needed. But not anymore. Now she's my enemy.

That word, "enemy," flashes in my head like a strobe light, altering all of my memories. I see past her lies now, her manipulations. I see Mother for the puppet master she always was, and I see the strings that she pulled to make me dance. I have to cut them off. Even if the sudden loss frightens me.

I've put all of my faith in Arthur, the only one who has told me the truth, the only one who has ever escaped her, and I can only hope he doesn't betray me again.

There are so many people tripping over each other at the Underground stop, and everything is dirty, nauseating. I hold my breath as we push through the crowd. The trains are tiny and packed, and Arthur and I are smooshed together by the door for several stops. With my ear pressed against his chest, I can almost hear his heartbeat, and for a moment, that relaxes me. The rush, the noise, the strangeness of this all melts away, as if I'm fourteen again and hiding behind the guesthouse with him, escaping from the world around us.

When a seat opens up, though, Arthur gestures me to it.

We get out at Sloane Square and step out into a bustling, traffic-filled street. A grassy area with a few tall trees rests in the middle of the streams of cars, but everything else about this square is urban and commercial, with shops and banks everywhere I look. I have to keep close to Arthur, practically on his heels, as we maneuver through the crowds.

A few blocks over, we enter a stretch of stately townhomes and smartly dressed people. In my jeans and thin black sweater, I don't stand out too much, but I still draw stares with the layers of black eye shadow and dark red lipstick that I put on this morning for Ben's benefit. I realize, with an unnerving jolt, that I want to be invisible, after so many years of engineering my appearance for these second glances. I run a finger over my lips, smudging off most of the lipstick, and tuck my hair under my sweater, hoping that will help.

Arthur has given me his map with Ben's address circled, and we find our way to a neighborhood of almost blinding-white townhouses arranged in crescent circles, gleaming in the morning sun. Arthur stops me as we get closer to Ben's street.

"You ring the doorbell," he tells me. "I'll wait here. People won't be as suspicious of a girl on someone's front stoop."

"What do I do if someone answers?" I ask.

He smiles. "I'm sure you can figure that out."

I don't know if I'm supposed to be flattered or insulted by that comment, so I let it go.

Ben's street is one of the most beautiful I've seen: a block of white houses bordering a park of almost astonishing green. The trees grow wide and tall, cutting off the view of what must be a garden inside, surrounded by black bars to keep the unprivileged out. Flowers spill out from the window ledges around us, creating beautiful tapestries all the way up the four-story buildings. I find Ben's number painted on a white column, take a deep breath, and walk up the stairs to the sun-dappled front door.

I can hear the faint echo of the doorbell chiming through the house when I press the button, but nothing else. I press it again thirty seconds later and knock on the door, but still no one comes to answer it. Collingsworth must be at the office, and I know from Ben that a maid only comes on weekends when he's away at school. The house is empty and ours for the taking.

I see a few people on the sidewalk as I shrug and walk back down the steps, but no one's looking at me.

Arthur and I duck behind the row of houses without a word, then creep through an alleyway of private garages until we get to the back of the third house. We sneak down a side path and find a solid wood back door. No one on the street can see us as Arthur jiggles the lock.

"There's no way they don't have a security system," I whisper to him.

"You didn't get your boyfriend to give you the code?" Arthur sneers.

I sneer right back. "That would have been a bit suspicious."

"Don't worry." He takes a long, thin file and slides it deftly into the crack between the door and the frame. "Have you forgotten I'm my father's son?" he asks with a bit of a half smile that takes my breath away.

He gets the door open and runs inside before I can respond. I find him at a control panel on the wall, fiddling with wires inside. His father clearly did teach him the tricks of the trade.

I take a moment to absorb the details of the house where Ben grew up. We've entered into a kitchen and breakfast room, and everything is modern and clean and sterile, all startling white and stainless steel. Pots gleam from their cabinets, and a gigantic stove fit for a chef takes up most of the center island.

Arthur stops fiddling with the wires, closes the control panel, and turns to me, a proud smile on his face. "Now we just need to find—"

There's a flash of white from the panel, so quick I almost miss it.

Something's wrong; I can see it in Arthur's eyes.

"What is it?" I whisper, looking around, wondering if someone is going to come attack me.

"Silent alarm," Arthur says, his voice strained and quick. "His system's more advanced than I'm used to. We don't have much time before the cops get here."

We separate, running through the house in a whirlwind. I find myself in a den with leather sofas in front of a ridiculously large television and a portrait of Ben as a young boy on the mantelpiece. I glance at it for only a second, but I recognize those hazel eyes in his younger, rounder face.

Whatever we're looking for, it won't be in such a routinely used room. I run up the stairs two at a time, hunting for the largest bedroom of the house. The second floor is all small bedrooms and an office, where I find Arthur going through the drawers of a large desk.

I run up the stairs to the third floor, and finally I find a large room with a sitting area and a king-size bed. I rifle through the small desk there, but its drawers are empty.

Among the photos of Ben at various ages sitting atop the desk, though, there's a photo of someone else I recognize. I pick it up and stare at the girl with long black hair. She's the one who drew the picture of the tree that Ms. Elling had me look up in the yearbook. The student from the same year as Mother whose husband had been shot.

A boy stands beside her, and they both beam out at the camera, pressed closely together. That must be her husband.

I unclasp the back of the frame with fumbling fingers, and the photo falls on the desk, revealing the writing on the back that I hoped to find. *Rose and Adam Travers.*

A wail shatters the silence outside, and it's growing louder. I stuff the photo in my bag and run for the stairs, Arthur meeting me at the bottom before we burst outside.

CHAPTER 33

We bound out the back door and run through the alleyway. Once we hit the sidewalk, I pull Arthur into a walk and stuff the files he carries into the bag I took from Mike's flat. I grab his hand as a police car speeds toward us, turning my head and smiling innocently at him. His eyes are still panicked, but he sends a quirk of a smile back. The car whisks right by us.

I drop his hand and quickly direct us to Hyde Park, where we lose ourselves in clusters of trees and crowds of people sitting on the lawns, soaking up the rare sunshine that makes the day warmer than it's been in months. Only then do I breathe a sigh of relief.

Arthur sighs, too, and glances down at the bag I carry. "I don't think I got anything good. The files are just tax returns from the first years of Collingsworth International, but I doubt he'd put anything useful in them about how he developed the avatar. And if he realizes that's what we took—"

"He'll know what we're looking for," I finish for him. "We have to figure it out quickly, then."

"What'd you find?" he asks.

"A photo."

He looks at me with raised eyebrows but says nothing.

I sit down on the nearest open bench, its wooden slats warmed by the sun. It rests along a wide dirt path with dozens of people strolling past, and it has a view of a large lake in the distance. "You look through the tax files," I tell him, taking them out of my bag.

He nods, sitting beside me.

I take the photo delicately, looking down at the two people Collingsworth wanted to display on his desk. The only other people besides his son.

It was a stupid thing to grab, I think as I examine the two smiling faces. Maybe Collingsworth was friends with Adam and wanted to remember him. Maybe I only took this photo because I was drawn to their expressions, these two people clinging to each other as if the other was the only thing they would ever need in this world. Adam has hair almost as black as Rose's. His face is round and his eyes are small, but the way he holds on to her and the way he grins out at the camera—there's something beautiful about it.

I look over at Arthur, who sighs as he shuffles through the tax forms on his lap. He's a study in concentration, his brow furrowed, his dark brown eyes narrowed and piercing. He doesn't even notice me looking at him.

I remind myself that he has great reason to be focused, and if I don't focus myself, my life could very well be in danger.

I glance back at the photograph, shifting away from Arthur. He feels too close.

And then my focus shifts. I don't see Rose and Adam anymore. I see what's behind them. Because there, just visible in the background, is something else I recognize: the house in Loworth that so enchanted me on my first visit to the village. That narrow, foreboding house looks more polished in this photo. There is no sign of the unkempt yard or the creeping vines slithering up the walls. This is the house in a happier time.

I flip the photo back over. *Rose and Adam Travers.* Adam. The name of the male avatar.

"I've got a clue," I tell Arthur, drawing his eyes from the tax forms. "We need to go to Loworth."

"Loworth? You're sure?" he asks, glancing at the photo in my hands as I stand up.

I nod. "How do we get there?"

He stands up as well. "A train to York and a bus from there would be the fastest option," he says, leading me out of the park. "How much money do you have?"

We take another foul-smelling, crowded subway ride to King's Cross, where everyone seems in even more of a hurry than we are. We spend the bulk of my cash on two economy tickets to York and rush onto the three o'clock train.

CHAPTER 34

The two hours it takes to travel back up the country make me want to stick needles up my fingernails just to give me something else to focus on. I can't sit still. I pace up and down the aisles, earning the curious glances of the other passengers and the glare of the ticket collector.

"Are you going to tell me why we have to find this Travers person?" Arthur asks me for about the tenth time.

I can't talk about it, and I shake my head firmly. The idea forming in my mind is too strange to speak out loud.

I try to take in the world out my window, but I barely notice it. If I were to paint anything right now, it would be a swirling mass of confusion and color on the canvas.

Or maybe it would be Ben's face in all its variations from the pictures on Collingsworth's desk. The rounded baby face thinning to the face of the man he almost is. Those unchanging hazel eyes.

I try to push Ben from my mind. I don't want to think about him. I don't want to wonder what he's feeling now that he realizes I've left him.

Finally, *finally*, the train pulls into the York station, and we bound off and look for the bus connection that will take us to Loworth. The five-thirty bus, the last bus of the day, is sitting at the curb, as if it's waiting for us. I smile so widely when we spot it that I know my cheeks will ache. Arthur looks at me, his eyebrows raised, as if he's never seen me before. We make it on just as it releases a loud squeak and gets ready to move.

The bus lumbers along at the slowest pace imaginable, and the world outside grows dark: a cloudy night with only a sliver of the moon visible. When I look out the window, all I can see is a reflection of my own face and Arthur beside me. It would make a good portrait, a study of a girl on the cusp of something she doesn't yet understand. My eyes are big, and my skin looks even paler than usual. Arthur catches my eye in the window, and for a second, I think I see something in his expression as he looks at me. Something intense and warm. Like he never wants to stop looking at me. I feel the scratchy wool of his coat graze my arm. My breath hitches in my throat, and I look away.

"We'll be there soon," Arthur assures me.

As soon as we reach Loworth, I'm running off the bus into the night, and Arthur is hurrying to catch up with me. I scurry through the slanted paths of the cemetery, only slowing when the house comes into view. It's just as haunting as I remember it, its narrow body shooting up to the sky, covered in ivy and surrounded by a cluttered yard.

I plant my feet in front of the door and stare for a moment at its old cracked wood and the blackened window on top of it.

"Do you want to tell me what's going on?" Arthur asks from behind me. His voice isn't the mocking one he has adopted with me lately. Its softness nearly breaks me.

"Just follow my lead," I order, not looking at him.

I finally knock on the door, three swift knocks. I notice the doorbell late and ring it, too, for good measure.

An older woman, someone in her sixties, at least, opens the door. Rose Travers would not be so old, and part of me is relieved that I don't have to face her right away. I'm nearly trembling.

Whatever the woman expected, it wasn't two young people on her porch. "May I help you?" she asks, looking at me curiously.

"I'm here to see Rose Travers," I say, straightening my shoulders.

"I'm sorry," she says, though it's clear from her sharply etched smile that she's not. "Mrs. Travers doesn't receive guests."

"I think I know who killed her husband," I say bluntly.

Her mouth drops open.

"Do you think she'll see me now?" I ask with cutting politeness.

The woman, a maid or housekeeper, I'm sure, doesn't know what to do for a moment. Finally, she ushers me in. "You can wait in the library," she whispers. "I'll—I'll see what can be done."

She leads me through a dark entryway into a large room. The shades are drawn, and even when she snaps on the overhead light, there isn't much to see by. I make out the shape of bookshelves lining the walls, their contents barely visible between the carvings of the wooden doors. The wall with a dormant fireplace has no shelves but is covered instead with abstract swirls of dark color. I step closer to find they are oil paintings in unframed canvases, clustered so closely together that the wall has disappeared behind them. They have such a gloom about them; they must be Rose's.

"What do you mean, you know who killed her husband? What's going on?" Arthur asks, his voice low and urgent.

"Collingsworth did. With Mother's help," I tell him, my back turned to him as I continue to examine the paintings.

Finally, I turn and look at him to find his mouth almost open in surprise. I nod, answering his unspoken question. "I'm sure of it."

Before he can ask any more questions, there's a loud bang from somewhere above us. And then a rush of footsteps, someone's bare feet running down stairs. I turn toward the closed door and brace myself.

The woman who bursts through it is no longer the happy girl from the photos. Her bright blue eyes have sunken into her skull and are surrounded by deep wrinkles. Her skin is almost a translucent white and looks papery thin to the touch. Her cheek-bones threaten to cut right through the surface. She must only be around thirty-seven years old, but she looks on the brink of death. She wears a white nightgown and robe, which sag from a fragile, thin body.

But her long, thick black hair, the hair that invites your touch, identifies her clearly enough. It hangs down to her bare feet.

She stops at the sight of me, her hand flying to her mouth, resting there.

"Daughter," she whispers. The word practically leaks from her throat, her voice is so rusty.

It takes me a moment to realize what she's said, and I shake my head. "No, no, I'm sorry. I'm Vivian."

Rose shakes her head right back at me, her gaze still transfixed on mine. "My baby," she says, her tone incredibly insistent.

I look to the maid to find her gaping at me. "Oh, Lord," she whispers. "You *are* her daughter."

CHAPTER 35

Beside me, Arthur is flicking his eyes from Rose to me and back again. "Maybe you better explain what's going on," he tells the maid.

Rose answers, and she looks right at me as she talks. "You were stolen from me. When you were just five months old. It was a month after they killed my husband, your father, and someone came back to the house and took you." She steps forward, a little closer to me. "I couldn't find you. You were just . . . gone."

My confusion melts into horror, swiftly followed by a reflex of denial. I can't be her daughter. *Mother* is my mother.

But in the next moment, I see—really see—Rose's blue eyes. They are almost the same deep blue as my own, and, just like mine, they are a touch too far apart. Her face has the same heart shape as mine, her mouth turns up in the same bow. As she looks at me in shocked happiness, I recognize my raised eyebrows in hers.

It's true. This ghost, this madwoman, is my mother. Our resemblance is too strong to be denied.

But . . . how? I can't even sort through all of the questions and exclamations swirling around in my mind.

She steps forward, hesitates, then rushes to me, and I almost take a step back as she wraps her arms around me. "My baby," she murmurs. "My baby girl." And then she's sobbing, and I stretch my arms around her tiny frame to hold her up.

We stand at this stalemate for several minutes. She will fall if I let go, but everything about me wants to run away. I don't want this history. How could I be her daughter? How could Mother not be my mother? I feel as if the world has flipped upside down once more, and everything is chaos. Everything I have done, the person—the *people*—I have twisted myself into, has been for that woman in New York, because she was my mother. She was my blood, my family. But everything I thought I knew is wrong.

And now, just after I've repudiated my identity, I discover a new one. An identity that has been mine all along. That has been robbed from me.

I glance at Arthur, whose shifting expressions match my shifting emotions. He finally settles on sympathy as he meets my gaze, and that sympathy makes me wince. It's sympathy for the years I've lost, thinking that a manipulative murderer was my mother. And for the loss of my father. Because he is the one who was killed all those years ago. Those bright, shining people I found in the photo on Collingsworth's desk were the parents I always should have had.

I disengage myself from Rose's arms quickly, and she staggers before righting herself. I watch her, shaking my head. "No," I say. "It's not possible. It doesn't make sense."

Rose opens and closes her mouth, shocked. It's Arthur who says my name softly, trying to pull me back to myself. I look at him. "Mother wouldn't have done that," I say, my voice a high-pitched, pleading thing. "She wouldn't have stolen me away from my family."

He doesn't say anything, but I can read his eyes. Because of course she would. She always taught me that if you want something, you should take it. So she took me. I was just a baby, and she took me.

I look back at Rose. My mother. She's as much a victim as I am.

"Where have you been?" she asks, her voice cracking and creaking.

I clear my throat, unsure of my voice. "I've been living with— with a woman I thought was my mother. In America."

"Who? Who is she?"

"Morgana Whitfield." I spit the name out. "She knew William Collingsworth."

Rose nods absentmindedly for a moment, and then suddenly, she blinks. "I know him, I think."

I stare at this woman, imagining myself turning into her. Imagining her holding me as a baby. Nothing makes sense, and my breath rises unsteadily.

I try to focus on the questions I originally came here to ask. I have to. "Your husband was Adam?"

She nods slowly, and then her expression clears. "William was one of his friends at Madigan. When Adam and I married, and we moved here, William would visit us. When this house was filled with light." She looks to the heavy drapes covering the windows, like she doesn't know why they're closed. Suddenly, she rushes to the fireplace and plucks a framed photo off the mantel. "See, here. This is Adam, and that's William." Adam looks the same way he did in the photo I found on Collingsworth's desk, with black hair like mine and a pleasantly doughy face. He towers over Collingsworth, that miniature Ben. I focus on him now. My father. This man who was my age when I was born. And when he was killed.

I look back up at Rose. "I think William and the woman who raised me were the ones who broke into your house."

"And . . . Adam? They killed Adam?" she asks, her voice sharp, thin.

I nod, swallowing hard.

She draws in a harsh breath and looks up at the ceiling, as if there are answers there.

"What happened that night?" I ask.

"We never found out," she answers, still gazing at the ceiling. "Not really. The police finally decided that some addict had come in looking for prescriptions. There had been another break-in a few villages away around that time. We don't know what the thieves took from here—I never found anything missing. Or why they killed Adam." Now that she's started speaking, her words come out in a rush, tumbling over one another. "So the police thought some addict had come in and Adam had surprised them, and they never found any evidence. With our baby in the next room. They killed my husband with our baby in the next room, and then a month later, someone came in and took her—you—and everything was dark, so, so dark." She stops, pressing the back of her hand to her lips, staring at me with wild eyes.

The maid, who I realize now must actually be Rose's nurse, takes her by the shoulders. "Look at me, love. That's it. Deep breaths." She waits as Rose gasps for air until her breathing finally slows and she closes her eyes.

"After my parents died," she says finally, slowly, opening her eyes, "my life became all about waiting for you, always waiting for you to come back to me."

"What he was like? My father?" I ask, my voice hardly more than a whisper.

She nods, as if she'd been expecting the question, and takes another deep breath before answering. "He was kind and caring. He could light up a room just by walking in it. He lit up my whole life. And he was smart. He knew computers so well that all kinds of high-profile tech companies in London and in America were offering him internships and jobs that summer—that summer that he was killed. He had been working on this idea that he said would change the way kids grew up, but I never got to find out what it was. He was going to be something big, special. But more than all that, he loved you. Even before you were born, even though we were so young. He loved you."

She reaches out again for my arms, and I let her pull me close, but not before I shoot a glance at Arthur.

It really is true. Collingsworth killed my father. His own best friend. And the woman I thought was my mother helped him. While I was in the next room.

I shiver, and Rose's grip on me tightens. "Someone came a month later and took me?" I ask, and she nods.

I close my eyes, trying to construct the timeline that's forming in my mind. Collingsworth and Mother robbed the house after the had graduated from Madigan. I was four months old. Adam must have developed the avatar program, and they stole the codes for it from this house. Collingsworth killed Adam and then cut Mother out of the deal as well.

Ben is only five months younger than I am, so his mother must have been heavily pregnant with him at the time. Ben must have been born right after the robbery. I imagine Mother standing over my crib the night my father was killed, staring down at the new life before her. Had that image twisted in her mind with her need for revenge against Collingsworth once she heard about his betrayal? Somehow, she came to believe that I was the answer, that I would be the one to ruin him. Just like her uncontrollable, incoherent periods of rage, this delusion was a symptom of her madness. The madness I tried so hard to ignore.

Everything clicks into place, and I open my eyes. Before I can censor myself, I tell Rose everything I know about the woman I thought was my mother, my anger building with every word. As I recount my childhood, she sinks into the sofa, looking up at me with round, horrified eyes.

When I have told her everything about Collingsworth and Ben and the journey that led me here, she pushes herself off the couch and hugs me. I'm nearly thrown off balance by it, because there's nothing weak about her now. Her arms are strong as they enfold me. "It's not your fault," she whispers. "You're not a bad person, I know it."

I close my eyes and will my tears to disappear, taking a deep, shaky breath.

Arthur has retreated to a corner of the room, leaving Rose and me as much space as possible. He has taken in my story with impassive eyes—a stark contrast to the emotion skittering across Rose's face.

I step out of her hug and try to regain control. "Is there anything—a fingerprint, maybe, or a scrap of clothing—that the robbers or the kidnapper left behind?"

"The police looked for weeks, but we couldn't find anything."

"We can't stop them without evidence," I mutter, trying to think of something, anything that might help.

"You're the evidence," Arthur says softly.

My eyes snap to his.

He looks at me with a gentleness I haven't seen since we were children. I suddenly have to remember to breathe. "Do a DNA test to prove that you're Rose's daughter, and it will be clear that Morgana stole you," he says.

"We should go to the police right away," Rose murmurs.

I nod. But there are questions I need answered first. "What was my name?"

"What?" Rose asks.

"My name. The woman named me Vivian. What did you call me?"

She opens her mouth, but it takes her a few tries to get it out. "Sarah."

Sarah. What a soft name. A name for a girl who worries about getting her homework done in time for class and making sure her clothes are in fashion.

I don't feel like a Sarah. I don't look like one. It unsettles me.

I think of Ben, wondering if he would have fallen in love with that Sarah version of me. He deserves someone more like her.

I sigh. He has to be panicking about where I am, wondering if I'm safe. I have to let him know not to worry. "Can I use your computer?" I ask. "I need to let Ben know I'm okay and tell him to stay put for a few days until all of this dies down." I owe him that much, at least.

Rose nods, gesturing at her nurse. She brings me a laptop, and I settle down at the desk in the corner to use it while she hurries to the kitchen to see if there's anything she can offer me to eat.

When I log in to my school account, I see I have several emails from an irate administration and one email from Ben, with the title "Help." I open it, a sinking feeling in my stomach.

Vivian, your mother's got me. She's going to take me to our cottage. She'll kill me if you don't come, and she'll kill me if anyone calls the police. Please come. Ben.

CHAPTER 36

The room is spinning. I grab the edge of the desk to keep myself from falling over. My knuckles go white, and, for a moment, they're all I can see.

"Viv? Viv, what is it?" Arthur asks, a frantic edge in his voice. He leans over me to read the email, then slams his palm on the desk.

"She has him. My—Morgana, she has my . . ." I don't know how to complete that sentence.

Arthur grabs me by the elbow when I bolt up out of the chair and turn to rush out the door. "Stop," he insists. "Your mother—Morgana—she just wants to draw you in. She'll kill you if you go, Viv. You can't let her manipulate you like that." The severity of his brown eyes burns into me, and I flinch from the heat.

"If I don't go, she'll kill him."

"If you *do* go, she'll kill him! And she'll kill you, too."

"I can't let him down. I have to try to rescue him."

"That's what she *wants*!" Arthur exclaims, shoving a hand through his hair. "Viv, Ben might not have even written that email. You have to think carefully about this."

I am thinking carefully about it. I'm thinking that Mother is no longer an ocean away but just a few miles, in the cottage that I thought was my refuge. I'm thinking that she isn't even my mother at all, but a stranger—a criminal—who stole me from a house of love and kept me captive in a house of hate. I'm thinking that the boy who never did anything wrong except fall in love with me is about to be killed. I'm thinking that if I don't do something right this instant, I'm going to despise myself for the rest of my life.

"I *have* to," I tell Arthur. My voice comes out firm and unyielding.

"You care about him." The look in his eyes is guarded, but I can hear a break in his voice. Pain. I don't quite understand it, and I don't have time to try.

"So what if I do? Are you going to help me or not?" I don't need his approval, and he knows that, but I have to admit that I might need his help.

Arthur stares into my eyes, the way he does when he wants to see inside my head. He must find my determination, my sincerity. Finally, he nods. "Let's go."

Rose brings out a tray loaded with cheese and crackers, but the smile falls off her face when she sees us heading out the door.

"I'm so sorry, but we have to go," I tell her in a rush. "We'll be back soon, I promise." *I hope*, I amend in my head. She nods, confused, and I follow Arthur out of the house.

The wind whips around us, freezing my cheeks and turning Arthur's a ruddy red, as we run to his car in the bus station parking lot. The cracked leather passenger seat is cold, and Arthur's heater isn't enough to combat the chill. I clench my hands into fists and stare out the window as we speed out of Loworth and onto the narrow road of the moors.

The clouds over us darken as we approach the stone facades of the Madigan campus, which is still as proud and imposing as ever. Arthur screeches to a stop outside the gate, and we both fling ourselves out of the car, running out onto the moors.

The rain starts when we are only just out of sight of the school. It's only mist at first, but then the drops grow bigger, pelt down harder. By the time we're halfway to the cottage, the rain is coming at us sideways. It feels like running through an assault of tiny knives, but I don't slow down. All I can see is Ben's face, open and trusting as he told me he loved me.

I should have told him the truth. If I'd told him about Mother's plans and how dangerous she was, he would have stayed in hiding. How did she even find him? I'm sure Helper had everything to do with it. And if he's with Mother at the cottage now, our situation will get a whole lot worse.

I stumble on a clump of dead heather, and I hit the ground palms-first, the jolt traveling up my arms. Arthur pulls me up and onward. We can't stop. Not now that we're so close.

I have no plan. I don't know what to do when we reach the cottage. I can only hope that I can somehow distract everyone enough for Ben to get away.

We slow when the smudged outline of the cottage appears through the rain and the darkness. There's a light inside: a fire. The light from its flames dances through the window.

For a second, the reality of what's happening hits me, and I nearly double over in pain. The place where I let myself escape from everything, the place where I put up my sketches, the place where a boy told me he loved me, as if I deserved that love, has turned into something terrifying. I don't want to get any closer.

But I force one foot in front of the other, and Arthur and I creep forward. We say nothing, both of us too busy trying to hear anything that will rise above the whistling wind and give us a clue as to what we are about to come up against. But I can make out nothing.

We crouch to the ground to stay out of sight of the windows, and I hold my breath as we slither like snakes up to the structure, the heather scratching holes in my clothes. I don't feel anything. Everything in me is focused on that cottage.

Suddenly, there's a shout, and someone pulls me up by the back of my sweater. "Got one!" a voice yells. Arthur hits my captor in the stomach, hard enough to make him buckle forward and let go of me, and I scramble away. Helper. He holds his middle and looks up at Arthur. His mouth drops open. "Boy," he whispers. Arthur doesn't answer. He just springs up and attacks him again. Behind me, the door opens with a swift creak, and then there's a strange metal sound. A sound I should have been expecting.

I turn slowly and find that the woman who raised me is pointing a gun right at my head.

CHAPTER 37

All I can see is the shiny black metal of the gun. Everything else goes blurry, but the gun is still in sharp focus.

"I knew you'd come for this worthless boy," Mother says, her voice mocking. Cutting.

Behind me, everything has fallen silent except for the thud of the rain on the muddy ground.

Mother jerks the gun, gesturing me forward, and I can finally look up at her face. Her lips are twisted into a cruel smile, making the heart-shaped mole on her cheek more prominent. She is familiar and unfamiliar all at once. "Come inside. Look how well we've treated your boyfriend."

I feel Arthur step up behind me, the warmth of his body radiating along my back. Like he's trying to send me strength.

Mother points the gun at him, shaking her head with a cold smile on her face. "Just Vivian," she declares. "Though I am glad to see you, Boy. Your father has been having a devil of a time trying to find you. It was much easier to find Ben. His friends were all too happy to speculate about where he might have gone. You're lucky you've never had any friends."

"Go to hell," Arthur spits.

Mother says nothing, her smirk never wavering. "Come along, Vivian."

I take a deep breath and step forward. She moves aside so I can get in the door. "If you try anything," she tells Arthur, "I will shoot her. And I imagine after all these years of devoting your every breath to her, you don't want that." Arthur says nothing in response as she steps inside with me and closes the door.

Ben is tied to a chair over by the hearth, which houses a meager fire. A gag covers his mouth, and his eyes are wild. My stomach practically falls to the floor when I see him there, and blood rushes to my brain, making me dizzy. I did this to him. I'm the reason he's in danger. And I hate myself for that.

I run to him, kneeling at his side. But I don't touch him.

"Of course you were stupid enough to fall in love with him," Mother says with a laugh.

"No," I answer, turning to face her. I can't look into Ben's eyes. "I'm not in love with him. You've made me incapable of love."

"I have protected you from it, you mean." She gestures with

her gun for me to move away from Ben, and I rise and shuffle over a few steps, keeping my eye on the weapon.

"Yes, love can dismantle, and all that bullshit," I say, rolling my eyes to show my disdain. Fear claws at my insides.

She blinks at my harsh words. "Why did you come here, then, if you don't love him?"

"Because I care about him. I can't let you kill him."

She looks at Ben, a crazed smile of triumph on her face. She truly is a lunatic. "I have told him all about you. I told him your mission, how you have manipulated him, how you crowed about victories on the phone to me. I suspect he hates you now."

I look back at Ben and see in his eyes that she's right. They're filled with venom as they pierce into me. I have broken his heart, just as his father did to—Morgana. I have to start thinking of her as Morgana. She is not in any way my mother.

"So you have your revenge," I say, turning back to her. "You've hurt him the way you were hurt. You can let him go."

She laughs, a laugh that is too high and too loud, as if I've told a particularly good joke. "You still think all of this is just about revenge for a broken heart?"

"No," I answer. Anger battles the fear inside me, and right now, anger is winning. "It's also about the programming codes for the avatar. The codes that you stole."

Her eyes widen. "What did you just say?" Her voice quavers, and I see that I have shaken the calm control right out of her.

"I know everything. About Adam Travers. And Rose. My real mother."

Her face, always pale, turns even whiter.

There is a sudden shout and sounds of a scuffle outside. I look out the window, horrified, hoping Arthur hasn't been foolish enough to start a fight with his father.

The door bursts open, and a man I've only seen in old photographs is pitched into the room, struggling with Helper.

"Collingsworth," Morgana breathes, confirming my suspicion. Her hand fumbles with the gun for a moment as her eyes go round. No one moves as they stare at each other. Collingsworth tries to take a step forward, Helper's arms still holding him, and that seems to wake Morgana up. She points the gun at him and gestures for Helper to get out of her way.

He does, leaving the cottage and closing the door behind him. Despite the sudden change in situation, I want desperately to go outside and make sure Arthur's all right. What is going *on* out there?

Collingsworth holds his hands up at his sides. He's an older version of Ben, though his jaw isn't quite as square and his hair has receded, leaving a shiny white dome on the top of his head. He has Ben's hazel eyes, and they widen as they take in the barrel of the gun aimed right at him.

"Morgana," he says with uncertainty. "I knew it would be you."

She keeps the gun pointed at him, but her hands are shaking. She looks more rattled than I have ever seen her, her eyes wide and unblinking.

"What are you doing here, Will?" she asks.

"Never mind that. Morgana, just let my son go." Collingsworth spares a glance at Ben, who's taking in the scene with the most horrified eyes I've ever seen.

"How ugly you've gotten." She glares at him, pointedly looking at his balding head.

"We've both grown older, Morgana."

She winces. I know how much she hates her gray hair, which grows so quickly that, no matter how rigorously she dyes it, her roots begin showing within days.

But her confidence returns almost immediately. She hadn't been planning on confronting her old enemy today, but she will take advantage of the opportunity now.

"You ruined my life," she declares, her booming voice filling the cottage.

I take the smallest sidestep toward Ben, hoping to evade her attention. She turns the gun on me in one fluid movement and shakes her head.

Collingsworth flicks a glance toward me. But at the moment, I am unimportant.

Morgana turns back to him and continues. "You broke my

heart, and you ran away with our money. *My* money!" He opens his mouth to protest, but she cuts him off. "It was my idea in the first place, so that all the little girls who grew up like I did could have a friend, someone to talk to, someone who wouldn't judge them!" Her rage is rising, and she has to close her eyes to calm herself. "It was a brilliant idea, and it was all mine."

It's the first time I've ever heard Mother talk about her childhood, and I realize why the money is so important to her. She created the Ava. She created something personal, something beautiful, and it was ripped away from her.

"I was the only one with the connections to transform your character into a business," Collingsworth says, his voice measured and reasonable. Like he's making pleasant conversation over tea. I have to admire him for that.

"Of course," Morgana says with a sneer. "All's fair in love and war. Your precious little motto."

He knows her well enough to say nothing.

"I had to go back home to my mother empty-handed. Do you know how she treated me then? I was supposed to come home with a rich husband, the whole reason she sent me to this school, but instead, all I had to show for myself was a broken heart and a stolen baby. She thought I was being stupid, so stupid. Nothing I did for that woman was ever enough to drag her out of the poverty she'd sunk herself into with her furs and her diamonds and all the trappings of an aristocratic lifestyle we couldn't afford after my father died. She threw me out of the house, the damned bitch. But not for long.

"I came back. And he helped me kill her," she says, gesturing outside to Helper. "I couldn't stab her to death or strangle her with my bare hands, the way I wanted to. We had to be sneaky. Cutting her brake lines was his brilliant idea."

Collingsworth continues to stare at her calmly, no trace of surprise on his face. My stomach turns.

"I lost you and I lost Ava and I had nothing but that baby," she says, pointing at me without looking at me. "So I made her into my own avatar. I taught her how to shift her personality to fit any target, and I set her on your son."

Her own avatar? I feel my face turn deathly pale, and spots whirl in front of my eyes. Collingsworth looks at me, a long, penetrating look. "That was why you took her? To transform a *living child* into an Ava?"

Roaring fills my ears, and I can hardly hear her when she replies. "I made her the ultimate Ava. No one else could create an Ava so perfect. Which is why that money belongs to me."

I know now what Arthur was trying to tell me all those times when he asked me if I knew what Mother had turned me into. I thought I was a weapon with skill and agency, but I'm something more insidious than that. I'm an avatar. A living, breathing avatar; a deadly shell of a human, controlled by someone else. He didn't have the heart to tell me. He knew how much it would hurt.

Collingsworth raises his brow, which is now slick with a sweaty sheen, but his voice remains cool and collected. "I was the one who befriended Travers, who discovered how good a programmer he was. I was the one who mapped out the house."

"And I was the one who actually went into the house when you were too much of a coward! I had to go in with *him*," she gestures out the door to include Helper, "to steal the damn program! So that we could be partners, just the two of us, the way you promised."

"It had to have been you. They would have recognized me if they saw me!" he cries, throwing his hands out to suggest innocence. "They hardly knew who you were!"

"And when Adam discovered me, I was the one who had to kill him! You told me he wouldn't be there, but you lied. You knew he'd be there all along. Of course he would be—he'd never leave his beloved Rose and his beautiful baby. You wanted me to kill him so that you could walk away with the whole business. I earned that program with the blood on my hands."

"*You* killed him?" I gasp before I can stop myself. I see the scene in my head: Morgana, the mousy girl from the yearbook picture, holding this gun in her hand, pressing it against the temple of a young man—my father—and pulling the trigger. My stomach turns again, and I think I'm going to be sick.

She doesn't even glance my way. She's too wrapped up in this showdown with her enemy. I take another sidestep, but no one pays me any attention.

"I'm sorry," Collingsworth says, bowing his head. "I shouldn't have taken the code. I was a foolish boy."

"And what about my heart? Are you sorry you broke that? Are you sorry you got your damned slut of a girlfriend pregnant while you seduced me?"

I take another step.

Morgana grabs something off the wall, and it takes me a moment to realize what it is: the ripped old picture, the "Me and him" photograph that I found when I first came to the cottage. "We used to be happy," she says, shaking the photo at him. So it was her. She is "me," and he is "him," and this cottage has a more twisted history than I could ever have imagined.

"You used me!" she continues. "I loved you, and you used me! I *killed* for you, and you didn't even care! His blood is on your hands, too!"

Another step.

"I know. I know, I'm despicable. That's why I named the male avatar Adam, just so I could be reminded every day of what I did. I swear. But please, Morgana, don't take this out on my son!"

Another.

Her face twists in a cold grimace of a smile. "I knew your son was the only thing you cared about. I knew he was the only way to get to you. I *was* just going to have Vivian marry him and clean out his trust. But watching you die will be even better revenge."

Ben catches my eyes now, his gaze frantic. I creep closer to him and quickly clutch at the ropes binding his hands.

"What the hell do you think you're doing?" Morgana asks behind me. Her voice is the same cold and deadly one that I've known all my life.

I close my eyes and drop the rope, turning around slowly.

She raises the gun and points it at me, aiming for my heart, and no one makes a move. I know Collingsworth won't help me, and Ben can't.

I have no one to rely on but myself, as always. I straighten my shoulders and glare at her. "You won't kill me," I assert. It's a bluff, of course. I thought she was capable of murder, and now I have proof of it.

She raises her eyebrows, almost amused. "You are not my daughter. You are the daughter of the golden couple. Of perfect, artistic Rose and the boy who would do anything for her. She had everything I would never have."

"So you took me," I whisper, "because you were jealous."

"And now you're useless to me. And you know too much."

I'm not scared anymore. I'm *mad*. Rage builds inside me at this madwoman who stole the life I was supposed to have. Who raised me to hate and fear love. Who used me like a weapon and made me hurt everyone I ever cared about.

Surely she's not surprised that the weapon she built has finally turned on her. Like Frankenstein, she created a monster she couldn't contain.

Without even thinking about it, I lunge forward. And a shot rings out.

CHAPTER 38

I look down at my chest, waiting for the pool of red to appear. I can't feel the bullet lodged in me, but I know that's just from the shock. The pain will come soon enough.

But when it comes, I don't feel it in my chest. I feel it in my arm, and it isn't as blinding as I expected it to be.

I watch in horror as Morgana falls forward in front of me. There is a mass of blood and hair on the side of her head. One of her arms reaches out toward me, lying there pale and lifeless on the ground. I step back, away from her outstretched hand. She can't touch me.

I realize then that it wasn't one shot I heard, but two. One from Morgana's gun, a shot that seems to have torn out a piece of my upper arm. And another shot, just a fraction of a second earlier than Morgana's, from the policeman standing in the doorway, the policeman who must have snuck up to the cottage with his partners and subdued Helper outside.

Then, suddenly, everything is motion. Arthur bursts into the room just behind the policeman, staring at me with wild eyes. Collingsworth unfreezes and runs to untie Ben. Arthur runs to me, ripping off his shirt and wrapping it around my arm to stop the bleeding. "Is she dead?" I whisper, though I already know the answer.

He looks back at Morgana's lifeless form. "She's dead," he assures me.

And then he shocks the hell out of me by gathering me roughly in his arms and kissing the top of my head. The surprise of it eclipses the pain, and for a moment, I feel only that same shower of sparks that his touch has given me before. I stand frozen for a second, but finally I bring my good arm up and wrap it around his middle. I lean my cheek onto his broad chest and close my eyes.

Two more cops burst into the room. After Collingsworth gets his son free, they trap him in handcuffs. He doesn't protest, though Ben tries to pull the policemen off. "He didn't do anything! He was trying to save me!"

Ben isn't even looking at me, and I can't blame him. After everything I've done to him, he must never want to look at me again.

"He contacted us when he received the email you copied him on," one of the new cops tells Ben. "He confessed to being an accessory to murder and armed robbery."

Collingsworth doesn't say anything, but he looks soberly at his son as they drag him off.

"Miss?" one of the policemen says, standing in front of me. "We need to get you to a hospital. Can you walk?"

I nod, pulling my head away from Arthur's chest. Shuddering, I step around the body and crimson blood of the woman who raised me and let the policeman lead me out to the car. Arthur stays with me the whole time, keeping his arm around me.

A policeman has wrestled Helper to the ground outside, and Helper grimaces at both of us as they handcuff him. His eyes pierce into me from their crevices, and he looks more demon than man. But they push him into a car and drive off, and I can breathe again. Arthur watches, but says nothing. He just helps me into another car and gets in beside me, holding my hand.

"You did well," he says finally.

I nod, my throat too thick to say anything. There's a lump there, like I'm about to cry. Though I don't have any idea what I should be crying about. She's out of my life forever. She took so much from me. I should be satisfied.

It must be the pain, I decide. And the shock. I lean my head on Arthur's shoulder and try not to think anymore as we hurry to the nearest hospital. Somewhere during this strange journey, he has become the one thing that comforts me. Just like he'd been when we were children. And instead of pulling away, he rests a careful arm around me and keeps me close.

The wound is mostly clean, they tell me, though the bullet tore off a chunk of my skin and some muscle. I lie on a stark white bed with scratchy sheets, a bandage wrapped heavily around my upper arm. There's an IV in my wrist, and the sound of the slow drip of pain medication fills the room. I drift in and out of this world.

Every time I wake, groggy and confused, Arthur is there. He doesn't leave my side. He sits in a chair by my bed, and when a wave of pain crashes through me so intensely that I want to scream, I reach out my hand and he takes it with both of his.

It takes me two full days to get back to normal, though I wince any time I try to move my arm. Arthur has no news about Morgana. Every time I close my eyes, I see her body lying there, the side of her head bleeding out on the stone floor of the cottage.

The police keep coming in to talk to me, but Arthur has staved them off while I've been in and out of consciousness. When Arthur is being interrogated somewhere else in the hospital, a bumbling man comes into the room and asks for my

statement. I tell him everything I know and everything I suspect, and he says they have Collingsworth in custody, as well
as another man whose identity they are still trying to uncover,
who I know must be Helper. Though Morgana is, in his words,
"no longer a problem," they will do a DNA test on Rose and me
to corroborate my story. A single word on a piece of paper will
tell me what I already know: that I am Sarah Travers, and I have
been loved my whole life without my knowledge of it.

My doctor, a middle-aged man prone to nervous smiles and
clicking his pen repetitively, says he wants to keep me another
night to make sure my wound heals properly. I'm confined to
this scratchy bed for only a few more hours.

As soon as he comes back from his questioning, Arthur wraps
his hand firmly around mine once more. He won't let me go
this time.

There's a knock on the door, and Ben enters. It takes me a moment to recognize him within the grim reality of this hospital
room. To notice the pale pallor of his face and the tired droop-
ing of his eyes. He is not the king of confidence here. He's just
a boy, and, thanks to me, he's all alone.

"What are you doing here?" I ask. My words are harsh, but my
voice is soft.

Arthur looks back at me and, squeezing my hand, gets up and leaves the room without a word. Ben watches him go, a flicker of confusion and hurt in his eyes.

The door closes behind Arthur, and Ben shifts his weight from one foot to the other, taking in my bandages and the IV hookup. Finally, he looks at my face. "I had to see if you were all right."

I sit up and resist the urge to smooth back my hair. It looks abominable, I know, but I shouldn't care. I'm no longer playing Morgana's game. "You've got to have so many questions."

He nods.

Silence fills up the corners of the room. He doesn't know where to start. I wait.

"You never loved me, did you?"

I blink. I didn't think he would start there. I figured he'd be too preoccupied with his father, trying to discover how this man he knew his whole life could have hidden such a history from him.

Ben steps forward, his hazel eyes locked on mine.

I owe him the truth, at the very least. "No," I say simply. "It was all a manipulation. But I *did* grow to care about you. A lot. And everything I did was to make sure you didn't get hurt anymore."

He drops his eyes, but not before I see the pain flooding them.

"I think I could have loved you, if I weren't—if I were normal. You were my safe haven," I whisper. "As screwed up as that sounds. But, no. I'm sorry. I'm not in love with you."

He nods at the ground, and we're stuck in silence again.

"How's your father?" I ask finally.

"I don't know what to think of him anymore. I always knew he was a bastard, and now I know he's a thief, too. But he, you know, he came for me. I thought that blind-copying him on that email was just a shot in the dark, but he showed. He's the one who called the police, even though he knew getting them involved would probably mean his arrest. He confronted that woman and risked his life for me. I just—I don't know."

I don't know what to say to him.

"They said that the guy they stole the programming from is your real father. That you were kidnapped when you were a baby."

I nod.

"Then it's your money. My dad stole the legacy that's rightfully yours."

I look away. I hadn't thought of that. "I don't want anything to do with it," I declare. "That money has blood on it."

He doesn't say anything, but I see him step forward again out of the corner of my eye. I sigh and look back at him. "I guess everything's going to be different for you now."

He nods. "I'm going back to Madigan. In light of everything, they're willing to ignore my absence this week. Oh, and they're dropping the drug charges against you, too. Claire woke up and told them you had nothing to do with it."

Claire. A sharp pain lances through me. With everything that happened, I'd forgotten about her. "She's all right?"

"She's fine, except for having to have her stomach pumped. She's just down the hall here, if you want to see her."

I nod, tears filling my eyes. We're both surprised to find them there, I think.

"What will you do? Will you come back to Madigan?" he asks.

"I—I don't know." I look down at my hands clasped over the covers and wait for him to ask me not to come back. For him to tell me that he never wants to see me again.

"You should," he says after a moment. "You shouldn't let her take everything away from you."

I look back up at him in surprise, tears spilling down my cheeks now.

He leaves with a quiet goodbye, and I do my best to wipe away the tracks my tears have made. I know if I go back to Madigan, I'll see him again. But it won't be the same. He used to look at me like I was someone worthy of love and care. Now seeing me will only remind him of everything he's lost. Including his heart.

I know it's for the best that he knows the truth. But that thought still hurts.

"You have another visitor," Arthur says, appearing at my door a few moments later. There's something strange but soft in his tone, and I look up as my mother—my real mother—follows him into the room.

She's like a bird freed from her cage: unsure of her movements and wary of everything. Her long black hair looks ratty and unkempt but still beautiful. Her eyes dart around the room, but then she rests them on me, and she rushes to my bed. "My darling girl," she cries, taking my hand gingerly.

I let her take it, biting my lip. Arthur leaves us alone.

It takes me several minutes to assure her that I'm all right and to finally say what I've been wanting to say. "I don't want anything from you," I tell her. "I mean, any money or anything like that. If you get any payout from Collingsworth especially, I don't want it."

She curls her lip, her distaste at the thought of that mirroring my own. "I would give any of that money to charity. Money won't bring your father back, and I don't think we need it at all." She pauses. "I won't give you anything but my love," she tells me.

"I don't know how to love," I admit to her. "Not anymore. Morgana beat that out of me."

She draws in a breath, then bites her lip and looks into my eyes resolutely. "Then I'll show you."

I nod, unable to say how grateful I am.

"Is there anything I can do for you right now?" she asks.

I answer without hesitation. "Can you help me up? My friend is down the hall, and I need to see her."

She gives me a frail arm to lean on as I swing my legs over the side of the bed and rise slowly. My muscles feel a bit weak from all the stress and the medication, but they'll hold me fine.

I shuffle down the hall on my mother's arm and ask a nurse what room Claire is in.

I take a deep breath before the closed door of her room, and my mother squeezes my arm for support.

I knock quickly, and a faint "Come in" seeps through the door.

Claire is sitting in a chair by the window, a notebook in her lap and a pen in her hand. As soon as she sees me, she jumps up, tossing the notebook and hurrying to throw her arms around my neck.

I'm so surprised that I find I'm bracing myself for attack, and I will my body to untense. She pulls away before I can hug her back, but she's smiling radiantly at me. "I didn't want to bother you until you were all better, but I wanted to see you so badly! You have to tell me everything—the stories are just so crazy."

She notices my mother in the doorway for the first time. She makes a strange apparition there, her black coat contrasting so sharply against the otherworldly paleness of her skin. I'm in no state to catch anyone's eye in my shapeless robe and disheveled state, but Rose is striking.

Claire looks at me, a question in her eyes. "Your mother?" she asks softly.

As soon as I nod, she's across the room and hugging Rose. Rose seems less shocked by this than I am, and she gives a small crack of a smile as she hugs Claire back.

"I thought you were going to die," I tell Claire. I assumed my voice would sound warm, happy. Instead, it's as scorching as the heat of a fire. "I held your head in my lap and thought you were going to die."

Claire blanches, looks down. "My parents are putting me in a rehab program. They weren't even mad. They just—they were actually worried about me." She pauses, a smile sparkling on her lips. Like she can't believe it. Her expression darkens again, and, still staring at the floor, she tells me, "I'm sorry."

The flames lick at my throat. "You should be."

"Sarah!" Rose hisses.

Her use of that name draws both Claire's eyes and mine. "Sarah," Claire repeats, savoring it as she looks back at me. I wonder if I look anything like a Sarah to her.

I close my eyes. What would Sarah do in this situation? "I'm sorry," I say. "I know it's not your fault. I—I should have noticed. I should have done something, said something. I didn't think. I'm just glad you didn't die."

Claire seems to find this amusing, and she half smiles at me. "I'm glad you're glad I didn't die?"

I nod. She doesn't realize how big that is for me.

CHAPTER 39

They release me that afternoon, and I'm led into the shining world outside. Rose has gone home to prepare a bedroom for me, and Arthur is the only one left with me now as I sign the discharge papers, though I make him leave the room when I put on my jeans and the shirt that he brought me from Madigan to replace my bullet-torn one. I let the orderlies wheel me out to the front of the hospital and step out into a dreary, cool afternoon.

"Where do you want to go?" Arthur asks.

I consider this, looking out into the parking lot and the village beyond. Everything is unfamiliar and new. I feel like it suffocates me, makes my chest tight and nervous.

"Can we go back to the cottage?"

Arthur raises his eyebrows at me, and I know it's a strange request. But I have to see it again.

He leads me to his car. Without a word, we drive the winding roads back onto the moors, and I look out at them eagerly. They're home to me now, I realize. This wild place, the mist clinging to the wide expanse, the wind-battered trees: It's home.

It's growing darker now, night throwing a chill on the land. We come upon the stone structure of Madigan, its lights shining out into the gathering darkness, inviting us in. But as soon as I step out of the car, I turn away from them.

We wander down the hill and into the wild, helped by the light of the moon, only slightly dampened by the clouds drifting over its surface. The night is calm, almost eerily quiet. There's only a breeze ruffling the heather, not the full-blown whistling wind I'm used to.

I move faster.

I stop when I catch the first glimpse of the cottage's black shadows. Arthur steps closer to me, almost touching but not quite. "Are you sure you want to go in?" he asks.

I nod and force one foot in front of the other. I'm here, and I'm not as fragile as I feel. I can face this place.

It's still an active crime scene, so we can't enter. But I can shine a flashlight into the window and look inside. They removed

Morgana's body, of course, but harsh yellow tape cordons off the area where she fell. I think I see a dark outline on the floor, like a bloodstain, but I look away quickly before I can confirm.

My drawings are still on the walls, though, and all of the candles and warm blankets are still there. If I put a good fire in the hearth and come out here with my sketchbook in hand, it will look almost exactly as it used to.

It's still mine.

Arthur gently places an arm around my shoulders, drawing me into his embrace. "Are you okay?" he asks softly.

I nod. "I think I will be." I let myself lean against him, let him support my weight a little bit. I feel like I'm fourteen again, when Arthur was the singular strength and warmth in my life. I didn't realize how much I needed that back then.

I force myself to step forward. "I'm sorry," I murmur without turning around to look at him.

"For what?" he asks.

"For touching you. I know you don't feel that way about me."

He places his hand on my arm, gently turning me to face him. He stares at me, his deep brown eyes concentrated on mine as if he's trying to figure something out. Before he can say anything, though, the question that I've wanted to ask him for so many years bursts out of me. "Why?"

"Why what?" he says.

"Why did you leave me after I told you I loved you?" I feel suddenly dizzy, my head swimming. But now the words are out, and there's no taking them back.

"What do you mean?" he asks.

"You know what I mean. You left me. You didn't even say goodbye. Why?"

"Because you wanted me to," he says, his voice harsher now. "You told Morgana everything. About our spot behind the guesthouse, about my poetry. It was all a game, one of your little practice tests. And I fell for it."

My mouth drops open as he accuses me, those warm brown eyes turning cold, his jaw set in defiance. As if he's facing an enemy. I scramble to understand his words, my mind sprinting to re-create the past. How could he see me as an enemy when all I did was fall in love with him?

"I'm sorry," he says, and all of a sudden, the Arthur I've come to know in these last couple of days is back. "I know it wasn't your fault. I know she made you into that person. I just couldn't stand the thought of you laughing about me with her. It was real for me, no matter how much of a joke it was for you."

I shake my head, my thoughts clearing as I figure out exactly what Morgana did. "She played you. And me. I didn't tell her that we'd fallen in love, or anything about us. She must have been spying on us, letting us get close so she could rip us apart." It's all so clear now, and I wonder how I could have missed it. Morgana, the woman who taught me how to manipulate everyone around me, had done the same to me so easily. She raised me with a boy I was never supposed to talk to, but she made him my whipping boy because she knew hurting him would hurt me. She made me care for him. And then she sent him away so I would know the pain of a broken heart, so I would use that pain to become the weapon she wanted. I was a fool.

I step closer to him so that he can see the truth in my eyes. "It was never a game for me."

He studies me for a long moment. "You really loved me?" he asks.

I nod, not trusting myself to speak. He pulls me in for a hug, and I bury my head in his chest. His heart is beating as loudly as mine. "I'm sorry," he murmurs. "I'm so sorry."

We stay locked together for several lingering moments, his arm securely around my waist, our pulses racing. "Viv?" he asks, pulling back so he can look me in the eye. "What do you want to do now?"

What do I want? The words taste strange as I swirl them around my mouth, feeling their edges with my tongue. I can do what I want. But what exactly is that?

"I want to graduate," I say finally. "I want to get to know my real mother. And then I want to see the world." I don't know exactly what I want from the world. College, maybe, or to sell my art on the banks of a river somewhere. Something. And I can do it. I can make a life for myself, a life all my own.

I am not dangerous anymore. I'm not some avatar. I'm whatever I want to be.

Arthur nods, like he was expecting that answer.

I look at him seriously, making sure he's listening. It takes everything I have to ignore the sudden weakness in my knees, the dryness of my throat. I have to say this. I know that with every particle of my being, though the strength of the knowledge shocks me.

I clear my throat and force the words out. "I want you to come with me."

He definitely wasn't expecting that. He shifts to face me full-on and stares into my eyes, searching. As I watch his brown eyes grow even darker, my breath catches in my throat. My lips part, and before I realize what's happening, he has stepped forward, wrapped his arms tightly around me, and is pressing his lips against mine.

It feels like sunrise. Like that moment when bolts of golden light shoot through the gray haze of the world. When the sky turns pink and red and orange—a riot of color over the bleakness of the moors.

I kiss him back, pressing my lips against his with a desperation I can't measure. My arms are around his neck, pulling him as close to me as I possibly can.

I open my mouth wider, deepening the kiss, and the image of the golden circle of the sun rising above the world fills my mind.

We pull away only when we have to catch our breath, and I lean my head against his chest. I'm still not close enough.

"I've tried—all these years, I've tried to fall out of love with you." His voice is uneven, his breath ragged. "I tried to tell myself that you used me, that I was nothing but a plaything to you. I tried to hate you."

"You certainly seemed to, when I came here," I murmur into his shirt.

"It was a good show. But really, my plan was to help you run away, to escape. I got us fake passports when I went to London, just in case. I've been trying to save you ever since you got here, but I could never figure out a way." With my ear against his chest, I feel his heart beat faster. "I love you, Vivian. I always have."

There's a pause, and I try to sort out what I am feeling. "I don't know if I can love as other people love. Not anymore," I say slowly. "I don't know if I can give you back everything that you need."

He draws back and looks me in the eyes. "We'll take it slow," he assures me. "I think you'll be surprised, Viv."

I like that idea. I like the idea that I can surprise myself, that I can grow into someone different, someone better.

"Call me Sarah," I tell him.

ACKNOWLEDGMENTS

First off, thanks so much to my family. Mom, you always, always encouraged me to work hard for my dreams, and I can't thank you enough for that. Dad, you've shown me unconditional love and support. Thank you for everything.

To Greg, for telling everyone you've ever met about your writer sister. I love you, and I'm so proud of you, too. And to Jenn, for being more like a true sister than just a sister-in-law. And, of course, to Lucy and Jimmy, for being the absolute cutest niece and nephew in the world.

To my incomparable grandmother, Liz Ghrist, for being a perfect example of a smart, well-traveled, strong woman. And to Lahoma Moore, Granny, the sweetest woman I ever knew.

Thanks so much to Denise Delaney and Ross Netherway for putting me up in London every year so I could traipse around the city. Denise, thank you for having your hen party in York so that I could go visit the Yorkshire moors and be inspired to set the book there. Without you, this book wouldn't have happened.

And to my wonderful critique group: Angélique Jamail, Shirley Redwine, Brenda Liebling-Goldberg, Lucie Scott Smith, and Gabrielle Hale. You've rooted for this book from the beginning, and I'm so grateful for the helpful comments and critiques you've given me along the way. Extra thanks to Angélique and my other high school creative writing teacher, Carolyn McCarthy, for teaching me all the rules of writing. And how to break them.

I have to thank all of the friends who've cheered me on, even when I couldn't go out because I was revising or researching what happens when you get arrested in England: Nic Buckley, Karan Lodha, Allison Maffitt, Valerie Grainger Henderson, Jen Chang, Curtis Sullivan, Jenn Richards, Drew Rossi, Adam Yock, Lee Mimms, and Erin Nelsen Parekh.

I'm also indebted to the YA community in Houston and online. All of you readers, writers, and bloggers have been so supportive, hilarious, and wise. Thanks for all of the book recommendations, encouragement, and commiseration.

Thanks to my agent, Alexandra Machinist, for being so excited about this book that you pitched it out the next day. You've helped make my dream come true.

And thanks to my fabulous editor, Elizabeth Tingue, for the critiques that have made *I Am Her Revenge* so much stronger. You've understood this story from the very beginning, and you actually made me excited to revise it, which has to be a first. And to Ben Schrank and everyone at Razorbill and Penguin for believing in this book.